WHEN LOVE WAS BLIND

How Judith wished that the Duke of Sutton could see how much the world thought of him. How she wished the duke could see how much his friends cared about his plight. How she wished he could see how much his servants hoped he would get better. How she wished he could see how handsome and winning he still was. And above all, Judith wished the duke could see how very much in love she was with him.

But the duke could not.

And until Judith could make him see what she saw, she knew she could never say yes to him. . . .

MARJORIE FARRELL was born in New York City and currently resides outside of Boston, Massachusetts, where she is an assistant professor teaching psychology, writing, and literature to adult students.

Miss Ware's Refusal

by
Marjorie Farrell

A SIGNET BOOK

Dedicated to my father, who introduced me to Barnabas Barty, and who like him is "only an Amateur Gentleman after all."

With thanks to my daughter, for all her encouragement and support.

SIGNET
Published by the Penguin Group
Penguin Books USA Inc., 375 Hudson Street,
New York, New York 10014, U.S.A.
Penguin Books Ltd, 27 Wrights Lane,
London W8 5TZ, England
Penguin Books Australia Ltd, Ringwood,
Victoria, Australia
Penguin Books Canada Ltd, 10 Alcorn Avenue,
Toronto, Ontario, Canada M4V 3B2
Penguin Books (N.Z.) Ltd, 182–190 Wairau Road,
Auckland 10, New Zealand

Penguin Books Ltd, Registered Offices:
Harmondsworth, Middlesex, England

Published by Signet, an imprint of Dutton Signet,
a division of Penguin Books USA Inc.

First Printing, April, 1990
10 9 8 7 6 5 4 3

 REGISTERED TRADEMARK— MARCA REGISTRADA

Printed in the United States of America

AUTHOR'S NOTE

Jane Austen's *Emma* was published in 1816. I apologize to her and to my readers for advancing the publication date to the fall of 1815, for the purposes of my story.

1

J udith awoke with a start. Outside her window she could hear the cries of early-morning vendors and the clatter of milk wagons. The street sounds that characterized the city would not reach a crescendo until later, but the chorus of bakers and watercress girls was startling enough to one who was used to being awakened by the sun and the rooster from the home farm.

Gradually the unfamiliar furniture took shape and the street sounds faded into the background of consciousness as Judith savored the sweetness of waking in her own bed in her own house, free to rise when she wished and not in answer to the demands of others. The small bedroom, with its worn furniture and faded curtains, looked luxurious at the moment. She could hear Hannah starting breakfast, and Stephen whistling as he dressed. After a few minutes she got up, and having splashed her face with cold water from the pitcher, she pulled her wool shawl around her shoulders and opened the curtains. Her bedroom overlooked the backyard, a tangle of grass and weeds, with two old rose bushes on either side of the door. The weeds and the roses were enjoying that last spurt of growth that occurs in early autumn. The weeds were high and turning from green to a deep red. The roses were sending out long shoots to reach the more distant sun, a few last pink and yellow blooms flung open. Like the sudden shooting up of flames from a dying fire, thought Judith, and then she turned quickly to dress and help Hannah with the breakfast.

Her brother was already down in the small room at the front of the house that served as both morning room and dining room. He was engrossed in the *Morning Post*, and Judith stood on the threshold and cleared her throat. Stephen peered over the top of his paper and then jumped to meet her as she moved toward him.

"Judith! I thought you would still be sleeping. Come in, sit down.'' Stephen smiled at his sister and said, ''You don't know how good it is to have you here.''

''If there are two happier people in this city, I would not believe it,'' replied his sister. ''We have waited a long time for this.''

''Yes. And I believe it has been a much harder time for you. At least I was my own man at school.''

''No,'' replied his sister, ''my first position was a nightmare, but I was lucky Mrs. Hastings found me a place with the Thorntons. They treated me almost as a member of the family, and were as sad to see me go as I was to leave them. But no matter how kind a family, the governess is still betwixt and between. I am happy to be free!''

''Well, sit down, my dear, and relish your freedom.''

''For a day or so.'' Judith laughed. ''Then I will set to work on this house, and perhaps find some way of bringing in a little money.''

''I wish you would not, Judith,'' said her brother. ''I am making enough to support us both, and I want you to rest and have time for your painting.''

''Oh, I shall take advantage of every moment. I have learned how to do that,'' Judith said. ''But I want to contribute something to the household. I know that you will be a successful barrister someday, and we will be living on some fashionable street in Mayfair, but for now your salary covers only necessities. I don't want to be a burden, and besides that, if I can bring in something from sewing or—well, I don't know quite what—we can get to the theater and opera. We could buy books.''

''Books! I can just see us, squeezed out of here already,'' teased her brother, remembering his sister's bedroom at the rectory.

''I will try to restrain myself.'' Judith smiled. ''When must we leave?''

Stephen glanced at the clock on the sideboard. ''In a few moments. Now what do you plan to do with yourself this first week?''

''I thought Hannah and I could investigate the pantry and go out for supplies. And since the Thorntons were most generous in their going-away present, I might try to find a circulating library, or even a booksellers, and treat myself to a novel. Where would I go, and how would I get there?''

"Hatchards is one of the most popular. You could take a hackney to Piccadilly and then walk. Are you sure that you want to go by yourself?''

"Oh, yes. I will have to get used to finding my way around, so I might as well start soon. It will be scary, but exciting. I haven't been in London since we visited Grandfather years ago.''

"I am not sure it is the thing for you to go alone. Shouldn't you take Hannah with you?''

"As my abigail?''

Brother and sister looked at each other and laughed at the thought of their tall, distinguished-looking companion acting as a lady's maid. Hannah was a distant cousin who had come to work for their father, the vicar of Cheriton, after his wife had died.

When the vicar himself had passed away, and Stephen was up at Oxford, Judith was forced to find work as a governess. Hannah had gone to live with her sister and brother-in-law. It had not been an ideal situation, for Hannah was so used to being in charge of a household that it was hard for her to sit back and watch someone else carry the keys. All three had been relieved when Stephen, having settled in this small house, had written and offered Hannah a place with him. Terrifying as it was for her to leave the countryside, where she had always lived, she jumped at the chance to be in charge again, and to "mother" the two she considered her own. Hannah was a woman of few words who rarely spoke of her feelings, but she was fiercely devoted to the Wares, and their laughter was full of their equal affection for her.

"No, Stephen, I think I am old enough to go about the city by myself. That is one advantage of being a young woman of no fortune—a certain amount of freedom. I will get along famously.''

"I hope so. Please be careful," Stephen said as he stood up and brushed the muffin crumbs from his coat. He was tall, like their father, but there the resemblance ended. His hair was thick and black, like his mother's, and he had her startling blue eyes. Judith, on the other hand, aside from her short stature, looked more like the vicar, with her reddish-brown hair and sprinkling of cinnamon freckles on her face and arms. Her eyes were hazel, with flecks of green, and her skin was fairer than Stephen's. She was small and quick in her movements, he tall and languid. To an unobservant person, they appeared not at all like brother and sister, but those who knew them well could see a likeness when they smiled. Then their faces showed both the sense of humor of their mother and the tenderness of their father.

Judith looked at her brother fondly. He was dressed well, in a coat of blue superfine that set off his eyes, and he looked every inch a confident professional. Three years ago he had been thinner and more unfinished-looking. Today, his shoulders filled his coat to perfection, his jaw was squarer above a cravat tied perfectly in a most conservative knot. He reminded her, in his seriousness, so much of her father, while looking so like their mother, that she impulsively reached out to him and was enfolded in an affectionate hug.

They both laughed shakily when Stephen released her, and Judith wiped her eyes with the corner of her napkin as she watched him out the door. Then she squared her shoulders and turned toward the kitchen.

A few days later, after hours of cleaning and inventory and shopping for everything from brown sugar to curtain material, Judith was ready for her first expedition into London. She was dressed in a wine-red kerseymere round gown, which brought out the chestnut highlights in her hair. It was a plain dress, but nothing to be ashamed of. Her gray pelisse was worn, but she was satisfied with her appearance. She knew that she was no beauty. In fact, without an indefinable something, a combination of humor and lively intelligence that brought her face alive, she might have been categorized as plain. But between the strength of her personality and her love for rich colors, no matter how worn her clothes, Judith always had a decidedly attractive air.

She set out, with Hannah's admonitions to be careful ringing in her ears. In the country she had been used to taking long walks in her hours off, and she was eager to explore some of the city on foot. Today, however, because she only had a few hours, she decided to treat herself to a hackney to and from Hatchards.

The store was on Piccadilly, and for all her self-confidence, Judith was a little overawed by the exquisite young ladies who patronized the establishment. Most were accompanied by footmen, who followed behind, holding the latest romances from the Minerva Press for their mistresses, as they exclaimed over a favorite author's newest with their friends.

Although Judith was a voracious reader, and able to lull her critical faculties when engrossed in the latest popular novel, today she had only the money to buy one book, and she had decided upon Miss Austen's latest. She had just found *Emma* and was feeling the new pages and anticipating the enjoyment to come when she heard a familiar laugh. She looked up and saw the lovely face of Lady Barbara Stanley in animated conversation with another young woman.

Barbara was the daughter of Lord Richard Stanley, and the two young women had met at Mrs. Hastings' Seminary for Young Ladies. Judith had taken the younger girl under her wing, helping her over the initial homesickness. They had become quite close, despite the differences in age and rank, because of their shared sense of the ridiculous and the essential unspoiledness of Lady Barbara. Judith had spent one Christmas holiday and part of a summer with the Stanleys, becoming acquainted with Barbara's parents and her brother, Robin. For a few years they had written to each other faithfully, but Judith had not heard from Barbara for months and had not had an answer to her last letter. She had assumed that, with Barbara's come-out last spring and the differences in their circumstances made more marked, the friendship had faded away, as many schoolgirl friendships do, when the common surroundings and concerns give way to different lives.

Lady Barbara must have felt Judith's gaze, for she looked up just as Judith buried her head in the book, not wanting to risk a cool response from her old friend. Better to remember the old intimacy as it was than to embarrass both of us, she thought.

"Judith? Judith, is it you!"

"Hello, Barbara," she said hesitantly.

"However do you come to be here? Oh, how easily I might have missed you. Why did you never answer my last letter?"

Judith felt herself relax, and realized that she had armed

herself against rejection by her old habit of presenting a serious and emotionless countenance to the world, while keeping her real feelings hidden.

"I never received a reply to my last letter in April," she replied. "I thought perhaps you were too busy with your come-out."

"I did write, sometime in May. But you did not think I was too busy," Barbara said shrewdly. "You thought I had forgotten an old friend in the excitement of the new ones. I was concerned, not hearing from you. But we were so caught up in the progress of the campaign and in worrying about Robin's safety that I must confess I have had little time to write anyone."

"Was Robin at Waterloo?" Judith was afraid to ask anything further, since so many young men had not returned. But surely he had survived, since Barbara was not in mourning.

"Yes, and he was lucky enough to come home whole," replied Barbara, answering Judith's unspoken question. "There are many families who weren't so lucky. But, Judith, tell me how is it you are here in London? Surely the last time I heard from you you were still with the Thorntons in Somerset?"

"And so I was, until a week ago. You knew that Stephen and I had planned to set up house together? He is finally established as a fledgling barrister, and we are settled cozily into a small house on Gower Street. I have been busy helping Hannah set up the house, but I could not restrain myself any longer. I had to find Miss Austen's latest."

"That sounds just like you, Judith." Barbara smiled. "And would your next visit have been to call on old friends? Somehow I think not."

Judith blushed. "No, you are right. I would not have called."

"And I would never have known you were in London had we not met by chance. I could be very angry with you Judith, were I not so happy to see you."

"I would have sent you a note," protested Judith. "I just did not want to presume on an old friendship."

"Judith, I could shake you. You haven't changed a bit. You are still the oddest combination of intelligence and hen-wittedness that I have ever met. Did you ever consider you were depriving me of your company, rather than sparing me? I can just see you, mourning the loss of an old friendship and never dreaming your friend might be missing you.''

"You are right, Barbara. I don't know why, but it is difficult for me to see beyond my experience of a friendship. I am only just beginning to realize what pride lurks behind my 'humility,' " Judith said ruefully. "I apologize."

"No apologies. I must have your promise, now, that you will call tomorrow."

"Not tomorrow," replied Judith, "for you could not believe the work that still needs to be done in such a small house. But I promise I will call early next week. Is Tuesday convenient?"

"I will expect you early," Barbara warned. "We have a lot of time to make up for. Give me your direction and I will send the carriage."

"Oh, no," protested Judith, "that won't be necessary. I can take a hackney."

"I insist. John Coachman will be at your door at eleven o'clock. That way we will have almost a whole day together."

"Are you sure eleven is not too early?" Judith teased. "Will you not still be tired after yet another assembly or evening at the opera?"

Barbara laughed. "This is only the Little Season, so I attend only two functions a night, not four or five," she teased back. "I will be up long before you arrive. I am so happy we met. I have missed my dear friend. I must go, but I look forward to Tuesday."

Judith smiled her farewell. "Till Tuesday."

She watched Barbara rush off with her companions in a flurry of pinks and primrose. Her own dress, which had satisfied her as being rich and simple, now seemed only dark and plain. She would not have exchanged it for a less-becoming but fashionable pastel, but she did feel a bit like a moth in a flock of butterflies. A beautifully marked moth, but a different species all the same.

I do wish I could be consistent, Judith thought. I am not interested in living Barbara's life. I know I would not be happy with endless socializing and I despise the superficiality of the *ton*. Yet I feel twinges of envy and inferiority with young ladies of fashion, while at the same time being critical of their empty lives. Judith smiled at her own ambivalence and proceeded to the desk to complete her transaction.

When she finally reached Gower Street, she was greeted with the smells of roasting chicken and the spicy aroma of warm gingerbread.

"Hannah, that makes me feel like a child again. I can close my eyes and be back in the vicarage."

Were Hannah the sort to blush with pleasure, Judith would not have known, for her naturally high coloring had been increased by her proximity to the stove. Although she turned away, Judith knew her too well to assume that she was not pleased. She moved over to the older woman and placed her arm around her shoulders. "We are blessed to have you with us, Hannah, and do not take for granted the fact that you have left your own family to help us set up house."

When Stephen arrived home, he brought with him an inexpensive bottle of port, and after a supper of chicken, potatoes, minted peas, and gingerbread with fresh cream, he and Judith toasted each other and their endeavor.

"Did you find your way to Hatchards, Judith?"

"Yes, and I found Miss Austen's latest . . . and a long-lost friend, Barbara Stanley."

Stephen was delighted to hear the details of their meeting. The one worry he had about their arrangement was that Judith would be deprived of any companionship of her own age and interests. He had the opportunity to socialize with his fellow workers, but Judith was on her own in a rather ambivalent social position. Although they were both the children of a gentleman, the vicar having been the younger son of a baronet, Stephen's place in society was much clearer. It was expected he would follow a profession, since there was no chance of him succeeding to the title, there being four male cousins ahead of him. Although he would therefore not be moving in the first circles of society, he did have the opportunity to socialize with gentlemen of his class. For Judith, it was more complicated. Aside from marriage, she had had no choice three years ago. Working as a governess had been preferable to accepting her only offer, from the local squire, twenty years older than she, and in need of a mother for his four children. Now that Stephen could support her, she was freer, but fit no place. Unless Judith found one of the wives of his fellow barristers a kindred spirit, she was again betwixt and between. Stephen trusted her resourcefulness, and knew that between her art and the house she would be kept busy enough. But busyness could not make up for the lack of companionship.

"Lady Barbara Stanley . . . I remember meeting her when we once picked you up from school. Did she ever stop growing, or is she as tall and weedy-looking as she was then?"

"She is no weed, my dear brother. She is now a goddesslike, lovely young woman, and I was rather overawed at first by her fashionableness. But she was genuinely happy to see me and invited me to call at the first opportunity."

"And will you?" Stephen asked.

"Yes. She is sending a chaise for me on Tuesday. I am ashamed to confess I thought she had quite forgotten me. She never answered my last letter, you know. But I found out today she had never received it."

"Ahem," Stephen said with pointed emphasis and looking questioningly at his sister.

"Yes, I know, I know. You deplore my tendencies toward humility. I suspect it isn't humility, Stephen, but my feeling of insecurity is quite real, nonetheless. Do you remember that Barbara had a brother who was a captain? Robin?"

"Yes, I remember you mentioning him after one of your visits. Is he still in the army?"

"Yes. He was not wounded in the last campaign, thank God, for I remember him as quite active."

"He was lucky, then, Judith. I see soldiers begging in the streets who are in pitiable states, lacking eyes or limbs."

"I am glad that you did not choose the army," said his sister. "I do not think I could have survived these last three years had I known that you were in constant danger."

"I was never interested in that kind of action. I would far rather put my energy to work in the courtroom. It was necessary to stop Bonaparte, but I do not wish to see us forgetting what led to his ascendance in the first place. We can't turn our backs on Europe now that we are at last the victors. Well, enough politics for tonight! Let's sit in front of the fire and enjoy *Emma*."

2

Barbara returned home after her meeting with Judith feeling that something very valuable had been returned to her. Her intimacy with Judith had eased her loneliness at school and helped make up for the lack of a warm and responsive mother. The countess, by no means a neglectful parent, was, however, like many women in her position, rather removed from her children. Barbara relied mainly on her brother, and she and Robin were very close, having drawn together for comfort and support, but his seven years seniority meant he was gone just at the time Barbara needed him most. She left for Miss Hastings' feeling awkward, gangly, and homesick. Judith, who remembered her own first weeks, was quick to respond to Barbara's silent but obvious unhappiness. What could have been only a brief relationship blossomed into a rich friendship. Both girls shared a self-reflectiveness and intelligence that enabled them to laugh at their adolescent agonies even as they suffered them. The social distance between them was not a barrier. Barbara loved hearing about the small, cozy vicarage in Hampshire, and Judith's unworldly but adored father. Judith, on the other hand, was fascinated by Barbara's life, which alternated between Ashurst and London. And both of them were impatient with the limitations on their lives as women. They resented their brothers' greater freedom, but swore to each other they would never marry just to gain the greater freedom as a married woman. They dreamed of marriage with men who would treat them as equals and appreciate them for their intelligence as well as their beauty. If either of them would ever be said to be beautiful, a development they despaired of! They read Mary Wollstonecraft secretly and imagined themselves setting up house together. Judith, in addition to her painting, would learn German and Italian and support them by translating, while Barbara worked on her music. Somehow, in their fantasies, their dreams of romance and independence seemed not incompatible.

Despite their dreaming, they were both in touch with reality. They knew that Barbara would make her come-out. They knew too that Judith would not, and that it was less than likely that she would ever marry, the selection of eligible men in Cheriton being rather limited. There was the baronet, and a few gentlemen's sons from the surrounding neighborhood who treated Judith like a sister. When the vicar died suddenly and Judith was forced to cut short her last year at the school, she and Barbara swore to maintain their friendship. They had successfully done so for a few years. Barbara had read between the lines of Judith's letters and felt the old anger at the lack of opportunities for women.

As for herself, she had wealth and position, but except for Robin, no one to whom she could reveal her ironic view of the world. The few occasions upon which Barbara had spoken plainly had taught her it was safer to appear thoroughly conventional if one wanted to keep one's friends. To have Judith back in her life was like recovering a part of herself.

On Tuesday morning, therefore, she woke early, with a feeling of excitement, like a child who is anticipating a special outing. At first she could not identify the source, and then she realized that she would have a whole day to herself. No calls to make, no shopping to do. A rare luxury.

When she walked into the breakfast room, she found Robin already there, reading the newspaper. There was no footman about, for both the Stanleys preferred to live more informally than their parents and took advantage of their absence to be more relaxed. Barbara served herself eggs and ham and muffins from the sideboard, and Robin looked up from his paper.

"You are up early this morning," he teased. "I am sure you were not in earlier than two last night."

"I hope you weren't waiting up for me," Barbara laughed. "Weren't you also out?"

"No, I had planned to go to the Beckwiths' assembly, but I was tired, so I sent my apologies and had a quiet night here, losing to Devenham at piquet."

Barbara tried not to react to the viscount's name. All the men she had met in London had not diminished her feeling for Robert

Chase, Viscount Devenham. He had grown up with them in Kent, and was the heir to the large estate bordering Ashurst. Several years younger than Robin, he had been at school while Robin was on the continent. Now that Robin had returned, he had resumed his habit of treating the Stanleys as his second family.

Although Dev was only a few years older than Barbara, he teased her like the younger sister he considered her to be. Barbara, however, was afraid she was more than a little in love with him. She had tried to talk herself out of it, for he was hardly the serious partner she and Judith had fantasized. He was charming, boyish, and apparently frivolous, although she knew that he was also a responsible landlord and loving son.

She had no illusions that he looked for more in a woman than any other male of her acquaintance. He would more likely amuse himself with the demimonde before he settled down with some seventeen-year-old, fresh from her first Season. Barbara was sure that he had no knowledge of what she disparaged as her "schoolgirl infatuation": in fact, he seemed blissfully unaware of her as a woman at all, and had, over the years, come to her for sisterly advice regarding his affairs of the heart.

"Are you doing something special today? Or did you come to breakfast early just to watch the eggs get cold?"

Barbara was jolted out of her daydreaming, and blushed as she realized that Robin was repeating his question for the third time.

"Do you remember Judith Ware, my good friend from Mrs. Hastings'? She visited us one summer, and the last Christmas you and Simon came home on leave together. It was the year of the big snowstorm, and we were all housebound. Remember you and Simon taught us to waltz?"

"Yes, that nice little wrenlike girl? I thought you told me she left school to work as a governess?"

"She did, after her father died. But she has a brother who is now in London studying law. He sent for her, and I met her by chance at Hatchards and invited her to spend the day with me."

"So you have been reunited with an old friend, and I fear I have lost one," replied Robin.

"Simon?"

"Yes. He has been in London for almost a month now and will not admit anyone. I have tried for weeks, Barbara, and he just sends his butler back with apologies that he is not in to visitors. He seems to be living in the expectation that his sight will return."

"But I thought the surgeons told him he was permanently blind?"

"Yes and no. There was no damage to his eyes, Francis told me. They speculate that the head injury irreparably damaged whatever part of the eye conveys images to the mind, but since they cannot see the injury, there was initially room for hope. Simon is holding on to that for all he is worth. But he sits all day in the library, looking at nothing. He is eating little and has lost almost a stone since he came home, according to Francis. I am worried about him, and don't know what to do. I can't very well force my way in and drag him out."

Barbara placed her hand on Robin's arm. "Do not give up, Robin, keep going back. Even if he refuses to see you now, you may eventually wear him down. And he has to be taking it in, on some level, the fact that you have not given up on him."

"I hope so, Barbara, I hope so. Well, I must be off. I will see you later."

Barbara sat over her last cup of tea until it grew cold, lost in thought. Of all her brother's friends, Simon, Duke of Sutton, was the one she felt closest to. He was the son of an old friend of their father's, and they had seen him many times over the years, on his visits to Ashurst. She had many memories of the three of them picking raspberries or racing their ponies. She had been allowed to tag along after her older brother and his friend, and they tolerated her as long as she didn't become missish. "Missish" meant being unwilling to bait their hooks for them, so Barbara had learned to close her eyes and quickly press fat, wriggling worms against the needle-sharp hook, sometimes impaling her thumb in the process, but never crying out. "Missish" meant worrying about her clothes, so Barbara had learned to kilt up her skirts and ignore scratches on her legs when they went berrying. "Missish," she thought, would also have been complaining about a twisted ankle, so she hobbled after them one day, until Simon, glancing back, noticed her grimace of pain and supported her the rest of the way home.

Had Simon not been so much like an older brother, Barbara might well have given her heart to him instead of to Dev. He was genuinely kind to all: servants, tenants, little sisters, and hero-worshiping young viscounts. Responsible and possessed of a true dignity, but not at all impressed by his own rank and fortune. In fact, she knew there had been a time when he had quite painfully questioned his wealth and position. At Oxford, both he and Robin had been influenced by radical thinkers. Indeed, it had been Simon who had first introduced her to Mary Wollstonecraft's writing. He had eventually come to terms with his responsibilities and sincerely believed that since he had been born into a particular place, he had a duty to use the influence he possessed for those who were less fortunate.

Simon was a serious man, albeit with a good sense of humor. And good-looking. Not Byronically handsome, of course, like Dev, or blond and elegant, like Robin. He was tall, and he had outgrown the gangliness of his adolescence without losing a certain ranginess. His hair, thick and sandy, and his light sprinkling of freckles counterbalanced the imposing quality of his rather hawklike nose and clear gray eyes. And now those eyes, which were always so direct and honest, looked out at nothing.

Barbara loved Simon as a member of her own family, and was as distraught over his injury as if it had been Robin's. Yet there seemed to be no way to reach out and help. If he would not admit his closest friend, he would certainly not admit her, even if it were appropriate for her to visit a man's house alone. And what was there to do or say? "I am so sorry, Simon. Come to dinner tomorrow night." Or, "Will you be at Lady Bellingham's? I'll save a waltz for you."?

Surely time will have a healing effect, she decided. Simon could not keep himself isolated indefinitely. Perhaps the thing to do was to go on waiting until he was ready to receive visitors.

Barbara left the morning room and settled in for her hour's practice at the pianoforte. Like most young ladies, she had been given music lessons and had been expected to develop a certain proficiency at the keyboard. What was not expected was that she reveal a genuine talent. She had gone far beyond the conventional, and her parents, in recognition of her ability, had finally hired a professional teacher. For her, music was both a calming discipline and a way to express emotion. Her range was wide enough to encompass Bach and Mozart, and now she was working on some new music, by Beethoven. She was busy working on a sonata she had just purchased, and as she worked out the fingering, she lost all sense of time.

When Judith was admitted an hour later, the butler was about to settle her in the morning room and summon Lady Barbara. "Milady is practicing, you see, and she often quite forgets about the time. I will inform her of your arrival."

Judith could hear the faint sound of the piano and impulsively reached out to stop Hotchkiss. "Let me go down. I have not heard Lady Barbara play for so long, and I would like to just listen for a while."

Hotchkiss pointed out the door, and Judith walked softly down the hall. The slow chords got louder as she drew closer. She opened the door quietly and sank into a chair. Barbara was so engrossed in getting the first few measures right that she heard nothing.

Judith was not familiar with Beethoven's work, and there was something about this new arrangement of sound that moved her in the same way as certain poetry or a painting by Turner. She wanted to get closer to the music, and so she walked over to stand a little behind her friend, watching Barbara's hands work out the best placement. Barbara, sensing someone's presence, stopped in the middle of a measure and glanced up.

"I am sorry to distract you, Barbara, but I couldn't resist that music. Whose is it? You play it beautifully."

"Oh, no, not yet. I am barely beginning to work out the fingering, much less the dynamics. Beethoven is much more difficult than anything I have tried before, and I am quite at sea."

"It was wonderful. I have not heard any of his music before. There is something about the music . . . I can't put it into words. He goes straight to the soul."

"Oh, yes, my friend." Barbara stood up and gave Judith a spontaneous hug. "It is so good to be with you again. You don't know how I have missed your insight."

"You have become an even finer musician than before. It is a shame that such a talent must be hidden, merely because you are a woman."

"I do work hard at it, but sometimes get discouraged. This piece is particularly difficult, and Signor Cavalcanti will have expected me to have learned this movement by Friday. Remember when we dreamed of becoming great artists overnight? Well, now I know how much hard work and discipline it takes. And you are right: as a woman, this music will never be my life. But I am determined to keep it a part of my life. Come, let's not stand here, but go into the morning room. I'll send Hotchkiss for some tea.

"Now tell me about the last three years, Judith," Barbara asked as they settled in. "They cannot have been easy for you."

"My first position *was* difficult. I was responsible for two terribly spoiled children. That I could have survived. But when their uncle started making advances and could not be convinced that I was uninterested, I decided to find another position. I was much luckier the second time. They had five children and all were a little harum-scarum, but the Thorntons are a warm, close family, and that more than made up for the occasional toad in my bed! They made me feel like one of the family, my salary was generous, and I had one half-day a week to myself."

"One half-day!"

"That is generous, my dear lady of leisure. And Lady Thornton was very involved with her children, so I seldom had full responsibility for them all at one time. At times I felt like a cousin who had come to help out, rather than a hired stranger. And one of my duties this past year was quite restful."

"What was that?" queried Barbara.

"Lord Thornton's older sister, Harriet, came to live with them. She suffers from a progressive eye disease that cannot be cured, and she is almost completely blind. I spent some of my day as her companion, walking with her and reading to her. She is a wonderful person, intelligent and independent, and much more accepting of her handicap than I could ever dream of being. We had long conversations on literature and life that reminded me of the talks we used to have." Judith smiled. "All in all, I was very lucky, Barbara. And I knew that it was only for a limited time. Now, that is enough of me. Your come-out was last year, and you are still not wed? Are you considered to be on the shelf yet?'' teased Judith.

''I'll have you know that if I was not the incomparable of the Season, I was quite the thing, despite my excess inches. I received no less than three proposals! In fact, I refused an earl last year.'' Barbara's eyes sparkled mischievously.

''An earl? Why did you refuse such a good match?''

''Well, if you must know, it was Julian, Lord Denver, and since he is but twelve years old, I told him I was flattered, but thought he deserved someone a bit younger.''

''Robbing the cradle proved too unconventional even for you, eh? However did this proposal come about?''

''We both met often in the park. He and I both share a rebellious streak. He was escaping his mama, and I was riding off some steam at mine. We agreed to be friends and support each other. We have visited the zoo together, and the water-works. I must say I have found him the most pleasant, most amusing male I've met in months. And he does not mind in the least my being bookish. He said, quite seriously, it might be very pleasant to have a wife with whom one could discuss politics intelligently.''

''Seriously, Barbara,'' Judith said after they had finished laughing, ''have you truly emerged heart-whole?''

''With regards to those proposals, oh, yes.'' Barbara bent her head over the teapot. ''More tea?''

'' 'With regards to those proposals'? So there might be someone who has not proposed whom you might have accepted?''

Barbara looked up at Judith and made a comically despairing face.

''Oh, Judith, I really have not admitted it, even to myself, but I am in a bad way.''

''Who is this heartless one? Don't tell me. He is years older and only looking for someone to run his household? No, no, he is a radical and does not even believe in the married state?''

''Oh, worse. He is everything I thought I despised. He is a top of the trees, drives to an inch, spars at Jackson's, gambles, and up until this fall flirted with the prettiest young debutantes.

He is, in short, utterly charming, utterly inappropriate, and decidedly not interested in a tall, musical lady.''

"And who is this villain?"

"Robert, the Viscount Devenham."

"Wasn't he the young man who was always hanging about the summer I visited you?"

"Yes." Barbara blushed. "We have grown up together, and that is why he never looks at me. And how I could form a *tendre* for someone so far from our old ideal, I'm sure I don't know."

"I remember him as witty and charming. A bit mischievous, perhaps, but he spoke quite responsibly about his tenants, did he not?" Judith also remembered him as boyish and suspected that the motherly side of her friend was drawn to the viscount. There was certainly no harm in him, she thought, but not much that could ultimately hold Barbara, who was essentially a serious person.

"Yes, he does take his duties seriously when he is at home. In the city, he has thrown himself into the social whirl. He is an only child, you see, and his father would not let him apply for a commission. He wanted very much to be in the thick of things, and feels it deeply that many of his friends went to war and he could not."

"So there is a reason for his apparent frivolousness."

"Yes. But I suppose what still bothers me is that he is not at all that paragon of virtue that we used to imagine for ourselves. He is most certainly not stupid, but I can't imagine having long conversations with him. How can one's heart be so inconsistent with one's head?"

"The eternal question, my dear." Judith laughed. "It sounds like he cannot see you as anything but Robin's little sister."

"Yes. And the worst of it is that this fall he has stopped his flirting, and is hovering around the Lady Diana Grahame."

"Who is . . . ?"

"Several Seasons out, three years older than Dev, and someone with whom, I am convinced, Robin was, and perhaps still is, in love."

"And the Lady Diana?"

"I don't know. I thought when Robin left for the continent they had reached an understanding. But he left in such a black mood that I was afraid for him. It seemed to me as though he were ready to throw himself into the most dangerous situation. Thank God, he returned unhurt. But he and Diana do no more than exchange courtesies now. She seems quite willing to let Dev make a fool of himself over her. Oh, I know I shouldn't say that, but she is much more sophisticated than he is, Judith. She is beautiful and glamorous, and if she has a heart to break, she keeps it well hidden.''

Barbara took a deep breath. "Well, I certainly needed to tell someone all that, didn't I? But it is a relief. I have been feeling all kinds of a fool for months.''

"It doesn't sound foolish to me. Devenham might not match up to our old schoolgirl fantasies, but we are both older and wiser. I doubt that either of us would be attracted to such perfection, even if it did exist. His attraction for the Lady Diana will surely pass, as these feelings of admiration for older women usually do.''

"I had hoped so, Judith, but there seems to be no sign of it. He hangs around her, always claims her for two dances as well as supper. She has not discouraged other admirers, but always demonstrates her preference for Dev. But this is too much of me! What are your plans, now that you are in London, Judith?''

"I intend to revel in my freedom, my friendship with you, and settle into a comfortable existence balancing housekeeping and painting.''

"How is your painting going?''

"It was difficult to find time for it these past three years, and so I almost feel as if I were starting all over again. But I have kept to my sketching, and now hope to work with watercolor again. I would love to attempt oils, but I am not sure but that my talent is for small things, and I intend to keep to a strict schedule. I would like to try to sell some of my work, if possible. I want to bring in a small income so that I am not completely dependent upon Stephen. He is quite likely to marry within the next few years, and I will not want to remain as the dependent sister.''

"And what about you, Judith? Do you no longer wish for a home of your own and children?''

"Yes, I do at times, Barbara. But it is unlikely to happen now. Perhaps if my father were still alive, there might have been some introduction into society. I come of a good family, but there is no money beyond my small settlement and what Stephen and I earn by ourselves. No, I have resigned myself to my fate . . . and indeed, it is not such a bad fate. I will paint, and I will be a doting aunt to Stephen's children and a doting godmother to yours, if you will let me."

Barbara could not deny Judith's analysis of her position. Her friend had been deprived, by her father's death, of the possibilities of meeting any eligible man. And as a single woman in London, keeping house for her brother, she would meet none but her brother's friends—and most of them too young.

"I am not going to allow you to hide yourself away. You are too intelligent and warm a woman to remain alone."

"Oh, no. I can guess what you are about to say. I will not presume on our friendship, and indeed, cannot continue it, if you cannot accept the differences in the lives that we lead, Barbara." Judith was adamant. "I have no money for the clothes that socializing would require. And truly, no desire for it. What you can do for me is to continue to be my good friend."

"And is a good friend to see you and encourage you to sink into obscurity? Ignore the fact that you enjoy riding and the theater and dancing? You do miss riding, I am sure, Judith. Must we see each other only over tea?"

Judith's eyes had widened at the thought of being able to ride again. "I do have an old habit. I am years out of practice, but if you could stand to be seen with me, I confess that I am sorely tempted. Oh, Lord, see how my good intentions go flying out the window when horses are mentioned. I was more upset over the loss of our horses than over any other change in our circumstances."

"Robin has several hacks in town, and I am sure he would not object to your making one of them your own," offered Barbara.

"It had better be an old hack for me. Oh, I will accept your offer. But not for the fashionable hours in the afternoon. My riding habit would not stand up to close scrutiny, and besides, I would not want anyone to witness me falling off the first few times."

"Robin rides early a few days a week to get in a good gallop, and I often join him. I'll talk to him today. And now that we have the riding settled, I'll have to convince you to come to dinner."

"I do appreciate your kindness, Barbara, but don't you see it would be awkward for both of us? I do plan to be earning some money soon, but right now there is nothing extra with which to replenish my wardrobe."

"I wish we were of a size. I have a closetful of dresses."

Judith laughed. "The alterations would cost as much as a new gown," she said, looking down at her small, rather thin self, and over at her friend's tall, full figure.

"I suppose you are right," Barbara said ruefully. "I am rather a 'strapping wench,' am I not?"

"You are goddesslike. And you certainly have grown more comfortable with your inches. You used to hunch yourself over, and now you carry yourself quite proudly."

"I have your encouragement to thank for it. I would have expired from loneliness and self-consciousness had you not taken me under your wing."

"I must admit, it was difficult," said Judith. "I had to stand quite on tiptoe, and even then my wings did not quite reach," she teased.

Both women laughed at the picture Judith had conjured up, for a most unlikely-looking protector was Judith.

At that moment, Barbara heard Robin's steps in the hall. She jumped up. "That's Robin. Wait here, I'll be right back."

Judith smiled at her friend's impulsiveness. Her come-out had not really changed her. She had acquired some town bronze, but was still the same Barbara: enthusiastic, generous to a fault, and unconcerned over the differences in their circumstances. She heard Barbara say, "Go in, Robin, and I will order more tea."

Robin appeared in the doorway. Judith had met him several times when he came to pick Barbara up at school, and then had spent part of a summer holiday and one Christmas vacation at Ashurst. She suspected—quite correctly—that initially Barbara had hoped they would be romantically inclined toward each other. But Judith's first impression had been that Robin was too handsome. He was tall and well-proportioned like his sister, and they both had the same wavy blond hair and light-blue eyes. He initially gave the appearance of languid elegance, and Judith had at first been rather intimidated. What saved him was his sense of fun and lack of pretense. His parents deserved the credit for those qualities in both their children. Lord and Lady Stanley were quite happy in their marriage, and although more involved with socializing and estate matters and each other than with their children, they were free of the snobbery of many of their contemporaries. They mixed with their neighbors freely, attending the local assemblies when in the country, and freed their children from an extreme awareness of class.

Judith had felt very welcome at Ashurst, and after she got used to Robin's good looks and stopped letting them prejudice her against him, he and she had become fast friends.

Robin stood for a moment in the doorway, and Judith took in the changes wrought by three years and the last campaign. Before, he had been slender, and now he looked filled out, although somewhat drawn and tired. His face was the same, and yet not. The laugh lines were there, but now there were other lines that pain and fatigue had left, and something of an edge to his smile. His face had gained in character, however, what it had lost in innocence.

Robin came toward her, his hands outstretched in welcome. She rose to meet him.

"Ju—I mean, Miss Ware, how lovely to see you again."

"Must I call you Captain Stanley? May we not go back to Judith and Robin?"

"You must call me Major Stanley."

Judith's face had subtly changed at the formality, and Robin laughed. "I've been promoted, is all, and of course you must call me Robin. You are such a young lady now that I thought I'd better start out more formal."

"You haven't changed at all, Robin. Still a tease. Come, sit down."

Robin sat and turned to Judith. "I hear you have come to join your brother here in London."

"Yes. I am still not quite used to my freedom, but it is wonderful to be here."

"And Barbara tells me you will be kind enough to help us exercise one of our horses?"

"You are as bad as your sister. Yours is the kindness, as well you know, I hope she didn't embarrass you into it?"

"Don't be foolish. Of course you are welcome to ride with us."

"I hope you have convinced her, Robin," Barbara said as she came back into the room.

"I think so. You will ride with us?"

"How can I refuse?" Judith said, relieved that they had pressed her.

"Now we must persuade her to come to the theater with us, and to an occasional dinner or musical evening," responded Barbara.

"I have been telling your sister, Robin, that I cannot enter into society. We are living on a small income, and I have no money to spare for the wardrobe even a little socializing would require. And if I had, well, it would make me most uncomfortable to be pushing myself in where I most certainly don't belong."

"But, Judith," protested Barbara, "you will never meet anyone. If you agreed to accompany us occasionally, you would be sure to meet some eligible young men."

"Surely it is better for me to accept where life has landed me and make the best of it," replied Judith, with a slight edge of protest in her voice.

"I think Judith knows what is best for her," interrupted Robin, "and we shouldn't tease her, much as we would enjoy her companionship. However," he continued gently, turning to Judith, "you might come to dinner here occasionally, and an invitation to the theater once or twice would not be inappropriate, nor make you compromise your resolution."

"I would sound the most ungrateful, unbending Puritan if I refused. But that is all. Please do not push me harder, for, believe me, my resolve is not proof against the kindness of friends."

"Agreed," said Robin. "And now I must be off. But we shall ride the day after tomorrow? At ten o'clock? We shall bring our nag to your door."

Judith smiled and nodded. After he left, she looked at Barbara and said a bit shakily, "Truly, I am grateful for such good friends."

"Judith, you must learn to receive as well as to give," said Barbara, surprising herself. "I never thought of it quite that way before, but, yes, that is it. You are a generous person, Judith, but friendship works both ways, and your pride keeps you from letting others give to you in return."

"You are right, of course," admitted Judith. "One feels somehow stronger when one is the giver. Oh, I am not explaining myself well, but I thank you for your bit of wisdom."

"I promise I won't push you, if you promise to remain open to an occasional entertainment?"

"Agreed," said Judith.

"Now, let me show you the garden. There are still some late roses. And then we can have a light luncheon and spend the rest of the afternoon telling each other all the details of the last three years."

3

Major Stanley was not the only one of his friends who had tried to see the Duke of Sutton. Simon was very popular. He was an excellent athlete, graceful dancer, and his valet never had reason to be ashamed of his appearance. But what made Simon so attractive was that his natural intelligence and dignity were combined with a genuine liking for most people. If he stood a little removed from the utter frivolity of *ton* life, he did so humorously, not cynically. He had served in the Peninsular campaign and on the continent, not because it was a dashing and fashionable thing to do, but because he saw it as a necessity. He had not been very romantic about the idea of war, and the reality of it only strengthened his wish to put his peacetime energies into eliminating some of its causes. He had planned to take his seat in Parliament upon his return and work toward reform, in both domestic and foreign policy.

He had been wounded on the second day of battle. Having had two horses shot from under him without sustaining an injury, he had begun to think that he might make it back unharmed—if he thought much about it at all. He had found, in his years of soldiering, that the first hour before the battle and the first fifteen minutes into it were the worst. Then, he was terrified. But as he was drawn into it, it became a job, something to get done. When you got caught up in the momentum, you were only present to what was happening directly in front of you: an arm lifting a saber, the body you were stepping over, the shell whistling by your ear. And so, when it happened, it happened quickly, and without him expecting it. Simon remembered leaning over a wounded friend, the Viscount Alderstoke, and then a sudden blow to his head, and then nothing.

When he awoke he was lying on a farmer's cart that smelled of turnips and onions and blood. He had been thrown on top of a pile of wounded and dead men. He was conscious of the

weight of an arm across his knees, and such unbearable pain
in his head that he groaned aloud.

The sergeant driving the cart turned at the sound and said
to his companion, ''Well, that's one wot still breathes. I'll be
surprised if one out of three survives this ride,'' and he flapped
the reins across the back of the cart horse.

Simon's headache and the jolting made him nauseous. He
opened his eyes slowly, afraid that light might make him even
sicker, and saw nothing. It must be the middle of the night, was
his first thought as he waited for his eyes to become accustomed
to the dark and begin to pick out shapes. This night seemed
darker than others, however, and nothing changed. The smoke
and no moon, he thought as he fell off into a state somewhere
between sleep and fainting.

When they reached their destination, a farmhouse on the edge
of the battlefield commandeered as a makeshift hospital, Simon
was jostled awake. He felt his fellow travelers being pulled out
around him, and felt hands reaching for him. He was willing
to walk, but somehow his limbs were not responding and he
allowed himself to be carried after a weak protest. He heard
a voice say, ''Here's one who'll likely make it. He's covered
in blood, but he's got all his arms and legs, not like the other
poor devils.''

Simon's eyes opened and he was ready to smile up into the
eyes of whoever was leaning over him when he realized that
it was still dark, even inside wherever it was that they had
brought him. Surely there is at least a candle, he thought, and
he pulled himself up from the floor to look around. Nothing.

''Where are the lights?'' he started to say, and felt a hand
on his shoulder. ''Steady, sir. There's a wall behind you. Here,
let me help you up.'' Simon's eyes closed involuntarily as his
head exploded at the movement, but once he was upright, the
pain and nausea subsided. He heard a voice near his ear and
felt something warm near his face. ''Can you see the lamp now,
sir?'' Simon turned toward the voice and said almost inaudibly,
''No.''

''Dr. Shipman, over here,'' said the voice.

Simon heard steps approaching and an impatient voice saying,
''What is it, Lieutenant? I am just about to operate. I don't have
time for men like these who will be walking home.''

"I think you should examine him just for a moment, sir."
"All right."

Simon felt the doctor's hands probe gently around his skull. He winced as the hands started to wipe some of the blood away. "He has sustained severe blows to the head, but we knew that. You are quite lucky, Captain. A little closer to the temples and you would not be here. As it is, you will have a head like you have never known. Give me the lantern, and I'll check for concussion.

"Look directly into the light, Captain."

Simon passed his hands over his eyes as if to see if they were open. "I can see nothing," he said quietly, realizing that the warmth he had felt near his face was the lantern and that all that was reaching him was its heat, not light.

The doctor lifted the lantern and leaned closer. He moved it left and right, and into Simon's face until he drew back from the heat.

"That is why I called you over," whispered the lieutenant.

"Quite right, John. What is your name, Captain?"

"Simon Ballance. I am attached to Wellington's staff as a dispatcher."

"Do you remember anything about being wounded?"

"Nothing. I saw a friend of mine and dismounted to help him. There was so much blood. His legs were gone." Simon shuddered.

"Yes," the doctor said gently.

"I was leaning over him and then something hit me from behind, as though someone were driving down with a rifle butt. I was conscious of nothing until I awoke in the cart."

"And could you see anything then?"

"I thought it was a dark night—smoke from the battle-field . . . No, I couldn't see. But there is nothing wrong with my eyes. The blow was from behind."

"The blow was from behind, yes, but it looks as if you were repeatedly struck on both sides of your head. Sometimes, we are not sure how, blindness can be caused by internal damage to the brain. Your eyes work, but your brain can no longer receive the message."

"Blind? I can't be blind," protested Simon. "If my eyes are uninjured, then surely my sight will return when I recover?"

"Sometimes—and again we are largely ignorant in this area—there can be a spontaneous return of sight. But I will not give you false hope; it happens very rarely. It would be better for you to accept your blindness and adjust to it."

Simon's face contorted with pain as his head started pounding. It was like being on the rye fields of Waterloo, only the fifty-pounders were inside his head, and he lost consciousness, thinking, I can see that line of cavalry preparing to charge, so I can't be blind.

"Let him sleep. Give him a small dose of laudanum now, and when he awakes, as much as he needs to cope." The doctor turned away to resume his makeshift efforts to save limbs and, failing that, lives.

When Simon awoke hours later, he could not, at first, remember where he was. Slowly he oriented himself: he was lying on what felt like a dirt floor, on a folded blanket that smelled of horse. He could hear groaning around him, but not much else. He saw nothing. The pounding in his head had lessened, and he pulled himself up on one elbow. He felt stronger and wanted to get up and walk, to ease the stiffness in his legs and back. He also needed to relieve himself.

"Is there anyone there?" he said softly, for some reason afraid to raise his voice in the void that surrounded him. He sensed someone stirring next to him. Simon turned toward the sound. "Hallo, are you awake?"

"I am now," answered a cultured, rather annoyed voice. "What do you want?"

"What time is it? Where is the doctor?"

"I don't normally carry a watch into battle," said an amused voice. "But about ten minutes ago I heard a cock, and it seems to be getting lighter, so I would guess close to five. The doctor collapsed about an hour ago, after being up for two nights straight."

"I need the privy. Could I impose upon you to take me?"

"Said doctor relieved me of the better part of my left leg, as you can plainly see, and I haven't had time to come up with a false one, Captain. You look well enough to get there on your own. From what I understand, we are just using the back of the barn."

Simon had flinched at the man's words. "No, I can't see that your leg is off. I can't see at all. I'm sorry," he said, and his voice trailed off.

"Oh, God, what a comedy. Here am I, able to see every bloody body in the bloody place, and here you are, all right and tight, sound of limb, and you can't see a bloody thing. And for that," he muttered under his breath, "you may count yourself lucky."

The man reached out his arm and gripped Simon's shoulder, squeezing it in sympathy. "What is your name, Captain?"

"Simon Ballance."

"Mine is Peter Carstares. Lieutenant. How were you blinded? I would never have known it from your eyes."

"I was beaten by a rifle butt. The doctor last night said that the damage seems to be internal. But I am not permanently blind," said Simon hastily. "He said sight can return when the head injuries heal."

"You are quite lucky, then."

Simon was growing more uncomfortable. "Is there no one around who could take me out?"

"The staff is all asleep, and I doubt the Second Coming would wake them. The rest of us are drugged or, like me, incapable. We are too far from the door for me to guide you by voice. You'll have to wait until someone wakes up."

"And if they don't soon?"

"You'll mess yourself, as we all have done."

Simon had never felt so helpless. His head had begun to ache again, and he felt alone in a void with only a disembodied voice next to him. He remembered there was a wall behind him. He turned and groped for it, and pulling himself up to face it, he fumbled with his breeches. He urinated, he hoped, against the wall. He felt around for his blanket and lay down, only to feel it get warm and wet as the stream ran from the wall across the floor. He was humiliated, and tears slipped from the corner of his eyes as he stretched out, trying to ignore the dampness under his head. Eventually he fell into a troubled sleep.

The next few days slid together into one hazy wakening from laudanum-induced nightmares of the battlefield to the real nightmare of groans and screams, and the smell of blood and vomit and piss and excrement. When there was a lull, orderlies did attempt to maintain cleanliness. Simon was led outside a few times, but more often than not, he and the rest of the men lay in soiled clothes and bedding. He was dirty and smelly and thirsty, and maintained his sanity by repeating to himself that it would not last, and by talking to Peter. They talked about their homes, Simon describing the Sussex Downs and Peter waxing eloquent about the Yorkshire moors. Peter was the eldest son of a gentleman with a small estate. He had been stationed in London, so he and Simon had mutual acquaintances. Peter kept up an amused commentary on their situation and described the layout of the barn for Simon. This he found helpful when the orderlies had the chance to guide him outside, since they were constantly forgetting he couldn't see, and he found himself tripping over legs and banging his shoulders on the door. No one could have guessed it from his demeanor, but he was terrified. He felt, with every step, that he was about to fall from a great height. He returned to his filthy blanket gratefully, for it, at least, was known.

There were moments, however, when Peter would groan in his sleep, and Simon would be pulled out of his own hell. One night Simon woke to a choking sound next to him. He groped for Peter.

"Are you all right?"

The choking sound stopped, but Simon was too worried to let it go.

"What can I do, Peter?"

"What can anyone do?" whispered Peter. "Dammit, I am not a vain man, but what woman would look at me now? I may as well sit at the side of the road and beg."

Simon, convinced that at least his own incapacity was temporary, was more sympathetic to Peter's state than his own.

"And it hurts," Peter sobbed suddenly. "I can *feel* the rest of my leg, but it's not there."

Simon lifted Peter's head onto his knee and smoothed back his hair, softly and rhythmically, as though he were a child. There was nothing to say, nothing to do but offer the small comfort that he could. They both fell asleep, Simon propped against the wall, arms around Peter. When Peter awoke, he blushed at the memory of the night before, but realized that he felt better for having let out some of his fears. And at least I can see, he thought. He wondered what Simon would be able to salvage of a normal life. As Simon stirred, Peter slid himself down into his own blanket, embarrassed by their moments of intimacy, and pretended to sleep.

4

The next morning, Simon was shaken awake by an orderly. "Wake up, Captain, you're to be on your way home today. All those who can walk are being sent into the city in two hours. I'll take you to the pump to clean up."

"What about Lieutenant Carstares?"

"Nah, he's not well enough yet. He'll go into Brussels with you, but stay there until he's strong enough to get about on crutches. Come on, then."

Simon washed as thoroughly as he could, although it seemed rather pointless, since he would have to put on his filthy uniform again. Perhaps in Brussels there would be clean clothes. At the thought of clean clothes and warm water and soap, some of his depression lifted. There was a world outside this fetid barn, and although he couldn't see, he was going home. He hadn't realized how much he wanted to until now.

This time the traveling was easier. He and Peter were transported in a wagon filled with clean straw. The men were smelly, but awake, and for the most part, not in pain. Peter said, "There's four of us. You, no sight, me no leg, Smith missing an arm. And another, I don't recognize, shot through the lung. What a sight we are, but at least we're out of there."

The hospital in Brussels, though makeshift, was paradise compared to the farm. There were, of course, too many wounded and too few doctors, but many ladies had remained and volunteered as nurses. There were real beds, there was soap and water, and clean blankets. First there was a general stripping. Filthy clothes were burned and the men given clean pants and shirts. Odd sizes, of course, collected from everyone in the city. But clean.

Simon had no idea what he looked like. Probably ridiculous, he thought, since the sleeves of his rough cotton shirt hung down over his hands. His pants, on the other hand, were made for a smaller man and barely reached his ankles. He didn't care.

Peter was taken to a different room, so Simon was without his running commentary. He spent the first day being scrubbed and deloused, and it wasn't until the next morning that he was approached by any of the medical personnel. He was lying on a pallet, having insisted that he did not want to take a bed from the more seriously wounded, when he heard voices. One, speaking heavily accented English, came closer.

"And what is wrong with this man, Sergeant?"

"He is blind, Doctor."

"What is your name, Captain?"

"Simon Ballance."

"Ah, a French-sounding name."

Simon smiled. "There is a Norman ancestor somewhere, but it is well and truly a British name."

"How were you injured, Captain?"

"A rifle butt. All I can remember is the first blow to the side of my head."

"Stand up, sir."

Simon rose and the doctor offered him his arm. "Come, I wish to examine you myself," he said, and led Simon into the adjoining room and sat him down in a chair.

"Can you see anything, Captain?"

"Nothing yet, but my headaches are becoming less frequent, and the doctor at the field hospital assured me that in cases like mine, sight could return at any time."

"Hmm. Yes, that can happen, but very rarely. Did the doctor explain the reason for your blindness?"

"He seemed to think that the force of the blow led to internal damage."

"I have some knowledge of this kind of injury myself, although I am not an oculist. We do not know much about the eyes, but it is speculated that damage to the nerves can cause permanent blindness even if the eyes themselves are unharmed. If the nerve is severely affected, it will not recover. You have headaches, then?"

"Yes, and I still do, although they are not as severe."

"And you still do not see light or shape?"

"No." Simon hated to admit this, as though he were giving the doctor information to use against him.

"My opinion is that if the nerve were going to recover, it

would have begun to do so. I may be wrong, of course, but
I think the force of the blows was enough to do permanent
damage. I will not offer you false hope: I believe your blindness to be irreversible."

"I cannot accept that," said Simon, clenching his hands on
the side of the chair.

"I understand," the doctor said gently. "But the sooner you
can accept it, the sooner you can begin your adjustment."

"When can I go home?" Simon asked. "I feel it wrong that
I am taking up space when those more seriously wounded are
still lying out in those filthy field hospitals."

"There is a ship leaving in two days. I suggest you begin
to move about a bit, to restore some strength in your legs."

"Has my household been notified?"

"Yes. We dispatched the names of this group yesterday, so
there should be someone to meet you at Dover. Is there anything
else I can do for you, Captain?"

"I would like to visit a friend before I leave. Where is
Lieutenant Carstares? Can someone take me to see him?"

"I will make sure of it."

"Thank you, Doctor."

Simon stood up and reached his hand in the direction of the
voice. "I would appreciate it if you would take me back now."

The next morning he was approached by an orderly.

"Captain Ballance?"

"Yes."

"The doctor asked me to take you upstairs to visit your
friend."

Simon's face lit up, and he took the orderly's arm. He was
led to a large room with pallets and makeshift beds lining the
walls.

"Simon!" Peter's voice was warm and welcoming. "My,
we are elegant this morning, Captain," he teased. "You will
be setting a new style when you return to London. An interesting
combination: homespun and black superfine."

Simon turned toward Peter's voice and said, "I'd venture a
guess you look no more stylish than I do."

"You are right," Peter admitted. "They dressed me in black

velvet knee breeches. Sliced up the side over my bad leg, of course, so we both look rather like scarecrows. It is good to see you.''

Simon cleared his throat, which had suddenly grown tight.

"I've only come to say good-bye, Peter. I leave for Dover today.''

"Don't say it, Simon. I promise that as soon as I'm hobbling about, I will come to London. We will go out drinking and bore people to death with our war stories.''

Simon reached out and Peter grasped his hand. "I will miss you, Lieutenant,'' Simon whispered.

The orderly led him back to his room, where he sat and waited to go home.

5

The trip from Brussels was crowded and tedious. Simon felt his frustration and anger building. Not to see meant more than helplessness. It meant a sort of starvation. No sights to take one's mind off the crowded traveling conditions. No view of fields and trees on which to rest one's gaze. Just hours and hours of darkness. He found himself beginning to listen more carefully. When they passed through towns or stopped to change horses, to alleviate his boredom he would try to identify at least one activity going on around him.

The boat trip was easier. Simon had always been a good sailor, and he had himself led up to the rail, and stood there a long while, breathing in the clean scent of salt air, letting it cleanse him of the smells of battle.

When they reached Dover, he began to panic. Who of his household would be coming to meet him? Had they been told of his injury? With the crowds, how would they find him, since he could not see them?

The pier was a confusion of sounds. As they walked down the gangway, Simon could hear voices from the shore.

"There he is, Jimmy, there's your dad!" And although civilians were supposed to wait, he could hear them rushing up. One—a woman, he could tell by the rustling of her skirt—pushed by him to reach her husband. He could hear them behind him, the man and the woman, crying and laughing at the same time.

The sergeant who had Simon's arm asked, "Who should I be looking for, Captain?"

"I think that my secretary will be here. He is a young man, tall, with black hair. My valet may be with him: short, stocky, balding."

The sergeant looked at Simon in surprise. A secretary and a valet? This unassuming young man? It was obvious that Simon was well-bred, but he had never pushed himself forward or complained the whole trip.

He saw two men fitting Simon's description separate from the crowd. They were waving slowly at first, and then frantically, to get Simon's attention. As the sergeant steered him in their direction, he heard them call out, "Over here, your grace. He seems fine, Martin, why doesn't he look at us?"

Simon heard Francis' voice and turned toward him, looking not at him, but to the left. As Francis lifted his arms to wave, he suddenly realized what a "head injury" might have resulted in. The sergeant with Simon—no, *leading* Simon—mouthed the word "blind" as they drew closer. Francis felt his stomach turn, and he and Martin looked at each other in dismay.

"Is that you, Francis?" he heard the duke ask.

"Yes, your grace," he answered, stepping to Simon's other side. "We are very happy to have you home."

"Not half as happy as I am to be here. Do you have a guinea on you? Could you give it to the sergeant here? He has been most kind to me this whole trip." Simon turned toward his guide. "Thank you, Sergeant, for all your help."

"I can't take anything, Captain—I mean, your grace."

"Of course you can. I know it was part of your duties, but I appreciate your patience more than I can say."

"Thank you, your grace. Good luck to you," said the sergeant, and saluted before he walked away, fingering the gold coin in his hand.

"Now, Francis," Simon said, "take my arm and get me home. Is Martin with you?"

"Yes. Right here, sir."

"Good. You must be speechless at my attire, Martin, which, I understand from a friend, is an odd combination of the rustic and formal. But there was nothing else in Brussels. Indeed, I have begun to think homespun could be the next style. I might stay with it," teased Simon, trying to put them all more at ease.

Martin laughed, along with Francis, as Simon had meant them to.

"Did the letter tell you anything of my injury, Francis?"

"All we heard was a slight head injury, your grace. We were not prepared for . . ."

"Blindness? Just as well, for it is not a permanent state, Francis. I was very lucky that my eyes escaped injury, and I am convinced a few weeks at Sutton will restore me."

Francis' face lifted as he heard Simon's words, and he led him toward the coach.

They arrived at Sutton in the afternoon. A stableboy had been posted at the gate, and ran up the drive to alert the servants when he espied the coach. They all lined up in front of the house, with Mrs. Wolfit, the housekeeper, at the head.

Francis climbed out and handed Simon down. The duke looked unharmed. Thinner and older, of course, but with no sign of injury, and all of them, who held Simon in great affection, wore smiles of relief. When Francis took the duke's arm, however, and led him over to Mrs. Wolfit for a greeting, it became obvious that Simon could not see.

"He's blind," muttered one footman, only to be nudged on the arm by the one next to him.

"By God, you are right," said his attacker after a moment.

Simon heard the whispering and could guess what was being said. He had never considered himself a proud man, but he must be, he decided, or he would not feel this degree of humiliation. It had been hard at the hospital, his feeling of helplessness, but there were others around who were also helpless. Here, among able-bodied civilians, he felt on exhibit.

He walked toward the house, lost in self-consciousness, and almost tripped on the first step. Francis was not used to guiding a blind man and kept forgetting that obstacles hardly noticeable to him were not there for Simon until he hit them or tripped over them. The pain in his foot brought Simon back to his surroundings. After all, he had grown up here; he ought to remember what he couldn't see. He set himself to count the steps up, and then the steps to the door.

Inside, it all became too much for him. He did not want to make the effort of moving around his own house so carefully; he wanted to move freely. He realized now that at some level he had been expecting that just the arrival home would restore his sight. Instead, coming home had only reminded him of what he could not do, of the mobility he had lost. Instead of resting his sight on the Downs, instead of drinking in the warm red brick of Sutton, instead of smiling into the welcoming faces of his staff, he was standing in his hall, feeling like a stranger. No one around him had been in the hell of Waterloo. No one was limited. He was where he had longed to be, and he felt he didn't belong.

I'd rather have lost my leg like Peter, he thought bitterly as he pushed down his rage and frustration. His face took on an expression of aloofness foreign to his nature, and his voice an ironic tone, as though he were removed from all of this. As he indeed was. Simon retreated, and left the Duke of Sutton to cope with his life.

6

July passed slowly for everyone at Sutton. The staff was ever on the alert for the duke, ready to help him from one room to the other, beginning to realize that any small thing out of place, like a chair not set back after sweeping, became a hazard for a blind man. Francis found it impossible to interest Simon in what had occurred during his absence. Anyone asked to explain the heaviness that hung over the house would have said they were waiting, waiting for Simon to return. For although his body was certainly present and although he was as polite and considerate as ever to his servants, he himself was elsewhere, also waiting. Every morning he would open his eyes slowly, thinking, This will be the morning. He only went for walks around the house. Francis suggested a ride in his curricle, and Simon refused. The neighbors who came to call were turned away. Mrs. Wolfit had free rein with the house, but when in residence the duke had always listened and made suggestions when she talked over a decision with him. Now he just nodded and said in his removed manner, "I'm quite sure you have made the correct decision, Mrs. Wolfit."

"There is no heart in him," she told Watkins, the butler. "He is like a shadow of his former self."

The cook wore himself out, first cooking all of Simon's favorites and then experimenting with the latest continental specialties. Simon sent back both his compliments and half the food on his plate to the kitchen. He had lost weight immediately after Waterloo, and since his return he had been losing more, so his clothes were beginning to hang on his tall frame.

One morning in the beginning of August he called Francis into the breakfast room.

"Francis, I wish to return to London."

Francis' face lit up. This was the first sign of interest he had seen in the duke for weeks.

"And when do you wish the house opened, your grace?"

"Immediately. I intend to follow you in a few days in the coach. I have decided it is time to consult with a specialist. My headaches are almost gone and I haven't seen a physician since Brussels. An oculist will be able to give me a better notion as to when my sight may return."

"Do you wish me to make an appointment, your grace?"

"Yes. Then I won't have to waste any time when I arrive."

"Yes, your grace."

Francis and Martin had discussed the duke's optimism about recovery and, in fact, had consulted with the local physician, for they had no idea whether the duke was denying a permanent handicap, or indeed correct that his sight would miraculously return. Dr. Howes, who had treated the duke's family and household for years, listened thoughtfully.

"It is true sight does return in some cases, but very rarely, Francis. If the duke still sees nothing, no shapes or shadows, I am quite sure that this is a permanent condition. I think he is holding on to hope as long as he can, and I don't think at this point we should try to take it from him. I am old enough to know people need to protect themselves from some things they are not yet ready to face. From what you have told me, he has adjusted to his blindness only as much as is necessary. I think he is afraid to take the next step, which would mean facing what he can never do again, and finding out what he is capable of."

Francis had agreed with the old doctor and never pushed the duke to receive visitors, go out more, or make estate decisions. This visit to a specialist, thought Francis, may be a sign that he wants to find out, one way or another. I hope so, for none of us can live in this limbo much longer.

Simon followed Francis up to town two days later. Once again he was thrown into a state of disorientation, in what were familiar surroundings. This time, however, he was better prepared, and within a day or so was moving about the town house more easily. It was a good time to be in the city for someone not interested in socializing. Most of the *ton* were still in the country, and would gradually return for the Little Season. Enough of Simon's friends were around, however, that the tray in the hall was rarely empty of cards. All were turned away politely but firmly. Those who were mere acquaintances did not return, but a few old friends, like Robin, persisted. But the staff, however much they deplored Simon's decision to isolate himself, were a loyal and protective group, and so even a close friend like Major Stanley was turned away repeatedly.

Simon's appointment with the royal oculist was on his second week in London. Francis accompanied him and led him into the examination room. The doctor probed Simon's skull and then moved a candle close to Simon's face, and then away, then from side to side. There was no response. Simon blinked, not at the light but at the heat, and he stared straight ahead the whole time, not tracking at all from right to left.

The doctor sat down opposite the duke. "Your grace, what did the doctors in the field hospital tell you?"

Simon repeated their diagnosis.

"I can only agree with them, I am afraid. I think the blows to your head were enough to cause permanent damage. Your headaches are almost gone, and yet you still see nothing?"

Simon nodded.

"The best advice I can give you is to begin to accept your blindness. There are many things you are still capable of doing. You are young; you have your health, a position in society, and the money to obtain all the help you need. You can still live a very full life. I urge you to do so."

Simon stared blankly to the right of the doctor, not even attempting to follow his voice. He could no longer maintain his denial in the face of a specialist's diagnosis. Weeks had passed, and he still saw nothing.

"Thank you, Doctor. Could you send my secretary in?"

"Of course. And believe me when I say that I am sorry I cannot give better news. You could, of course, seek another opinion."

"No, I am finished with opinions," said Simon. "Francis?"

"Yes, your grace?"

"Take me home."

Simon said nothing on the ride from Harley Street. Francis was happy that the waiting was over. Maybe this final word would free the duke to resume his life again.

The next day, however, was like preceding ones. Simon refused visitors and spent much of his day in the library, staring into the fire as though he could see the flames. There was no way he could imagine resuming his former life. The *ton* valued money and physical perfection. Even though he despised the superficiality and hypocrisy of many of his peers, his position required that he socialize. That he go to the theater, the opera, attend assemblies, and dance with the latest crop of young ladies.

But now, how could he move through an evening knowing that people would be staring and gossiping, some with malice and others with pity? Of the two, Simon preferred the former. And it would not all be behind his back. It would be right in front of his face, and he would not be able to see it. The doctor's advice seemed laughable. By the end of the week, however, he was finding it difficult just to sit.

He had taken the diagnosis in, and while there was still some irrational hope that he would prove them all wrong, he was beginning to become more aware of his surroundings, and indeed, beginning to be bored by inactivity and lack of stimulation. The numbness of the previous months was wearing off.

He paced the library, running his finger along the back of the big leather sofa. At the end of the week, he found himself running his fingers over the backs of his books and, realizing even that comfort was denied him, hurled one onto the floor. Then it occurred to him that although he couldn't read, he could be read to. Surely that would help to pass the time until . . . Simon wasn't sure until what. Until this nightmare passed and he awoke to find it only a dream.

He rang for the butler and summoned Francis.

"Yes, your grace?" Francis noticed a difference in the duke. He seemed more pleasant, and not off in a black musing.

"Francis, I want you to hire me a reader."

"A reader, your grace?"

"Yes, Francis, a reader," Simon repeated, with that edge to his voice which had been there since his return. "Someone who could spend a few hours a week helping me pass the time."

"Very good, your grace. How would you like me to go about it?"

"Place an advertisement in the *Post*. You will know how to word it. I am sure there is some retired clerk out there or some young tutor who wishes to make a little money. I will start with two mornings a week. You can interview the first applicants and then bring me one or two that seem most suitable. And, Francis, I want a stranger. Is that clear?"

"Yes, your grace, I'll see to it immediately."

Francis spoke formally, as though he and Simon had never had a more relaxed relationship as master and servant. He knew that Simon's resentment of his dependence on Francis showed itself in increased formality, and he tried not to take it to heart. He had taken Simon's cue, and was most impersonal, the perfect employee. But it was hard, at the moment, not to respond naturally. This was the first sign that the duke was beginning to accept his condition and starting to adjust to it. Francis forbore from pointing out that any one of Simon's friends would have been very happy to spare him a few hours. He sensed it would seem less humiliating to the duke to have a stranger come to the house as the first visitor. The fact that the duke would be paying for the service also made him less dependent. Francis went off immediately to draw up the advertisement and had a footman deliver it to Fleet Street that afternoon.

7

Judith was beginning to settle into her new life: breakfast with Stephen and then, on some mornings, a ride with the Stanleys. Occasionally she took a light luncheon with them and then returned home to help Hannah with the household. For a few hours in the afternoon, she was usually able to concentrate on her art.

She was pleased with her new freedom and the resumption of her friendship with Robin and Barbara. If at times she envied Barbara's description of an assembly or an evening at the theater, no one would have known. She was determined to stand by her decision to live within the constraints of her situation.

The only thing missing was the extra income she wished to bring in. At first, she had intended to sell a few of her sketches, or perhaps give art lessons to young ladies of the *ton*. But caricatures and oils were more popular than her delicate watercolors, and the cold reception she received at one small shop had intimidated her so much that she pursued it no further. Instead, she decided to wait until more people returned to town and ask Barbara to mention her availability as a drawing teacher.

Barbara, well aware of Judith's pride, was determined not to push her. What she was hoping to do, at the very least, was treat her to an early Christmas present and give her a new dress and an evening out at the theater. She knew that Judith wanted work and that teaching drawing would be the most appropriate source of income for her, and she fully intended to canvas her acquaintances in Judith's behalf. But when she opened the *Post* one morning and, avoiding the news, read the advertisements for amusement, she was intrigued by one which read: "Reader wanted two mornings a week for blind nobleman. Apply to Whithedd and Pierce, the Strand."

It must be Simon, she thought immediately, and jumped up to find her brother and confirm her guess.

Robin was in the library, at his desk, when Barbara rushed in, apologizing for the interruption but obviously intent upon speaking to him immediately.

"This had better be important, my dear sister, since I just lost my place in this column of figures."

"Robin, do you read the advertisements in the newspaper?"

"Barbara, this is beyond anything annoying. If this is all you came in for—"

"Hear me out, Robin. I read them for amusement, and look what I found in this morning's paper." She showed Robin. "It must be Simon."

"It is. That is the name of the family man of business. I can't understand why he thinks he needs to hire someone when he has got any number of friends who would be happy to read for him," Robin said rather angrily.

"Perhaps he doesn't want to be dependent upon the goodwill of friends. But this seems like a good sign to me, and it is perfect that he has advertised."

"Oho, I think we are getting to the source of your excitement."

"Judith, Robin! She read for a blind person in her last position, and she wants to earn some money and we would hear from her just how Simon is doing—"

"Slow down, my dear. The advertisement specifically requests that 'gentlemen' apply."

"Pooh! I'll speak to Francis and at least get her an interview."

Robin looked at Barbara thoughtfully. "If Francis is willing to recommend her for an interview, and if Simon is not set on a man, Judith might do very well. But haven't Judith and Simon met?"

"Yes. The last winter Judith was in school she came to Ashurst for the Christmas holidays. You and Simon were on leave. That was the year of the big snowstorm. Remember we were housebound for a few days?"

"I recall we gambled and danced and read aloud."

"It was lovely. And then, when we could finally get out, we went for a sleigh ride and you nearly overturned us in a snowdrift. But that was almost three years ago, Robin. Simon and Judith got on very well, but do you think that a ten-day acquaintance would stay in his memory for this long?"

"Probably not. There was no question of an attachment. We were all just good friends and companions. Judith would have been my little sister's friend from school, someone with whom he passed the time enjoyably, but not someone he ever asked about again."

"Well, he was foolish not to form a *tendre* for her, but I am glad of that now, because I think she can safely apply for this post without being recognized. After all, he cannot see her. Should she give her real name, do you think?"

"Wait a minute. Judith doesn't even know of this yet. We can ask her tomorrow if she is interested, and in the meantime, I'll call on Francis this afternoon."

Robin was wrong. Judith had been reading the advertisements daily, hoping to find something that would only take up a few days of the week. That same morning, she had taken the paper from Stephen while he went to finish dressing, and the word "reader" had immediately caught her attention. When her brother returned to the breakfast room, she was copying the information down.

"Have you found something of interest, Judith?"

She looked up and smiled. "Yes, something for which I am ideally suited," and she passed over the paper.

"I hate to dampen your enthusiasm, but it specifically asks for a gentleman. And do you think it is quite suitable for a young woman to be closeted with a man for hours every week?"

Judith found herself becoming annoyed as Stephen tried to dampen her enthusiasm. She had begun to realize over the past few weeks that her brother was far more conventional than she, and occasionally overbearing! Of course, it came from his concern for her, but also from his view of the world. Stephen was determined to succeed as a barrister and, through hard work and, he hoped, an advantageous marriage, establish himself in a position more appropriate to their background. To this end he worked long hours, carefully building his reputation as a hardworking, trustworthy young professional. If he had ever, when younger, questioned the conventions as his sister had, he was certainly committed to them now. Things had changed for both of them after the death of their father, but Stephen, at least, had the hope of a better future—a future, moreover, which was in his own hands. He had no desire to jeopardize it by taking unfashionable stands, and he and Judith had already had some mild disagreements.

It was clear to Judith that she and her brother would always have a warm and loving relationship. They shared happy memories and an interest in art and literature, but on some serious questions they were far apart. For now, while Stephen was at the beginning of his career, she knew they could live together very comfortably. But she foresaw a time when her independence and more radical opinions would interfere with their easy domestic arrangement. As Stephen became successful, and when he finally married, she would be in an uncomfortable position. This realization made her all the more determined to find a way to earn some money and perhaps be able to put a little aside for the future.

"Surely my reputation is in no danger. To whom could it matter? And as for myself, what real danger could there be from an octogenarian, sightless earl or duke?"

"I suppose you are right. But I cannot like the idea of you again at the beck and call of some stranger."

"I am not applying for parlormaid, Stephen," Judith said, trying to tease him from his disapproval. "It seems an ideal situation. I would only be reading a few hours a week, and have plenty of time to myself."

"Well, apply if you want to. There is no need for either of us to fly into the boughs over it, since you haven't even interviewed yet. I *am* sorry to play the 'older brother,' but I only want to take care of you."

"And I appreciate that, Stephen. Now go, before you are late, and I will no doubt greet you with the sad news that they hired a gentleman, after all."

In the meantime, having finished his business with his own secretary, Robin set out for Simon's house. He was admitted by the butler and shown into Francis immediately.

"How do you do, Major Stanley." Francis greeted Robin warmly.

He could not but appreciate the major's faithfulness to his old friend, despite constant rebuff. "Please sit down. I'll let the duke know you are here, if you wish, but he has still not received any visitors.''

''No, I won't try to see his grace today, Francis. It is you I have come to see.''

Francis looked at the major questioningly.

''It is about the advertisement you placed in the *Post*. At least we assume it was you, since I know of no other 'blind nobleman' whose solicitor is Whitbedd. Why, in God's name, does Simon think he has to hire someone? I would be happy to read for him.''

''I know that,'' Francis replied. ''It does look like another isolating tactic. But I am convinced this will be a good thing. It is certainly the first interest in anything outside himself that the duke has shown in months.''

''Have you received any replies yet?'' Robin asked.

''I have no idea. This is only the first day of the advertisement. Whitbedd may have had someone apply, but has hardly had time to inform me.''

''Good, because I have found Simon a reader. She will be perfect.''

''She? The duke requested a gentleman.''

''Yes, I saw that. But would he not agree to interview a young woman whom you recommend?''

''Perhaps. Who is it you have in mind?''

''She is Miss Judith Ware. She and Barbara were at school together. She is what you might call a gentlewoman in straitened circumstances. Good family, but no title or money. She left school to become a governess for three years. In one household there was a blind woman, and Judith read to her.''

''Why is she now in London?''

''Her brother is down from Oxford, reading law. They have set up a house together and have only a small income. She is looking for a way to supplement it, and this position would be just the thing. I would feel reassured, Simon would have an excellent reader and Judith would have the extra income she needs.''

''It sounds commonsensical to me,'' said Francis. ''But the duke wants no one connected with his former life.''

''She would not have to reveal the connection,'' Robin said.

"She would be the plain Miss Ware, telling what, after all, is the truth about her background and never having to mention us at all. Are you free now? Shall we go over to Whithedd and see where he has got with this?"

"All right," said Francis. "This feels like it is moving out of my hands very quickly, but I can't see what harm it would do to present her case to the duke. If he refuses to see her, it does not radically change things, since we will eventually find a reader."

8

As Francis and Robin were finishing their conversation, Judith arrived in the city. She had taken a hackney to the Strand and stood in front of Whithedd and Pierce for a moment before going in. She inquired of the clerk in the front room if Mr. Whithedd or Mr. Pierce were available.

"Mr. Pierce has been dead for eleven years, miss," he replied with a look of disdain on his face, "and Mr. Whithedd can only be seen by appointment. I don't believe you have one?"

"No, I do not, but I did not think it necessary, as I am come to answer the advertisement Mr. Whithedd placed in the *Morning Post*."

"The advertisement for a reader? He wants a gentleman, I am sure."

"Yes, I know," Judith said patiently. "But I have had some experience with a blind person. Surely he could spare me a few minutes?"

"I will see," said the clerk, realizing from her tone that Judith was not to be easily discouraged.

A moment later, he appeared in the doorway.

"I am sorry, miss, but Mr. Whithedd says that this position would not be at all proper for an unmarried young lady."

Judith opened her mouth, ready to protest, but saw, from the clerk's expression, that she would never get past him or, indeed, the absurd rules that made it inappropriate for her to earn her living reading to some elderly nobleman. As the clerk gestured her toward the door, she said with a touch of irony, "Don't worry, I'll find my own way. Thank you for your time."

When the outer door closed behind her, she leaned against it for a moment and choked back a sob. It was ridiculous, of course, but she had, as usual, gotten ahead of reality, and pictured herself earning money for present pleasures and future independence. And to be turned down for some antiquated notion of propriety!

She was just about to move away from the doorway when she heard someone calling her name. She looked up and was surprised to see Robin and another young man walking toward her.

"Judith, what are you doing here?"

"Making a fool of myself. I had read an advertisement in the *Post* for a—"

"Reader?"

"Why, yes! How did you know?"

"Barbara and I saw it too and thought of you immediately. It is perfect for you."

"So I thought. But Mr. Whitedd will not even see me. How can he think it improper for me to be reading to an elderly gentleman?"

"Elderly? Of course—you could have had no way of knowing. The 'blind nobleman' is Simon Ballance, Duke of Sutton. You met him at Ashurst one Christmas."

"Oh, Robin, no—not Simon!" Judith was distraught when she made the connection.

"Yes. I would have thought Barbara would have told you about it by now."

"No, she has never mentioned him." Judith did not add that she had remembered the duke quite well and had refrained from asking about Simon because she was embarrassed by her own interest.

"Judith," said Robin, "this is Francis Bolton, Simon's secretary."

"How do you do, Mr. Bolton."

"Let us all three storm Whitedd's office and convince him he has turned down the best candidate for the job," suggested Robin.

Fifteen minutes later, the three emerged triumphant. Robin offered to drop Judith off before continuing on with Francis. She accepted, "But only as far as Great Russell Street, Robin. I would like to walk awhile, it is such a lovely day."

When Robin dropped her off, Judith had at last some time to think. She had been so shocked at hearing Simon's name, and things had happened so quickly, that what she had done was just becoming clear to her.

Judith remembered Simon very well from her visit to the Stanleys'. She had been out riding and was returning to the stableyard when Simon and Robin had arrived, that Christmas three years ago. It was a dry, cold day, and the three of them were red-cheeked and invigorated. Robin had recognized Judith at once, and introduced the duke. That informal meeting in the yard, in the confusion of horses being unharnessed and baggage being lifted down—the young people stamping their numbing feet and laughing about the weather—set the tone of the next ten days. Judith forgot Simon's rank, as most were wont to do. He was good-looking, and his face was open, curious, and sympathetic, all at once. In his eyes lurked a sense of the absurd, which over the course of their visit she discovered they shared.

Judith was not returning to school with Barbara, but going on to her first position as governess. She had made up her mind to enjoy her last days of freedom, and did. Before the weather became worse, all four of them rode in the mornings. When they found themselves snowed in, they all seemed to forget their adult status and enjoyed parlor games and card-playing and endless conversations. Barbara's talent was obvious even then, so each evening they retired to the music room and ended the day with a quiet concert.

Judith had liked Simon immediately. But as the days went by, she realized that in addition to feeling he was one of the family, she was also attracted to him. They shared many opinions, on everything from politics to literature. Simon seemed to value intelligence in a young woman, unlike the young men of Judith's neighborhood. As the end of their stay drew near, she realized she was well on her way to being in love with the duke, a state she was determined to avoid. After all, she had resigned herself to her future: three years as a governess, and then London with Stephen.

In the abstract, not being a conventional young lady hurt not a bit, but never before had her straitened circumstances been brought home to her. Barbara would leave school and become part of the same social set at Simon. Had matters been different, Judith might have been doing the same. She might have looked forward to being introduced to Simon again, even dancing and flirting with him. But things were not different, and on the day before she was to leave, Judith awoke from a dream of waltzing with the duke with both pain and anger in her heart. She was very quiet at breakfast and shortly thereafter sought out the library for a place to be alone.

She spent some time randomly pulling books down from the shelves, and then she gave up. She could not concentrate. She moved over to the windows and stood gazing out at the gray day. The weather was becoming warmer and the snow was melting. The pristine whiteness was no longer. The snow was dirty, and Judith felt herself sinking into self-pity. But it is not fair, she thought. It is too hard. If I were a man, I would not have to become someone's servant.

She did not hear the door open. She was utterly sunk, and tears were beginning to slide down her cheeks.

Simon said her name softly and, when she didn't respond, moved closer and called her again. Judith started, and he apologized for disturbing her privacy. She muttered something and tried to wipe her eyes quickly with the back of her hand.

"I fear I startled you, Judith. Is something wrong?"

"No, no," she said, still facing the window.

"I do not wish to intrude, but it is clear you are upset. Can I help in any way?"

"No, your grace," said Judith, turning around.

"I thought we had agreed to be informal?"

"Yes, your . . . I mean, Simon. I am ashamed of myself. I was just indulging in a bout of self-pity. Our holiday has been so pleasant that I will hate to leave."

"You do not, I think, return to school with Barbara?"

"No, I have a position as a governess in Hertfordshire. My own school days are over."

"And do you not find that hard? Watching your friends go back to a carefree existence?"

Simon's ready sympathy touched Judith, and she lost all sense of decorum. Instead of hypocritically denying her anger, as a well-bred young woman should, she said, with a mixture of anger and grief, "Yes, I do find it hard. Had my father lived, I would have a home to go to. Might even have been brought out, had we petitioned a distant relative. But now, I must live among strangers until Stephen is down from school. I have never been so aware of the injustice in being female."

"I feel rather presumptuous in attempting to offer you comfort," said Simon, "but in a small way I do know how you feel. When I was younger, I felt very trapped by my position. I wanted the freedom to be myself, and not the Duke of Sutton. I was quite ready to chuck it all at one point and go live in a Godwin-like household!"

Judith smiled through her tears. "Surely your parents would have been horrified."

"They were already gone, which, I suppose, made it seem like a real possibility."

"Whatever kept you from it?"

"I decided that if I was born to a title, then perhaps a more useful thing to do with it than give it away to my third cousin was to use the influence I had for those causes I believed in. My ideas have modified a bit over the years, since the outcome of the revolution in France must needs give everyone pause, but I don't think I flatter myself in believing I have done some good. I have also developed a sort of philosophy over the years. I believe we are all limited in some way, after all, merely by being human. I think we find freedom in our acceptance of necessity. Of course, it is far easier, I realize, to hold to this philosophy in a position such as mine," said Simon apologetically. "If there were some way for me to help you, I would. But I could hardly take you under my protection without ruining your reputation."

Judith smiled at him. "Oh, there is nothing anyone can do, your grace. And indeed, I am being quite foolish. I have already made up my mind to what I must do, and this is only a moment of weakness. Three years is not forever, after all. I will see my brother occasionally and then I shall be free. I do not truly want to live the life of a lady of fashion. I just find myself, at times, wanting things that I don't really want, if that makes any sense at all to you?"

Simon nodded. "I do not find that hard to understand. And I admire you very much, Judith, and wish you well."

Judith left the library feeling comforted by Simon's sympathy. She left Ashurst the next day and relived the memory of that Christmas holiday many times. Until she had heard Simon's name again today, however, she had not been fully aware of how well she remembered him. In fact, she realized that

someday she would probably have questioned Barbara about
him, and that one of the reasons she had been happy to resume
her friendship with the Stanleys was a hidden hope that she might
one day meet Simon again.

I am no better than a schoolgirl, she thought. I suppose all
along I have been dreaming that we would meet again and that
he would immediately fall in love and rescue me from Gower
Street. And now I will be going to his house under false
pretenses.

Somehow it seemed all right to daydream occasionally about
bumping into Simon at Barbara's, or of Robin bringing Simon
along for one of their rides, for that would have involved no
deception other than pretending to have forgotten him, and no
action on her part. But to reenter Simon's life as Miss Ware,
taking advantage of his blindness, made her feel a bit guilty.
She had originally wanted the position thinking it was someone
else. She still wanted it, but was confused about her motives.
Was it only to be near the duke again? Could she not have kept
looking for another situation? But Robin was so sure that the
situation was ideal, since he would get firsthand reports on
Simon's progress. Robin had no second thoughts, but then Robin
had never been an impressionable eighteen-year-old who formed
an attachment to a good-looking, sympathetic duke.

Surely that is over, thought Judith. I have lived three years
on my own, and am, I hope, matured. I do read well, I certainly
care about the duke as a friend, and after all, he may well refuse
to interview me.

9

Two days later, Judith paid the hackney driver and turned toward the duke's town house. She hesitated, almost ready to jump back in the cab. Why on earth was she here? How could she have imagined this would work? Why had she been so impetuous and presumptuous? She heard the clatter of the horses moving away, and walked up the steps.

The young footman who opened the door stared at her rudely.

"Yes, miss? Do you have some business here?"

"I have an appointment with the duke," Judith answered tentatively. Perhaps Francis had not been able to get her an interview? "My name is Judith Ware."

Francis appeared from behind the footman. "This must be Miss Ware. Come in, his grace is expecting you. I hope you had no trouble getting here?"

"Oh, no. It is not that great a distance by cab."

"Before I bring you in to the library, I would like to speak with you myself. As the duke's secretary, I screen all applicants for any positions, no matter how highly recommended they come."

"Of course," replied Judith, and followed him into his office.

"Please be seated, Miss Ware."

Francis walked over to the window, his back to Judith. He seemed to be searching for words, and after a moment he turned back to face her.

"I am not sure you truly understand what this situation will be like, Miss Ware. I understand Major Stanley's concern for the duke and his frustration at continuously being turned away. I know why you yourself need and want the position. But I am not sure either of you realizes how different the duke is from what you remember. He has hidden himself behind the facade of his rank. He becomes furious at the least condescension. Or, I should say, cuttingly sarcastic, since that is his usual tone these days."

"I must confess to feeling some pity," Judith said, slowly. "Who could not? But I do not think I am here to bolster my sense of usefulness or virtuousness. I think I am aware of the danger in that. And, after all, I am mainly here for my own self-interest. I need an income, and am here to exchange my reading for it."

Francis visibly relaxed. "I am sorry, Miss Ware. It must sound rather presumptuous of me to question your motives. But I do not wish any setbacks from what I sense as the first progress in weeks."

"Mr. Bolton, your devotion is so obvious there is nothing to forgive. Now, what can you tell me about him, and this position, that will help me obtain it?"

Francis sank gratefully into a chair and leaned forward toward Judith. "You understand that the duke's face, his eyes, have not been injured?"

"Yes, Robin told me he looks the same as ever, aside from a scar from the initial blow."

"I think he finally is convinced of his blindness," Francis said. "But on some level, he still cannot accept what this means to him. So there are some days when he is himself: warm, cheerful, and sure that with time his life will return to normal. These days, however, are fewer and fewer, as the weeks go by and nothing changes. More of the time, he is withdrawn, rather bitter, and obviously despondent. He allows himself to be dressed. He breakfasts. I might read him the latest news, and then he shuts himself into the library for hours. He admits no one."

"What does he do in there?"

"I don't know. Brood. I suspect that a certain amount of rest and quiet has been good for him. He was still suffering from headaches when we arrived in London. But the fact he will still not go out or admit any of his friends worries me. His close friends, like Major Stanley, are faithful. But acquaintances tend to drop off after a while, and invitations decline. His estates are my responsibility, and the more he relies upon me, the harder it will be for him to resume control. And his place in politics? Well, the government has always managed to carry on without the contributions of honorable, intelligent, committed members." Francis smiled. "This desire for a reader is the first sign he has given of any interest in returning to life, and I don't want his first step back jeopardized.''

"Mr. Bolton, as you can see, I am no feather-witted, spoiled young beauty, and I am not likely to be scared away by the duke's moodiness. Nor am I given to doing things I do not intend to finish. I met the duke briefly a few years ago and remember his sympathy at a difficult turn in my life. I value that memory, and now I have a chance to do something useful for him.'' She stood up and looked down at Francis. "I assure you, although your acquaintance has been longer and more intimate, I share your concern and do not take this position lightly.''

Francis found himself looking up into serious hazel eyes that held determination and purpose. He blushed for his near rudeness, but as he started to stammer an apology, Judith waved her hand.

"No, no, don't apologize. I can only admire your devotion. If I have acquitted myself honorably, should we not go in to his grace? Will I need to give a reference? The Thorntons would be happy to vouch for me.''

"I think he will leave that in my hands, if he approves of you. As he has left everything, these past months.'' This last was said almost as an aside, and Judith looked at him more closely.

"Why, you must be exhausted, Mr. Bolton. You have obviously had to assume all responsibilities for the duke. And, I suspect, with little thanks from him at this time,'' she said shrewdly.

Francis started to protest, but seeing her genuine concern, he admitted that he was close to the breaking point himself, as much from his worry about the duke as from the extra work.

"Well, then, you now have some help,'' Judith said, extending her hand.

Francis took it gratefully and held it for a moment before letting it go and resuming his own air of competence again. "Let me bring you into the duke, Miss Ware.''

As she followed Francis down the hall, however, Judith wondered how on earth could she have sounded so confident that this was the right thing to do? So lost in her own nervousness was she that she sensed, rather than saw, him stop in front of the large, paneled library door. She stood behind him, cold and trembling. He knocked and then opened the door, motioning her to step inside.

The room itself was smaller than many libraries that she had seen, but that only added to its charm. It was clearly a room that had been much used. Books lined the walls, of course, but they also sat in small piles on the floor, and on the large oak desk in the corner. One bookcase to the left of the fireplace held folios and older volumes. These were the only shelves that looked neat. The rest in the room held books like a cornucopia, all the rich "fruit" spilling out, ready to be tasted. Clearly the duke was a great reader. Or had been, Judith corrected herself with a pang of sadness.

There was a red Turkey carpet on the floor, and the mahogany furniture seemed to reflect this red in its luster. A large leather sofa was placed in front of the fireplace, and in the corner of the sofa, seemingly gazing at the fire, sat the duke. He turned toward Francis as he heard them approach, looking not quite at him, but a little beyond.

"Your grace, I have interviewed someone I found very satisfactory for the position of reader. I told you she would be here this morning. May I introduce her to you?"

"And I asked you to advertise for a gentleman, not a lady, Francis," the duke said, quietly enough, but with a slight undertone of sarcasm. "Whatever made you consider her?"

"She was recommended by Whithedd, your grace, who knows of her brother. She has had some experience as a reader already, having been a governess in a family where there was a blind aunt."

"I hope I am not to be compared with a helpless woman whose preference was likely for gothic novels."

"Not at all, your grace," Francis said patiently. "But I did think it important you have a lively and experienced reader."

Judith was happy to see that Francis was not intimidated by Simon's rudeness. He approached the duke respectfully, but not fearfully. She had instinctively determined that taking his sightlessness as a given, and not something to be remarked upon sympathetically, was the best way to approach the duke. She was, however, becoming a little impatient at being talked about as though she were not there, although perhaps the duke was not truly aware of her presence?

"I was also considering," Francis continued, "this young woman's need. She is a young gentlewoman living with her brother, and she wishes to supplement their small income. If you give her the post, she will be able to obtain a measure of independence."

The duke seemed to listen with a different quality of attention to Francis' last remarks. For weeks he had been concerned only with his own immediate needs, and this reminder that others were also dependent stirred his dormant but innate generosity.

"Very well," Simon said, his voice less harsh, "I will meet her."

Francis beckoned Judith closer. She approached Simon and stood in front of him. It was her first sight of him in three years. As he turned toward her, she took a quick breath as his gray eyes looked straight at her as if they could see. She was sure he would extend his hand, laugh, and say, "It is Barbara's Judith, is it not? What is this masquerade about?" A scar running down his temple was the only reminder he could not see.

"Miss Ware, your grace."

Startled by Francis' voice, Judith gave a small gasp.

"I hope, Miss Ware, my face is not as intimidating as all that?"

"It is not your face which startled me, your grace. Indeed . . ."

"Yes? Indeed what?"

"The scar is hardly noticeable. It is just that I was convinced you could see me."

"I assure you, Miss Ware, I am truly blind, albeit temporarily, as my secretary may have explained to you. I find that one's other senses do sharpen, and I located you by the rustle of your dress and the smell of your perfume. I understand you have had some contact with a blind person before?"

"Yes, your grace. In my last situation, in addition to my duties with the children, I was also responsible for reading to an older sister of my employer. She wore dark spectacles, however, and it was easy to remember her . . ."

"Disability?" Simon's voice combined hauteur and shame, and, yes, even a tinge of self-pity, thought Judith.

"I was going to say her sightlessness, your grace. She was by no means disabled. In fact, she was only limited in the most obvious ways," replied Judith, her voice becoming stronger as she thought back to Lady Harriet. "She went blind gradually, you see, and had time to adjust herself."

"And what caused her blindness, Miss Ware?" Simon's tone was still somehow mocking.

"It was evidently some inherited weakness, since her father had lost his sight in the same way. There was no reason the doctors could discover, and no cure. She had the advantage of knowing it was going to happen, and prepared herself."

"Well, Miss Ware, my disability is only temporary. My eyes themselves have not been injured, and the doctors assure me that my eyesight may return spontaneously."

Judith gazed ruefully over his head at Francis, who shrugged his shoulders.

"You are indeed fortunate, your grace. In the meantime you wish a reader to ease the boredom?"

"Precisely. I find myself wearying of my own company, yet do not wish to go about society until I am myself again. What else can you tell me about yourself besides the fact you have been a governess? And have references, I presume?"

"Yes, your grace."

"Why don't you sit down, Miss Ware. Francis, you may leave us alone for a few minutes."

"Certainly," he replied, and gave Judith an encouraging look before he left, closing the door behind him.

"You need not worry about the proprieties, Miss Ware. You are obviously quite safe with me."

"I am not at all missish, your grace, nor am I a young lady of the *ton*. I have been in charge of my life these past few years. And Mr. Whithedd recommended you highly," Judith answered, a trifle sharply.

The duke could not help smiling. "I think you have got something backward, Miss Ware. Surely it is that Mr. Whithedd recommended you highly? Is it not usually the applicant who is to be judged?"

Judith laughed. "Of course, you are correct. Yet although I want a position, I would not work for anyone. I am at last free to make some choices."

"And how long have you not been free?"

"For the past few years, your grace. Since my father died."

"You have a brother?"

"Yes. Stephen has just started working in the City. He is a year younger than I, and has only come down from Oxford. We have been looking forward to being together."

"And have you not enjoyed being a governess?"

"In my last position, yes. Very much. I became quite fond of the whole family and they of me, and in some ways it was hard to leave. My first post, on the other hand, I was relieved to escape."

"Oh?" Simon's eyebrows lifted, questioning. "Don't tell me. There was a dissolute younger son who was not adverse to paying unwanted attention to a pretty young governess."

"Oh, no, your grace," protested Judith. "I am not that pretty," she said ruefully. "And it was a dissolute older man, the uncle of the little girl I was teaching."

"Ah, a variation on a very old theme." Simon's face was more relaxed, and he smiled. "Well, I don't mean to make fun of your very real trials and tribulations, Miss Ware. But you have a sense of humor about them. I congratulate you, for I seem to have lost mine. If I understand it correctly, you wish this position to supplement your brother's income?"

"Yes. I was able to save some money, but I do not wish to be a burden to Stephen. A little extra money will mean we could enjoy the theater or opera occasionally. And my reading is far superior to my sewing."

"An unconventional young woman. You are well-read?"

"Yes. And I must confess that your library, now that I have seen it, beckons to me quite as much as the idea of the salary. I hope you will consider me."

Judith sensed a sudden withdrawal. Simon had appeared to be relaxing into his former, charming self, but then his face became again cold and removed.

"I will, Miss Ware. You may start the day after tomorrow, in the morning. I will want you here for two mornings a week. We will try it for three weeks and see if we suit each other. I will leave Francis to settle the details of salary. Thank you for coming," the duke said, obviously dismissing her. He rang for Francis and, when the secretary returned, said, "I have decided to give Miss Ware a trial, Francis. I will speak with you later."

Judith got up, smiling rather tentatively at Simon, as though attempting to bring him back to their few minutes of warmth, and then remembered he couldn't see her smile or her quick curtsy. Francis gestured her out, and Simon turned again to the fire, as though he could indeed see it and was searching the flames for an answer to some important question.

Francis drew the library door closed behind him and gestured Judith down the hall. He sent the footman for her pelisse. They looked at each other for a moment and then let out simultaneous sighs of relief, releasing the tension of the past fifteen minutes.

"Well," Francis said, "you must have done splendidly."

"I was very nervous, and that sarcastic undercurrent almost did me in. I don't remember Simon, I mean the duke, ever speaking like that."

"No, of course not. But since he has returned home, it has become more and more the tone of every interaction. I think it serves as a protective device, and enables him to keep everyone at a distance."

"There was a minute or so when he did sound more like himself."

"Did he? Then you must have had some effect. Perhaps this scheme will work out, after all."

"I wish that above all things," Judith said. "But for now, I must go."

"We will see you soon again, then, Miss Ware?"

"Yes, Mr. Bolton, I am looking forward to it."

Francis walked Judith to the door and watched her down the street. Her warmth and intelligence had left an impression, and he thought to himself that under different circumstances she was the sort of woman who would have been attractive to the duke.

In the library, Simon lifted his head as he heard the heavy front door close. He tried to picture Miss Ware, but found he had no imaginative capacity for creating a face out of nothing; indeed, he seemed to be losing his memory for what familiar faces looked like. He was lost in a black void, seeing nothing but the occasional flickerings of his last sight of Viscount Alderstoke's blood spilling out over his hands, just before the rifle came down on his head.

10

Two days later, Judith was admitted by the butler, who took her wrap.

Francis emerged from his office to greet her with a warm smile. "His grace is expecting you, Miss Ware. I will take you in today, but Cranston will admit you in the future, since this is a busy time for me."

"Thank you, Mr. Bolton." Judith again found herself in a state of anxiety. In what mood would she find Simon? Would he have had any second thoughts about her employment? What had all seemed so simple in her imagination was in reality . . . reality. Something that existed of itself and could only be discerned from moment to moment. Something she could not control.

Simon was sitting in the same place on the sofa, dressed, or so Judith first thought, exactly as he had been on Tuesday. Then she realized he was wearing a different coat this morning, and there seemed to be an air of expectancy about him, as though he were more conscious of his appearance.

His head turned as he heard the door open, and when Francis announced her, he nodded in their general direction.

"Good morning, Miss Ware. Excuse me if I don't rise. You are prompt, I see. Or should I say, I hear. The clock just rang ten, and here you are. Please come in and sit down."

"Good morning, your grace." Judith could think of nothing to say in response to Simon's ironic reference to his sightlessness. His compliments were at odds with his voice. It was almost as if he had decided it was his duty to be read to. She seated herself nervously on the edge of the arm chair.

"Perhaps before you begin, you may wish to consider that our first meetings will be a trial employment to see if we suit each other. I may well find that your reading is not sufficiently dramatic, or restful, as the case may be. And you, to be fair, may find my present mood too much a burden. I hope you do not picture yourself as a messenger of fortitude and hope, Miss Ware?''

''I assure you, your grace, I am here as your reader, nothing else.'' Taking a deep breath to calm herself, she said, ''Do you have anything in particular you want me to read, your grace?''

''Since this is to be a trial period,'' Simon replied, ''I think we should start with self-contained pieces. I would not have you begin a novel and then leave me in the middle of a Radcliffe romance, never to find out whether the heroine is rescued from the diabolical monk.''

''Perhaps we might start with some poetry, your grace?''

''Just the thing. If you can read verse to suit me, I am sure we will deal well together. Unless someone has rearranged the shelves, you will find volumes of poetry to the left of the fireplace, starting''—Simon frowned as he attempted to picture the shelves—''at about my shoulder height. I will leave the choice to you.''

Judith got up and was soon caught up in the delight of browsing through old favorites and discovering new ones, as though she were at her favorite booksellers.

''This is a revelation, your grace,'' she said spontaneously. ''I would not have expected such a selection, and they all look well-read. You must be . . . .'' She paused, embarrassed by her blunder, and continued as naturally as possible. ''You must have been a prodigious reader. I am one too. It must be difficult to have lost what was obviously a great pleasure to you.''

''If you wish to remain, Miss Ware, I will have no pity,'' Simon said sharply. ''There is no need, after all,'' he continued, with a change of tone that Judith found profoundly disturbing in its self-deception. ''I am only temporarily deprived of the pleasure. Please, get on with your choice.''

''I beg your pardon, your grace.'' Judith continued to run her fingers along the spines of old friends. She suddenly stopped at a large, unbound folio and pulled it out. A ''Prospectus,'' yellowed with age, fell out. She picked it up and read the date: October 10, 1793. It announced that ten works of the author, William Blake, were published and ''on Sale at Mr. Blake's, No. 13, Hercules Blvd., Lambeth.'' She held two works in her hands, ''The Songs of Innocence'' and ''The Songs of Experience,'' and as she turned the pages, she exclaimed at the illustrations.

"You have discovered something," Simon said. "What book are you so intrigued by?"

"It isn't quite a book. It is an unpublished manuscript by a Mr. William Blake. I have never seen anything like this, your grace," Judith said in a delighted voice.

"They are engravings, Miss Ware. Mr. Blake's work is indeed unique. He etches with acid and then hand-colors each plate. He wishes to create works similar to a medieval manuscript. Do you think that he succeeded?"

"I have never had the privilege of seeing a medieval piece, but this book is surely one of the most beautiful I have ever seen."

"It seems to have chosen you, then," said Simon in his apparently constant dry tone. "Why don't we begin with Mr. Blake's poems."

Judith sat down and began to read in her clear, even voice. She looked up after each poem, surprised indeed that the duke had purchased this folio. The first poems were simple lyrics, almost bland in their "innocence," or so Judith thought. A few moved her by their very simplicity, but she could not but worry that Simon would be bored. And then in the middle of "The Little Black Boy," her voice quavered on: "And we are put on earth a little space / That we might bear the beams of love." She glanced up to see if Simon had noticed her emotion. There was a quizzing look on his face, and he asked, rather gently, "You seem moved by those lines, Miss Ware?"

"Yes, your grace. They took me by surprise."

Judith continued. And again, some of the songs she found too facilely optimistic, and then there would occur a poem, like the final one, that moved her more than Thompson's heavy style, and even more than Mr. Wordsworth.

"That poem ends the first octavo, your grace. Do you wish me to continue?"

"I think that will be enough for today, Miss Ware," Simon said quietly. "And what did you think of Mr. Blake's idea of innocence?"

"I am not quite sure what I think. Some of the poems seemed too innocent in their philosophy, and then comes a line or a poem that moves me as I have not been moved by other poets.''

"You are a reader of poetry, then, Miss Ware?''

"Yes, your grace, I am. I am a reader of anything and everything, but poetry is closest to my heart.''

"How do you like our contemporary bards? Or are you less acquainted with modern works?''

"Until today, I would have said that Mr. Wordsworth and Lord Byron were superior.''

"And after today?''

"I shall have to read more of your Mr. Blake. I will be interested to see how he treats 'experience.' ''

"Well, we will leave that question to be decided the next time you come. Until Tuesday then?''

Simon's face, which had been, for the first few moments of their discussion, lively and interested and open, as though he were truly present, closed down.

Judith rose and nodded, forgetting again that Simon could not see her. As she walked to the door, his frame, which had seemed to straighten and give some evidence of latent energy, slumped again as he resumed his position of "staring" at the fire.

She closed the door carefully behind her and, as the butler approached, asked to be shown into Mr. Bolton's office.

"I know that he is busy, Cranston, but I wish to inquire about my wages.''

Francis, who was indeed busy with what appeared to be an avalanche of letters and documents, lost his frown of annoyance at the interruption when he saw it was Judith.

"Thank you, Cranston. You may close the door.''

Judith stood until the door had closed behind her, and then she sank gratefully into the chair next to Francis.

"This is not such a simple thing as I thought,'' she said with her usual directness.

"No, it is not.''

"I actually feel ashamed of myself for deceiving him. And amazed at the deception should come so easily. It was all so much simpler in the abstract.''

"How did your first morning go? You were not with him as long as I'd expected.''

"He has not dismissed me out of hand. I think it went rather well. We read poetry, and there were some moments when he forgot himself and was caught up in the poems. But he so easily slides back into lifelessness. It is as though he were one of those new gaslights, flickering up, and then out suddenly, as the gas is turned down.''

Francis nodded in agreement. ''That is the way he has been since he returned to town.''

''Does he spend all day in the library? Does he never go out? How does he manage within the household?''

''He has gone out only once, when it was necessary to visit his lawyers. He is usually guided by one of the footmen, although he can make his way around the house pretty independently. But it seems to me that he does not want to be here. I think he removes himself so that the blindness will be less real.''

''I keep trying to imagine what it would be like,'' said Judith. ''Has he made no attempts at becoming more independent?''

Francis laughed. ''You know that as a duke, so much is done for one, blind or not. Your valet dresses and shaves you. You are cooked for and waited upon. You have a groom and butler and secretary. As I told you, he has learned to move around the house. He comes downstairs with little difficulty.''

''I wonder what a blind person is capable of?'' mused Judith. ''I am sure some of Simon's old life would be open to him.''

''Fencing? Hunting? Inspecting his estates? Assemblies?''

''His brain was not injured. I know he has always been politically active. Perhaps hunting is out, but surely he could ride with a companion? Dinners. I'll wager anything that a blind man could even waltz.'' Judith smiled at her own fancies. ''It is easy, is it not, to determine someone's life for him in his absence. Neither of us can know what it is like to be the duke. But he does have what many blind men do not: money, privilege, the ability to secure the assistance he needs to live an almost normal life. It is distressing to see how much he shuts himself off from.''

''Well, a little life is coming in the door with you, even if he refuses to go out the door and meet it.''

''Thank you for your time, Mr. Bolton. I had best go. I should not be in here too long or the servants may begin to suspect something.''

Judith rose, and Francis followed her to the door.

As he opened it, she said, "Thank you for answering my questions about salary, Mr. Bolton. I hope that I will prove a satisfactory employee."

"Until Tuesday, Miss Ware."

11

While Judith was beginning her position, Barbara was filling her days with her usual activities: shopping, morning calls, various assemblies, and, as often as possible, riding with her brother. On one of their early-morning rides without Judith, after warming their horses up, the Stanleys let them go from a sedate canter to an all-out gallop, something they had not enjoyed for a few days, having been held to Judith's less-experienced pace. When they pulled up, Barbara's hat was sliding off and her hair was coming down, but her cheeks were red and her eyes alive and laughing.

"Oh, Robin," she gasped, "I am quite out of practice. I have been behaving so well I'd quite forgotten what a real ride feels like."

Her brother laughed. "We both needed to clear the cobwebs out."

"What do you plan to do, now that peace seems to be won?" asked Barbara as they turned their blown horses back down the Row to cool them off. "Shall you return to Ashurst? Will you be able to settle down after soldiering for so long?"

"Lord, yes, my dear. I have had my fill of it. I intend to derive my pleasures from lesser adventures like challenging Father and experimenting with new farming methods."

"And do you intend to remain a bachelor?" Barbara asked in what she hoped was a light tone.

"And who are you to ask, my marriage-shy little sister?" he teased.

"Seriously, Robin, has no woman captured more than a part of your heart?"

"Isn't this a case of the pot . . . ?"

"But it is different for you, Robin. As a man, you have more choice—and a duty, as father's heir. I don't have the weight of an earldom hanging over me."

"What of your responsibility to yourself, Barbara? Have you never met anyone you care for?"

"I asked first." Barbara laughed. "I will answer honestly if you will," she said more quietly, suddenly occupied with untangling her reins.

"A challenge I can't refuse! Well, then, the answer is yes, there was someone. But we quarreled—how commonplace, eh? —and that was that."

"It could not have been as simple as that," said his sister. "If there was strong feeling there surely a 'commonplace quarrel' would not end it?"

"But it wasn't a small misunderstanding. I wished for a formal announcement at the end of my last leave. She refused. Oh, not me. She agreed to wed me. But no public engagement until I returned home safely. I think she did not wish to risk being tied to a cripple. And also," Robin continued bitterly, "she did not wish to curtail her many flirtations until I returned. Perhaps I was unfair in asking her to make that commitment then, but I wanted to know that I had her love supporting me and carrying me through. As it was, I made it through very well without it."

"Tell me, Robin was this woman the Lady Diana Grahame?"

"Yes. Did I make such a cake of myself that it was public knowledge?"

"Oh, no. I think it was only that I noticed the extra waltzes and 'accidental' meetings in the park," Barbara reassured him. "You were both certainly discreet about the degree of your involvement. I am sorry. I do not know her well, but I have always thought that, underneath her occasional wildness, she has a warm heart. Have you spoken to her since your return?"

"We have exchanged the necessary politenesses. I stood up with her once, but only because I could not have got out of it gracefully. The lady is most certainly not suffering from a broken heart. And neither am I. Who knows, I may fall suddenly in love with one of the Misses Stanhope!"

Barbara laughed with Robin, and some of the seriousness lifted from his face.

"And now you, miss. It is your turn."

"There is someone, Robin, but I fear it is a clichéd case of one-sided love," Barbara said lightly. "You would think I would have outgrown it by now. Perhaps I will retire to Ashurst with you, and we could challenge Father together,'' she said mischievously.

"I might take you up on that offer. And is that all you will tell me about the state of your heart? I think I was expertly outmaneuvered. Now tell me, how did Judith's first visit to Simon go?"

"It went well. He certainly did not seem to recognize her. They have agreed upon a few weeks' trial period to see if she suits him."

"How does Simon look?"

"Physically? Judith said thinner than she remembered him. But there is no disfigurement, as you know, aside from the scar on his temple. She said that when he looks at you it is hard to remember he cannot see. He is different, though. He has always been so open and natural, but now there is an ironic undercurrent to the simplest things he says. Francis told her that he has been this way since he returned."

"Does she think that the reading will help?"

"Well, it does not seem to hurt."

"And if our deception were discovered? What effect do you think that would have?"

"I think we are safe enough. The servants are ignorant of her connection with us, except for Cranston and Martin, and they are, like Francis, convinced that deception is necessary. If he does find out . . . well, at least his anger would be a reaction."

"Is he that subdued?"

"Judith says he is apparently convinced his sight will return. Underneath, she thinks he is beginning to realize it is hopeless, but he cannot yet face the truth. Yet, despite his blue devils, Judith seems to be enjoying herself. On her first day, she even discovered a poet she had never heard of, William Blake."

"That's famous. Thank God Simon was never one to be put off by a woman's intelligence. Her enthusiasm may carry the day, after all."

12

H ad she known, as she walked up the duke's steps, again trembling with fear and anticipation, that Simon had noticed, for the first time in weeks, how slowly the time passed—and that he found himself if not looking forward to something, at least expectant—Judith would have relaxed. As it was, when she was announced at the library door, Simon did no more than greet her as he had done on Tuesday. She did notice, however, that Simon held Mr. Blake's unbound work in his lap, as though he had been feeling it, in hopes the intricate designs would spring to life under his fingertips.

"Good morning, your grace," said Judith.

"Good morning, Miss Ware. As you can see, I wish you to continue with Mr. Blake's poems."

"Of course, your grace. Actually," she said, her enthusiasm breaking through her shyness, "I have been looking forward to it all weekend. I am eager to find out how Blake treats experience."

Simon held the folio out toward Judith, and she took it from him carefully. She began, and since Simon made no comments, she assumed she was reading clearly, and not too fast or slow. She forgot herself as "reader" as she was pulled into the world of the poems, a world of paradox and comment upon earlier songs. Had she been reading to herself, she would have read something like "The Tyger" over and over, in her delight at the language and the imagery.

When she got to the "Garden of Love" Simon shifted, turning in her direction and opening his eyes as though he wished to see her face and her reaction to this odd and, for a young woman, rather improper poem. After she had finished "London," she looked up quickly and thought she saw a tear running down Simon's cheek; she began the next poem as he surreptitiously wiped it away. Perhaps it was a reaction to his moment of vulnerability, but as she ended, he asked roughly, as though to see how shockable she was, "And what do you think of the poet now, Miss Ware? Are you shocked by his language? Did you blush at his mention of harlots?"

"Not shocked, your grace. I am, after all, old enough to know that harlots exist. But very moved and puzzled."

"Puzzled?"

"Well, at times I think I know what he is saying. And then I lose the meaning. He writes such simple lines that carry greater meaning than I can comprehend in one reading. And, I suspect, one would have to be Mr. Blake himself to understand all. He is surely an original, your grace. How did you discover him?"

"In my youth, Miss Ware, when I was just down from university, I fancied myself rather a radical young noble-man—not, of course, recognizing the inherent contradiction—and published some essays that gained me acceptance into radical circles. I frequented Joseph Johnson's shop, and he introduced me to Mr. Blake's writings, and eventually to Mr. Blake."

"You have actually met him? What is he like?"

"Not at all the fiery young Adonis that he sounds. He lives by his engraving, of course, not by his poetry. Many think he is a bit mad. I think he is a genius, albeit an eccentric one. And what is your opinion, Miss Ware? You don't seem as shocked as I would have expected a young woman to be."

"I must confess something, your grace. I agree with Mr. Blake about marriage."

"Do you truly see marriage as only a buying and a selling?" asked Simon.

"Surely in your circle, your grace, there is much marketing of daughters?"

"And sons, Miss Ware. Although I agree that women are in the most vulnerable position. But do you believe no one marries for love?"

"I think some do, in all classes. But far too often marriage is an economic solution rather than a freely chosen relation-ship. And in most cases, the woman loses."

"Have you made up your mind never to compromise? Would you not prefer an establishment of your own? Forgive me," Simon broke off, "I am becoming much too personal."

"You are forgiven, your grace. I was moved by these poems and could not have closed the book and discussed ideas only in the abstract."

"You are an unconventional young woman, Miss Ware. And, I suspect, not well-suited to being a governess. How on earth did you reconcile yourself to the demands of your position?"

"Not very easily, and sometimes not very well. I am always struggling, only sometimes successfully, to be true to myself and at the same time faithful to the demands of the life in which I find myself."

"That could be interpreted as mere resignation. Or as a 'Christian humility,' in the worst sense of the phrase."

"Someone once said to me," Judith replied hesitantly, "that it is up to us to find the meaning and purpose in the lives we have been given. I think that it is not passivity, but a sort of freedom."

Simon's face, which had been animated and open, became shuttered once again.

"Admirable philosophy. Given by someone in more enviable circumstances than your own, no doubt."

"Yes, you are right. But they seemed to come from a genuine struggle to make sense of life, and so I have always valued them."

Simon had obviously not remembered his own words. And while his advice to Judith years ago had sprung from a genuine struggle, it had also come from a young man with a warm heart and a wish to offer comfort. Simon had only had to reconcile his political beliefs and a natural inclination toward simplicity with assuming a privileged position in a society whose values were on the whole alien to his. Although he was keenly aware of the injustices around him, and active in his attempts to eliminate some of them, he had not personally suffered until now.

His hopeful moods were giving way more and more to the despairing realization that his sight would not return. He seemed to be slipping down into an interior darkness that seemed an extension of the physical lack of light. He felt half-asleep at times. The reading and conversation with Miss Ware woke him up, but only temporarily. Somehow he knew that to be awake would mean facing the painful reality of his life. He could find no good reason to do that, so he used sarcasm to protect himself, discovering within unknown reserves of a cold, bitter pride.

These he drew upon now. Judith felt almost physically chilled by his withdrawal, and his transformation from someone who resembled the old Simon into the marble statue before her.

"This has been an odd conversation, Miss Ware. I trust we will stay more with our respective roles of reader and listener. Until next time, then," and Simon rang the bell next to him.

"Yes, your grace," Judith said, taken aback by his abrupt dismissal. "I will see you on Thursday."

"Would that I could say the same, Miss Ware. Who knows what charms I am deprived of. Good day."

Judith flushed with embarrassment, stammered an apology for her careless phrasing, and Simon waved her away.

13

J udith hailed a hackney and directed it to Clarges Street, for she was to visit Barbara and take luncheon with her. She had originally planned to walk, but Simon's abruptness had hurt and she was glad of the privacy of the cab for a few minutes to compose herself. She was sure she understood his sudden withdrawals, but it did not make it easier to be the recipient.

When they reached the Stanleys', Judith was calmer and looking forward to the opportunity of telling Barbara about her first days as a reader. She was shown into the morning room, where Barbara joined her almost immediately. Barbara was experiencing that wonderful combination of calmness and strength that is the result of creative work, having just wrestled with a difficult piece of Mozart and won. Judith immediately began to relax in her presence, but not before Barbara noticed her pale face and red eyes.

"Did your second morning with Simon not go as well?" she asked.

"On the whole it went very well, Barbara. We had a discussion of Mr. Blake that reminded me of our Christmas at Ashurst. Simon seemed almost himself for a few minutes. But then something happens—he opens up and then very suddenly closes himself off. I know it is because of his coming to terms with his blindness—or, rather, not coming to terms with it— but it is still difficult to be on the receiving end of an unwarranted hostility."

Barbara nodded sympathetically. "I am sure even a little openness is a good sign, Judith. I hope you can overlook the coldness, for I think your being there is a first step in Simon's return to normal."

"Tell me what your plans are for this afternoon, Barbara, for I confess that if you are bent on shopping, I will come with you, just to cheer myself."

"I do need a pair of gloves, for we are attending the Stantons' ball tonight. Would you come with me, Judith?"

"I would be delighted. A little sifting through the scarves and stockings at the Pantheon is just what I need after this morning. And later you can tell me all the gossip so I am completely sunk into frivolity. I won't know anyone, of course, but I will enjoy the scandals just the same."

"The only scandal is likely to be Lady Diana's dancing exclusively with Dev," Barbara said. "Yet I should not be so catty. After all, I had always liked her before this year. She does not set out to steal other women's beaux. They just seem to fall at her feet naturally."

Judith was not sure how to respond. From what Barbara had already told her, the viscount had certainly never been a beau, so that Diana could hardly be accused of stealing him. But she could sympathize with her friend, for caring about someone did seem to make one illogically believe in or hope for a returned affection, and to watch the person one loved with another was certainly painful.

"I am sure from what you have told me Lady Diana is only humoring the viscount. If it is indeed an infatuation, she could hardly ignore him or treat him coldly, unless she had no heart at all."

"Do you think so?" Barbara asked eagerly. "I keep hoping that, but then that could be self-deception."

"I am sure that it is so," Judith said. What she was not so sure of was whether Dev would ever see Barbara as anything but a friend or a younger sister. Their relationship seemed to be too long-standing and familiar to be the sort that developed into a romance. But that was something Barbara could only discover for herself. Judith could sympathize with Barbara, for it hurt to discover that Simon had no memory of their easy companionship and few moments of intimacy at Ashurst. No inappropriate romantic fantasies had been entertained by the duke. He had gone off heart-whole, while Judith had developed a *tendre* for him. She had soothed herself to sleep after a particularly rough day with her charges by imagining what life might be like when she at last reached London. And the Duke of Sutton somehow figured in many of them. She would meet him by chance in the street and he would recognize her immediately. Or they would meet as dinner guests of the Stanleys, and he would invite her to a small gathering at his house . . .

Judith had never met any men who had aroused the same feelings. It had therefore been rather easy to imagine herself an independent young woman who had no desire to settle for a convenient marriage. After meeting Simon, however, she had begun to want something that she was barely able to define. She was even afraid to attempt to define it, for she suspected it was something few men and fewer women were able to have: a union not only for the purpose of creating children, but one that created for oneself the opportunity for affection and passion. "I was surely born in the wrong time," she would say to herself as she pushed away her fantasies before they developed further, before they took her into Simon's arms.

She shook herself out of her musings and, to rally Barbara's spirits, said, "Come, let us off to luncheon and then the Bazaar. Let us forget all men and their inability to appreciate the fine women under their noses, and revel in bargains."

Barbara was amused by the picture of her usually unfrivolous friend rummaging around silk stockings and scarves, and decided she must encourage any sign of willingness in Judith to indulge in activity "normal" for young ladies. At least she had a social life to counteract her tendency to pull too far back from society. But Judith could too easily become isolated. And so they both went off to an afternoon of giggling and gossiping and wild extravagance on Barbara's part and what felt to Judith like wild expenditure on hers. One pair of gloves to Barbara's three, a pair of cotton stockings instead of silk, and the largest but most treasured purchase, an Indian scarf shot through with gold thread that had been greatly reduced due to some small imperfections.

14

While the Stanleys were busy with the Little Season, Simon found himself sinking deeper into a frozen despair. He had been restless after Judith's second visit and found himself, for the first time in months, wanting to be outside and involved in some vigorous form of exercise. Instead of ringing for Cranston, he got up from the sofa, intending to find his own way to the door, and tripped over the coal scuttle, which had been moved by the parlormaid to light the fire that morning and not replaced. The contents spilled all over the carpet, and Simon ended up on his hands and knees, his clean breeches smudged with soot and his hands covered with ashes. A few weeks ago, a more hopeful Simon might have laughed at himself. He had no sense of the ridiculous left. He felt humiliated and helpless. He stood up and grabbed for the back of the sofa, unwilling to move again in any direction. He managed to find his bell and rang for Cranston, who, when he saw what had happened, moved quickly toward the duke, uttering solicitous phrases, which further fueled Simon's rage.

"Who is the downstairs parlormaid?"

"Betty, your grace."

"Give Betty her notice immediately. I cannot tolerate such carelessness."

"Yes, your grace." Cranston did not even think of asking the duke to reconsider. He was not a particularly perceptive man, but he knew that, at the moment, the employer whom the servants knew and loved was unreachable. Instead, there stood a man whose pride, so rarely in evidence, had been deeply wounded. Simon, who had been respected as an athlete and envied for his grace on the dance floor, was unable to move around his own home without tripping over something. He was paralyzed by fear of ridicule as well as injury. He felt eternally exposed, like a small child who has done something wrong and waits to be punished.

It was this fear of being exposed and not even knowing to whom one was exposed that kept him still. And in his stillness he could hear a humming, which grew more insistent and sounded like the shells that had fallen like hail and flattened the shoulder-high rye fields of Belgium.

"Your grace, may I take you to your room to change?" Cranston had been repeating this query several times before he finally penetrated Simon's withdrawal. Simon came back to himself, realizing that the smell of burned ashes was not from a battlefield, but from his own hands and knees.

"Yes, Cranston, you can take me up this time. I am afraid of what other havoc I might wreak should I try it on my own."

When Cranston had settled Simon in his room and laid out clean clothes for him, he went down and knocked at Francis' door.

"Come in," Francis said. "What happened? I heard the noise, but you seemed to be in control."

"The duke did not ring for anyone. I think he was going into luncheon on his own, when he tripped over the coal scuttle."

"I thought all the maids understood that everything must be in place in order for the duke to have any measure of independence?"

"They do understand, Mr. Bolton. But Betty must have forgotten to move it back after she laid the fire." He paused. "The duke gave me orders to sack Betty. Should I tell her, or will you, sir?"

Francis and the butler exchanged looks. "I do not know what to say, Cranston. We both know that under different circumstances the duke would never have given such orders. And yet I do not want to take any more responsibility from him. He has given over so much, both of necessity and otherwise, that I hate to go against his authority. Perhaps if I speak to him later to discuss his order, he may reconsider. Say nothing to Betty until I've spoken to the duke."

"Thank you, Mr. Bolton."

Francis waited until later that afternoon to approach Simon, who, having changed, refused any luncheon and had been sitting in the morning room, drinking brandy. Francis knocked, although the door was open, and Simon turned slowly.

"It is Francis, your grace."

"Ah, Francis . . . Come to determine what else the duke has collided with today?" Simon's tone was different: less sarcastic, but more resigned. Francis looked at Simon's strong hands as they held the brandy glass in front of him. There was a decanter and another glass on the table next to him, and he reached slowly and carefully for it, holding his finger in the glass as he poured to feel the level of the liquid. He held it out in Francis' direction.

"You see, Francis? If I confine my activity to sitting and drinking, I should do all right. Sit down, man. You must need to get a little drunk yourself. I have certainly kept you busy these last few months."

Francis reached out and took the glass from Simon. His fingers brushed the duke's and he could feel them shaking. All of a sudden he wanted to put his arm around him, as he would have done with his own brother. As though sensing this, Simon drew back.

Francis sat down opposite the duke. "Your grace, Cranston tells me you wish to have Betty dismissed. Did you want me to give her the usual month's wages?"

"What? Not done yet?"

"No, your grace."

"Well," sighed Simon, "that is just as well. Why should she suffer because of my helplessness? I overreacted this morning."

"I am happy you have reconsidered. Betty begged me to give you her apologies. Your servants care for you a great deal, your grace."

"Do they? I can't imagine why. I treat them no differently than most employers."

"It is not how you deal with them, although that is most generously, but who you are. All your staff wish you well." Francis was afraid to say more. The brandy had relaxed the duke, and some barrier was down. Francis stood up and placed his almost-untasted brandy on the table. He turned to go, and without thinking, he placed his hand on the duke's shoulder, attempting to convey his own affection and sympathy. He let it rest there for a moment and then turned quietly and left.

Simon sat still for a moment and then lifted his glass toward the door, as though in acknowledgment.

The next day found Simon in the same mood: having at last

given up hope, he was no longer placing the same barriers of irony between himself and others. He was more obviously hopeless, but also, in a strange way, more open and receptive, for hopelessness needs no protection. When Judith walked into the library, she immediately sensed the difference. There was no edge to the duke's voice when he greeted her.

"Do you wish to continue with poetry, your grace?"

"I will leave it up to you, Miss Ware. I have no strong feelings one way or another these days."

Judith began to search the shelves again. "I see you have *Clarissa* right next to *Tom Jones*," she said teasingly. "I am quite sure Mr. Richardson would not approve! Mr. Fielding would appreciate the irony, however!"

"Have you read both novels, then?" asked Simon.

"Yes."

"And which did you prefer?"

"Mr. Fielding's, of course," Judith answered without hesitation. "I find Mr. Richardson's heroines to be self-servingly virtuous, and in the case of Clarissa, quite morbid."

"You would not, I take it, write letters upon your own coffin in the event of being, ah, ravished, Miss Ware?"

"And what a poor-spirited woman she was, to be sure." Judith laughed. "And Richardson is so tantalizing in leading up to the seduction scene that I suspect him of wanting to titillate the reader's sensibilities. Fielding is a breath of fresh air in comparison," declared Judith, quite forgetting they were discussing subjects not considered quite the thing for young ladies.

She turned back to the shelves and said, "I see that you have several of Miss Austen's works. Have you read them all? Much as I admire Sophy Western, I find myself more sympathetic to women like Elizabeth Bennet."

"I am not acquainted with Miss Bennet."

"Of *Pride and Prejudice*? You have not read it? It is not her latest, but if it is new to you, I would enjoy introducing you to the Bennets, your grace. It is not an excessively long novel, and we should be able to finish it in a few weeks."

"As I said before, Miss Ware, I will go along with whatever you prefer. I have enjoyed Miss Austen in the past, and if you recommend this one, I will trust your judgment."

"Then let us begin, and I hope I can do justice to Eliza."

Perhaps because Simon and Judith were more familiar with each other, perhaps because of Simon's new mood, the next few reading days fell into a comfortable pattern. Judith would arrive and almost immediately open to the page they had ended on, and she and Simon would enter again into the life of the Bennets. They laughed together over the absurdities of Mrs. Bennet and argued in quite a friendly way over Darcy. Was he indeed insufferably high-handed in his treatment of Bingley and Jane—Judith thought so—or was he merely honest and candid in his appraisal of the Bennet family? Simon defended him stoutly.

"After all, he said nothing about them that Elizabeth did not know herself."

"But it is one thing to criticize your own family—quite another for an outsider to do it."

"Would you have refused him, then?" asked Simon as they came to the end of Volume Two.

"Yes. He gave her no indication of his feelings for her. And to begin a proposal by stating how hard he had fought his inclination . . . !"

"It seems to me," Simon said, "that Darcy's fault is one shared by many of my sex: the inability to put into fine words one's deepest feelings. And women seem to value words somewhat more than one's actions."

"There is some truth in what you say, your grace. I place more importance on friendships where I am able to utter my deepest thoughts, and tend to undervalue those who demonstrate their care in more practical ways. But do you not think that there is nothing more desirable than expressing oneself freely and without fear?"

"Do you realize, Miss Ware, our conversations range over subjects not generally discussed between men and women? Are you like this with everyone?"

"Oh, no, your grace. I can be quite insipid and conventional when I need to be. I generally speak my mind only where I feel safe."

"Safe? And do I seem safe?" There was an edge to Simon's voice that had not been there for days. "Does my blindness make me innocuous, then?"

"Your grace, no one looking at you could forget you are a man, and a handsome, vital one, despite your blindness. You no longer have the advantage of seeing yourself in the glass, so perhaps it is easy to doubt your attractiveness. Even as I spoke, I was marveling that I could speak so here. But by safe, I mean, able to be myself. Perhaps your blindness does have something to do with it," Judith said hesitantly. "Because you cannot see me, I do not have to worry about how I look. Women are always being seen and having to see ourselves with others' eyes. When I walk in here, I know if I express myself openly, you are not thinking either: She is quite beautiful, too bad she is a bluestocking, or the reverse: How boring, a plain, bookish young woman. I feel that you hear me first, and my beauty or lack of it cannot get in the way. I am sorry if this sounds like I am pleased that you are blind. Maybe 'safe' is not the right word? Maybe I feel equal?"

"And does a man have to be helpless for you to feel equal?"

"Oh, no," Judith protested. "I—truly I cannot explain this well. I believe every woman, whether she knows it or not, is somehow an outsider in society. You will, no doubt, not agree, and I do not wish to start a debate. I am only trying to explain what it feels like to be a woman."

"And an unmarried, poor one."

"Yes, I suppose that adds to it. Your blindness makes you an outsider too, despite your wealth and rank; that is all I meant. And in this room, surrounded by the words I read, we are quite outside the working-day world, and in quite another. I am groping for words that will not quite express what I experience. But, no, your grace, you are *not* safe," she ended vehemently. "And I must go."

Simon rose with Judith. "And are you quite plain or quite beautiful, Miss Ware?"

"Neither, your grace," replied Judith.

"Describe yourself to me, if that is not an intrusive request?"

Judith paused, wondering if her description would give her away. Well, her description would fit many women, after all.

"I am a little below average height, your grace."

"Yes, I can tell that from your voice."

"I have brown hair and hazel eyes, and I am afraid I am

cursed with freckles. In short, I am rather average-looking and not at all in fashion.''

''And were I to look in my own glass, what would I see?'' Until he asked his question, Simon did not realize how serious it was. The more obvious handicap of blindness was the lack of visual stimuli and his utter inability to find his way through his own house or city. Until this moment he had not realized how disorienting sightlessness was: when one sees another's reaction and sees one's face in a mirror, one's existence is subtly confirmed.

Judith answered hesitantly, ''You would see a man of above-average height with an almost handsome face and hair a bit longer than is fashionable right now.''

Simon was amused at Judith's matter-of-fact description of ''almost handsome.''

''Fine gray eyes,'' Judith continued.

''Staring blankly beyond you, I suppose?''

''Truthfully, your grace, you are quite good at locating someone by the sound of his voice, and looking directly at him. Let me finish. Your face looks rather drawn, and I would guess from the way your clothes hang that you are thinner than you used to be.''

Simon and Judith stood still for a moment. Then they both moved at once, she toward the door and Simon to ring for Cranston. Neither was able to say anything but an awkward good-bye, and Judith left quickly.

After she was gone, Simon brushed his hand through his hair, which was long, he realized, even for a windswept look, and shrugged his shoulders, amazed at how comfortably his coat moved with them. He was no dandy, but he had always prided himself on his quiet elegance. He rang again, to summon his valet.

''Martin, you have been very forbearing these past weeks. I'm sure I have tried your patience.''

''Oh, no, your grace,'' Martin protested.

''You are being too polite. My coats must have you despairing, and my hair. I want you to summon a barber and a tailor. Do you think you could persuade Mr. Weston to send an assistant here?''

Martin's eyebrows lifted so high in surprise that they almost met his hair. He had suffered even more than the other servants from Simon's lack of interest in his appearance. He had always regarded his master's simple, yet elegant appearance with pride.

"I am sure that he would be happy to oblige you, your grace. But would you not rather go yourself and have more choice?" Martin was hoping to get Simon out at last. On a trip to the tailor, he would be more than likely to meet friends.

"Choice of what? Colors? I cannot discriminate with my fingertips, Martin, and I trust Weston to send his best quality. I will not make a spectacle of myself in a public place, being led around like a performing animal."

"Yes, your grace. I will send a footman over right away." And Martin bowed his way out and then smiled at himself for continuing that now meaningless habit.

Even if he won't go out yet, he thought, at least he is back a bit to his old self, if he is concerned with the fit of his coats!

15

J udith's life had fallen into a comfortable pattern: two mornings a week with Simon, early rides with Barbara and Robin, and occasional shopping trips with Barbara. While there had been no miraculous transformation, Simon was at least involved in something outside himself if only for a few hours a week. He was clearly paying more attention to his appearance and had even allowed a footman to accompany him on some early-morning walks in the immediate neighborhood. Even this small bit of exercise had increased his appetite, and between gaining back a few pounds and his new wardrobe, he was beginning to resemble the old Simon.

After that one day of unparalleled closeness, both Judith and Simon resumed their lighthearted mode of conversation. Miss Austen's humor and gentle satire was just the thing to help them maintain a polite distance.

As they neared the end of *Pride and Prejudice*, Judith decided that if Simon said nothing, then she would directly ask him if she had secured the position. He seemed to enjoy their reading and their conversations, and she could not imagine him letting go of the one thing that occupied his week.

After a Thursday, with four days stretched before him, she often returned to find Simon sunk back into a passive hopelessness. There were times when her heart ached for him, but there were more and more times when she wanted to shake him out of his apathy.

This was one of the latter. It was a beautiful fall day, crisp and clear, and Judith had walked the last few blocks. She came in smelling of fresh air and iris, her exercise having intensified the smell of her light cologne.

"It is so beautiful out, your grace," she said as she picked up the book. "We should leave Elizabeth and Darcy inside Pemberley and go out for a walk." She had begun rather facetiously, but as she spoke, she realized she meant it. She could not bear another minute inside the library. Simon had hovered by the fire long enough!

She stood up and impulsively reached out for his hand. "Your grace, come out with me. I would go for a long walk and would like your escort."

Simon pulled his hand back and said, more coldly than he had in weeks, "You forget yourself, Miss Ware. If you wish to be outdoors this morning, instead of reading to me, I will excuse you and send a footman with you."

Judith was a bit taken aback by his tone, but she was feeling so delighted by the weather and, had she thought about it, so delighted to see Simon again after four days that she was not hearing him fully.

"Thank you, your grace, but I am sure it would be good for you to get out also. You cannot stay locked inside your library forever." Judith had completely and for the first time forgotten her place, and was speaking impulsively, as to a friend and not an employer. The walk had blown all the cobwebs out of her head, and she realized that there was a certain amount of energy that she toned down with Simon, as though he were an invalid.

There is nothing anyone likes less to hear than "It would be good for you." Simon was himself beginning to wake up to the fact that not only would it be good, but necessary, to pull out of the morass of self-pity, or soon completely drown in it. He was terrified, however, of taking the first step back into what would be a very different life. He could hardly admit to himself, much less anyone else, how frightened he was. Fear on the battlefield was one thing; there he had not been alone, but supported by others who were facing the same dangers. This was different. And he did not want anyone telling him what was good for him.

"I fail to see what business it is of yours, Miss Ware."

Judith was stung. To have been so close, and then to have him revert to this dismissive tone . . . it was hard to take.

"You are right, your grace. But surely you yourself must be tired of being such a hermit. I know you see no one but me. You cannot go on avoiding your friends and acquaintances indefinitely."

"And what do you imagine me doing with my old friends, Miss Ware? Shooting? Racing my curricle? Charming the ladies with my compliments on their appearance? Waltzing with them?" Simon's tone was biting.

"Of course I realize many of your former activities would be closed to you. But I am certain you could ride again. Your mind is not impaired: you have a seat in Parliament waiting for you, and the opportunity to speak out on all those issues that we have been discussing. And you have friends, I am sure, who miss your company."

"Oh, yes, I can just see myself being led like a child of five on his pony. I do not wish to be dependent upon others, nor do I wish to make a spectacle of myself. I would become a burden, and friends would be making excuses and I would find myself alone, as I am now."

"How can you be so sure? Are you God, to know exactly how your friends would react? Perhaps some would avoid you, and some, no doubt, would be initially embarrassed and ill at ease. But if you allowed them to work on their own frailties, perhaps they would become used to yours."

"You speak with such good sense, Miss Ware," Simon said sarcastically. "You cannot know . . . you have never experienced living in total darkness. You do not have to worry about walking into a lamppost, or a footman, or off an unseen step."

"It must be difficult, and I know I cannot fully imagine your experience, but you are lucky—"

"Lucky?"

"Yes. You have wealth; you are not reduced to begging on the streets, as so many soldiers are. You can hire me to read to you, or someone else to ride with you. You have a carriage and driver at your disposal. There have been other blind men who have made the best of their situation: Milton, John Fielding—"

"Miss Ware, you have said more than enough. I do not wish to be the Blind Duke of Sutton. I do not wish to be an inspiration to anyone. I wish to be left alone."

"Yes, I see. Alone, to revel in your self-pity. What of those close to you, who wish to see you happy?"

Simon shot up from the couch and felt his way behind it as

he walked toward Judith's voice. She felt his fury and realized how far she had gone. At that moment, however, she regretted none of it and stood her ground.

Simon heard her intake of breath and reached out to grasp her arm. His slid his hand up to her shoulder and shook her as hard as he could. She had spoken to him as no one had dared to, and he was outraged by her assumption that she knew what he was capable of when she had no real idea of what it was like to be without sight.

"How dare you speak to me like this, mouthing platitudes about how much I could accomplish, as though I were a trained animal." He shook her again. He was not shouting, but his quiteness was more frightening. "You play God, and you are completely ignorant of what it is like to be sightless."

Simon felt all the rage that had been smoldering for weeks flare up. He reached out to find Judith's face and, having found it, drew back his hand and slapped her. She finally pulled away and ran sobbing out the door, while Simon, amazed by his reactions, stood there a moment and then, forgetting everything, started to go after her, only to catch his boot on the edge of the carpet. This reminder of his helplessness set him off again, and he felt his way around the room, hurling books off the shelves and smashing the china pieces on the mantel. As he sank back on the couch, exhausted by his outburst, he became aware that he was making sounds like a child on the edge of hysteria. His rasping sobs subsided at last and he felt suddenly very old and very tired, so drained was he. He stretched out and fell asleep immediately, like a child after a tantrum.

Judith had automatically slammed the door behind herself. She stood shaking, one hand on her reddening cheek, and gradually became aware of the sounds from the library. Francis had come out of his office at the sound of the door and, seeing Judith's face, colorless except where Simon had struck her, walked over quickly.

"What has happened, Miss Ware?"

Judith had lost all control and sobbed out, "I have been so wrong to come here . . ."

Francis put his arm around her and led her into his office. "Martin," he said over his shoulder, "stay by the library door in case his grace should need you, but do not go in unless he calls." Francis sat Judith down, and sat facing her, holding her hands in his until she stopped sobbing. "Now, Miss Ware, tell me what happened?"

Judith looked up. "I lost all sense of the fact that I am an employee. I was so happy to be here and it is such a beautiful day that I started by suggesting a walk."

Francis' eyebrows raised.

"Oh, I know, not at all proper. I was just so tired of the duke's passivity, and angry at his self-pity that I spoke without thinking. I said that he could be out riding or walking, that he shuts out his friends, that he is wallowing in self-pity. I was outrageous, and am afraid I have done real damage." She half-rose as if to go back into the library.

"No, Miss Ware," said Francis. "Let him be. You said only what all of us who care about him have been thinking. I have been so harried that I must confess to wanting to shake the duke lately." Francis smiled at her and paused for a minute. "You know, this may have been a good thing, after all. A few weeks ago, the duke was confronted with his own helplessness and anger, and we all felt something of a change in his mood. I am sorry that this time it was you on the receiving end of his rage, but I am not sorry you provided it. Perhaps we have all been too careful."

"Do you think he should be alone right now?"

"I think the library is in more danger than the duke," said Francis. "Whatever is happening needs to run its course."

"I will never forgive myself if my interference has an ill effect. And I won't even know, for Miss Ware will certainly never be admitted again."

"Don't be concerned about that now. I will see you home and—"

"Oh, no," protested Judith. "I am fine now and will go back home myself."

"I will send a footman to the nearest hackney stand if you promise that you will be all right on your own."

"Truly, I will be."

"We have all been living in a quiet but heavy atmosphere, rather like the calm before the storm, as the saying goes. Now that the storm has broken, I think we will all experience some relief.''

''I hope you are right, for I can never forgive myself otherwise.'' Judith rose and averted her face as the footman summoned her.

Francis accompanied her down the front stairs and handed her in. He gave directions to the cab and stood quietly for a minute on the steps as it pulled away. He fervently hoped that he was right in his analysis of the situation.

16

When Judith arrived back at Gower Street, she went to her room after speaking briefly to Hannah.

"Please bring me some cold cloths, Hannah. As you can see, I have been careless. I stood too close to the cab door and have a small mark to show for it." Judith's voice was strained, but she was able to make herself sound calm.

She was sitting on the edge of the bed, holding her hand to her cheek, when Hannah knocked on her door.

"Now, what is this foolishness about you walking into a hackney door?" Hannah asked.

"Oh, Hannah." Judith started to sob.

The older woman sat down next to her and put an arm around her. "There, there," she murmured, "tell me what is wrong."

"I have been such a fool. So interfering and preachy. Simon was right."

"The duke is responsible for this?" Hannah lifted Judith's chin and looked at her swollen eyes and cheek in surprise. "Did he find out that you know the Stanleys?"

"No, no, not that. I was feeling so happy this morning. It was a beautiful day, and I just spilled over in my enthusiasm. I was so tired of seeing him sit there day after day. I thought . . . No, I didn't think, I just spoke. I encouraged him to get out and walk and ride, admit his friends. I even hurled Milton at him."

"The complete works?"

Judith had to laugh. "No, the great man himself, who 'lived a useful and creative life despite his blindness.' It was then Simon exploded. He shook and slapped me, and I ran out, leaving him throwing things. It was awful."

"Maybe you did something right," Hannah said thoughtfully. "You are bound to think the worst now, you are so close to it. I want you to rest for a few hours, and I will call on Major Stanley and have him inquire about the duke."

"Could you, Hannah? I would feel so much better if I just know how Simon comes out of this."

As Hannah closed the door behind her, Judith crawled under the covers and fell asleep instantly.

Hannah went downstairs to set the kitchen to rights before she set off to Clarges Street. When she arrived at the Stanleys', she asked for the major and was shown into the smaller drawing room.

Robin could not imagine any reason for Hannah to seek him out, and he entered the room with a puzzled look on his face.

"What can I do for you, Mrs. Webster?" he asked politely.

"It is not for me, but for Miss Ware." Hannah explained the situation.

"Simon struck Judith? I cannot believe it. He is the gentlest of men."

"She believes she gave him some real provocation, Major. Although, I must say I think it is just what he needed to be shaken out of his self-pity. For that is what the poor man has been suffering from, as well as his blindness."

"You may well be right, Mrs. Webster. I will give Simon some time to collect himself and go over this afternoon, and by God, this time I will see him. Tell Judith not to blame herself. I suspect that I should have done something like this weeks ago."

After Judith left, Francis walked over to Martin, who was still guarding the library door.

"Have you heard anything from his grace?"

"No, it has been quiet for the last few minutes."

"You may go about your work, then," Francis said. "I think it best we do nothing and wait for some sign from the duke."

Francis returned to his desk, where he had an unsatisfactory few hours, lifting his head at every household noise, waiting for the sound of Simon's bell. It was almost three o'clock when he heard his door open, and he turned, expecting to see Martin. There was the duke, standing quietly in the doorway.

"Your grace," Francis stammered, completely taken by surprise and at a loss for words. He rose and started toward Simon.

"You are here, then," said Simon. "I thought I heard your pen scratching away."

Francis stood still, holding his breath and wondering what Simon would say next.

"Come, give me your hand, Francis. I don't trust my memory of your office, and I've bruised my shins quite enough this morning, thank you."

Simon's voice held neither its earlier sarcastic undertone nor its more recent resignation. His expression was open, and his words humorous, not bitter. Francis felt an indefinable something, perhaps aloofness, that remained. But the barriers erected months ago seemed to be down. Francis moved forward and led Simon to one of the chairs opposite his desk.

"What can I do for, your grace?"

"No, Francis, you should rather be asking what I can do for you to repay you for your devotion these last months. I know I have been burdensome to my household as well as my friends."

"Never a burden, your grace. We have all been happy to serve you in any way we could."

"And you have. Perhaps too well," said the duke. "But I think it is time I resumed some of my responsibilities. It has been pointed out to me that I have neglected them long enough."

Francis was not sure whether the duke was still angry at Judith, and was hesitant to mention her name, when Cranston knocked at the door.

"Come in, Cranston."

"Major Stanley is calling, Mr. Bolton." Cranston was through his announcement before he noticed the duke. His face registered his surprise, but he did a masterful job of keeping it out of his voice as he asked, "Should I tell him that you are busy?"

"Send him in," said Simon before Francis had a chance to respond.

Robin entered quickly, expecting to find Francis alone, and eager to question him about Simon. "Francis, I—"

"Good day, Robin," Simon said coolly. He could imagine the expression on his friend's face. "Francis, we will leave you for now, but tomorrow morning I wish to sit down with you and review the business you have so capably handled in my absence. Cranston, could you bring us some brandy and soda? Robin, I beg your arm?"

Robin stepped forward eagerly and Simon placed his hand lightly on his friend's forearm and walked easily out the door. Only Simon knew the effort it took to appear nonchalant, while counting his steps and visualizing the hallway.

It will become easier with practice, no doubt, he thought as he counted off the number of steps he knew it took to the morning room.

Robin seated Simon and took a chair across from him. He searched his friend's face, looking for some sign of welcome, uncertain of how to begin.

"It is good to see you, your grace," he said, rather formally. "I hope I have not intruded. I have called before . . ." Robin hesitated.

"And have not been admitted, due to my stupid pride," Simon said. "You have been the better friend, Robin. I can only give as my excuse that I have not been myself these past few months. I feel like I have been lost in a darkness far beyond the obvious one. Thank you for your faithfulness. Other friends took me at my word after a few refusals."

"There is no need to thank me, Simon. I came because I missed you," Robin said simply. "Not out of kindness, but because you are like a brother to me and I . . . I would give my own eyes if I could . . ." His usual insouciance was quite gone, and his voice broke as he was speaking.

Both men rose, and the duke, putting out his hand and finding his friend, pulled him into a rough embrace. Simon kept his hands on his friend's shoulders after they pulled apart, and said shakily, "And let me look at you." He traced Robin's face lightly. "No scars, Captain? Nothing to drive the women wild?"

"It is Major now, I'll have you know," said Robin, trying to tease things back to normal.

A soft knock at the door made both of them pull back.

"Come in," said Simon, feeling his way back to his chair.

Cranston brought in the tray of brandy and glasses, and Simon dismissed him after instructing him to set it down in front of Robin.

"Robin, will you pour?" he said to his friend, who had gone to the window, his back to the room, to hide the tears that had risen. He was happy for the distraction, and busied himself with the glasses and liquor. Both men had been moved by their unprecedented show of affection, but were relieved to turn to a familiar ritual that enabled them to regain their composure.

They sipped their brandy in silence for a minute, and then a question of Robin to Simon about where he had been wounded led to an animated discussion of the battle. They forgot the time as they became engrossed in military strategy, until Robin, hearing the hall clock chime five, exclaimed, "My God, I must go. I am engaged to escort Barbara to the Stanhopes' tonight."

"Do not let me hold you back," said Simon, rising as he heard Robin move.

"I will be back soon . . . if I may," Robin said, still a bit unsure of his welcome.

"No, I think not."

Robin frowned and began to protest.

"I think it is time for me to return your calls," said the duke. "Would you join me for a drive in the park tomorrow?"

Robin was amazed and delighted. "I can think of nothing I would enjoy more."

"I confess to a selfish reason, my friend," Simon teased. "I need someone trustworthy to tell me when to bow and to whom, so I don't make a complete ass of myself."

Robin realized that however coolly Simon had made the request, he was, in fact, quite vulnerable, and it would require as much courage for the duke to face the public in Hyde Park as it did to face the French at Waterloo.

"Don't worry, Simon, I'll make sure you bow only to the prettiest young ladies and their mamas. They will be thrilled to see you back."

"Until tomorrow, then," said the duke.

When Robin left Simon's, he drove directly to the Wares'. Judith was awake, and sitting by the small fireplace in the parlor, dressed in her morning gown, which was rumpled from her nap. The mark on her cheek had faded, but her face and eyes were still a bit swollen.

"You look terrible, Judith," Robin said from the doorway.

"Robin! Did you speak to Francis? How is the duke?" Judith was trembling in her anxiety to find out the results of her outspokenness.

"I saw Simon, Judith," answered Robin. "He was in Francis' office when I walked in and he offered me a brandy and soda! Whatever you said to him has done nothing but good. It seems as if he is ready to take some steps back into his old life. In fact, he is calling for me in the morning."

"You are not funning me, Robin? You did actually speak to him? How did he look?"

"He looked like you and he have spent similar afternoons. His eyes and face looked tired, but there was an air of acceptance about him, and his sense of humor is intact. We were both quite moved at first. We have not talked since June. He asked to 'see' me."

" 'See' you?" asked Judith, puzzled.

"Yes, with his fingertips. It quite did both of us in, I can tell you. I must confess I could destroy a library myself. This shouldn't have happened to such a man."

"I know," said Judith quietly. "I have felt the same way. How did this excursion tomorrow come about?"

"It was Simon's idea. I think it is his equivalent of leading a cavalry charge." Robin laughed. "If he is going to return to society, he will do so with a vengeance. I think he wants to get the worst over quickly."

"Did he say anything about Miss Ware?"

"Not to me, nor directly to Francis. But I think you ought to go as usual on Thursday morning and see how he reacts. After all, he has not directly dismissed you, nor has he paid you. It would be quite natural to return to speak with Francis. I think it would look strange not to go."

"Oh, Robin, I don't know if I can face him."

"Knowing Simon, I am sure he is mortified by his treatment of you. He will have had time to think about it, and after all, he must be grateful to you for being the catalyst."

"Unless tomorrow is his first and last excursion. What if it doesn't go well?"

"Simon is not a coward, Judith. I don't think he will turn and run. He seems determined, and I think tomorrow is the easiest way to let society know he is back. And what could happen? I will be there to signal when to bow, and whom to speak to . . . and if there are rebuffs, well, Simon won't be able to see those who don't return his bows, will he?"

"So you do not think I made things worse?"

"On the contrary. I think the time was right for someone to confront him. I am sure he will ultimately appreciate your honesty."

"Do you think he will be appreciative by Thursday morning?" Judith asked.

"I am convinced he will welcome you back with a profound apology."

"I hope you are right, Robin. Thank you so much for going out of your way to reassure me."

"It was the least I could do." Robin rose to go. "After all, you have been responsible for returning my dearest friend to me." He took her hand and held it between his for a moment, and left quickly, unwilling to betray his feeling again today.

17

S imon's chaise, driven by his groom, pulled up in front of the Clarges Street house the next morning. Simon, dressed in his new dark blue coat, fawn breeches, and Hessians, sat next to him on the driver's box.

"I will hold them, Michael, while you call for Major Stanley. But ask him to be quick, for they are restless this morning." Simon's hands closed over the reins, and he felt his grays tossing their heads, pulling at their bits. He had lost none of his authority, however, and knew he had them under control. It was a good feeling, and when he heard Robin coming down the steps, he was tempted to hold on to his own horses.

"The major and I will be returning in a few hours, Michael. You can take a hackney back to Grosvenor Square," said Simon as Robin climbed up beside him. "I will have to trust this heavy-handed fellow with my horses' mouths." Simon reluctantly handed over the reins.

"Heavy-handed! If you are going to insult me this early in the morning, your grace, I'll have you bowing to lampposts before this ride is over." Robin flicked the whip over the horses' heads, neatly catching the thong, and they were off at a smart trot.

The park was fairly empty when Simon and Robin arrived, which was why Simon had picked the morning rather than the more fashionable late afternoon. He was determined to show his face, but he knew coping with the *ton* all at once would only confuse and exhaust him. This way he was likely to meet only a few friends and acquaintances, who would pass the word.

Robin pulled the grays down to a dancing walk, and Simon said, "You will tell me to whom I am bowing, but how will I know where to bow?"

"I hadn't thought," admitted Robin. "Why don't we do it by the clock? I will say, 'The younger Miss Stanhope at three o'clock,' and you will turn and bow and smile right into her eyes, and she will then tell everyone that your blindness was a false rumor.''

''By the clock it is, then,'' Simon agreed. And for the first half-hour he found himself bowing at two, and one, and four until Robin at last let the horses out a bit.

''Whew! How was that, Robin?'' Simon asked, relieved they were moving too fast to do more than tip the whip at an occasional rider. It was a strain locating someone by Robin's direction, and also suppressing the anxiety that surfaced at being seen while not being able to see.

''You did well, and for the most part were greeted with looks of pleased surprise.''

''Thank you for adding that, Robin. One thing I never realized was how much we depend upon seeing another's face. I feel quite in the dark, no pun intended, about people's reaction to me and just assume that they will be afraid or put off.''

Just then a horseman cantering by glanced casually at the chaise and, pulling up suddenly, turned his horse around and approached them, saying eagerly, ''Is that you, your grace? By God, it is good to see you.'' Viscount Devenham's voice was warm and enthusiastic, and Simon felt the tension drain out of himself.

''You were used to call me Simon, Dev,'' he said as he leaned toward the voice and reached out his hand. It was a little too far from the viscount, who nudged his horse up and shook it as though he would haul Simon off the seat.

''May I?'' asked the viscount. ''I haven't seen you since your return and I, er, we all wondered . . .'' His voice trailed off. As the younger, less-experienced man, he had been touched by Simon's friendliness toward him on various leaves, and had called twice since Simon's return. After two rebuffs he did not have the courage to face someone he admired to the point of hero worship. ''I did call, your grace, ah, Simon, but—''

''But you were turned away. I know. I have been rather blue-deviled lately. But I would be happy to receive you now, and to beg the favor of your arm at the next gathering we find ourselves at.'' Simon had decided that a matter-of-fact acknowledgment of his dependence on his friends would be best.

"It would be an honor," declared Dev. "Anything I can do to help, I will."

"Thank you, Devenham," Robin broke in coolly. "I can't keep the horses standing, so we will have to move on."

Simon felt Robin sitting stiffly beside him and turned back to give Dev a warm smile as they moved off. "You sounded rather high in the instep, Robin. That's not like you."

"He's too much like a young puppy, falling all over you."

"Yes, but I remember being his age," Simon said, "and following Lord Grey about. I must have driven him mad at times."

"And anyway," Robin continued, "you don't need his arm. You have mine wherever you need it."

"Oh, no, my friend. I will ask you for help often enough, but I do not intend to abuse a friendship. You must not hover about me or feel too responsible. I suspect it is going to be hard, but I must learn to ask for help whenever I need it, and from strangers too, at times."

"You can surely use one of your footmen?"

"Oh, I will, must depend on members of my household to get from one place to another. But I have been thinking about this, and it is not fair to expect them to be with me every moment, standing like statues, deaf and dumb, while I socialize. My friends will have to get used to my asking for an arm to dinner, and must also learn to refuse me when they have something better to do or someone prettier to escort. You must promise to be honest with me, Robin, for I could not stand to be a burden to my best friend."

"I am at your service whenever you need me, Simon. But I promise to tell you if that becomes burdensome or cramps my style."

"Is there anyone whom you are regularly escorting to dinner? I seem to remember you were quite a favorite with Lady Diana Grahame."

"Diana and I did enjoy a flirtation, but that is over. She seems to be occupied with Viscount Devenham at the moment."

"I see," said Simon, and thought he might have uncovered the reason for Robin's unusual impatience. From what he had observed months ago, Diana and Robin had been involved in something more serious than flirtation, although only those close to Robin would have guessed it.

"You have never been one to turn hermit, Robin. With whom are you amusing yourself these days?"

"Lady Amelia Lenox."

"Ah, Amelia. You are not looking for anything serious, then? I had thought you might have come home ready to think about setting up a nursery?"

"There is plenty of time to think about settling down. What of you, Simon? You have even more reason than I to think about getting an heir."

"Me? I hardly think I would now be attractive to any young woman, except perhaps a plain or poorly portioned one, and I do not want anyone's pretended devotion. No, I fear I will remain single."

"And let your cousin Richard inherit?"

"I admit I am disturbed by the thought of that irresponsible fool taking my place. But I do not want a woman's pity, Robin, and I fear it is pity and not love I am likely to inspire. I would always be wondering why my wife chose to marry a blind man."

"I think there are some who might marry you to become a duchess, and a few who might mistake pity for love. But you are no less lovable and attractive because you cannot see, Simon."

"Well, my head may agree with you, Robin, but my heart does not."

"Perhaps your confidence will return in time, Simon, and you will not let pride—"

"Pride? I am not proud, but shamed by my neediness."

"And isn't that a sort of pride, my friend?" answered Robin as he expertly turned the grays. "In fact . . . here, take the reins." And he thrust them into Simon's hands.

"I can't drive, you fool. I'll run into someone."

"I've taken the edge off them. There is no one in front of us. All you have to do is keep them pointed straight ahead." Robin handed Simon the whip and sat back with his arms folded. "We could sit here and argue, your grace, but I am ready for a bit of luncheon at the club."

"Damn you, Robin." Simon felt his horses' power through

the reins. "You are watching? You will tell me if I need to stop?"

"Of course, you gudgeon. Do you think I want to be killed in my prime?"

Simon touched the grays up to a slow trot. As long as he concentrated upon the horses' mouths, and not upon what might be in front of him, he found himself filled, not with fear, but with a rising exhilaration. He lifted them to a fast, steady trot, and Robin and he bowled down the path. His arms were aching from the unaccustomed strain, but he was not completely helpless, he realized, and he laughed aloud at the release. After a few hundred yards more he pulled them up.

"That is enough for one day, I think, Robin. It was wonderful to find I am not quite shut out from something I used to enjoy."

"Tomorrow we will ride, then," said the major, who was feeling as exuberant as his friend.

"Too fast, too fast. One risk at a time. And besides, tomorrow is Thursday. And I hope my reader, Miss Ware, returns. I have quite an apology to make to her."

18

The next morning Judith could not get herself to walk up Simon's steps. She walked the length of the block twice before she finally got up the courage to knock at the door. She fully expected Francis to apologize for the duke, and tell her that their deception was an abysmal failure.

When she was admitted, she saw that the library door was open. Francis quickly beckoned her into his office.

"I am so glad you have come, Miss Ware. I won't keep you. I only wanted to reassure you that the duke is most anxious to see you, and to tell you that you have wrought a transformation."

"Not I," said Judith seriously. "Perhaps I said something that helped the duke, but it could just as easily have harmed him. Are you sure he wishes to see me?"

Just then they heard Simon's voice at the library door, "Did I hear someone come in, Francis?"

"Yes, your grace. I was just taking Miss Ware's wrap."

"Send her in, then."

Judith followed Francis to the library. Simon was at the door, and as he closed the door behind them, she could feel her legs trembling as she turned to face him.

"I am so sorry, your grace . . ."

"I owe you a sincere apology, Miss . . ."

They both began at once, and then Simon put up his hand.

"You must let me say this. I have never lost control of myself before, Miss Ware. I don't know what you must think of me. I can only offer the excuse that I have not been quite myself these past few months."

He hesitated, and Judith replied, "Oh, your grace, I have been so ashamed of myself. I said unpardonable things to you. I had no right to take you to task as I did."

"You only told me the truth, which no one else has been

willing to do. And I thank you for it. I *have* been sunk in self-pity. And I am more fortunate in my wealth and position than many handicapped people. I have been very angry, Miss Ware . . . Oh, not at you, but at my helplessness. I am afraid that I hurt and scared you. I would like you to continue as my reader, but I would understand if you refused.''

Judith put out her hand. ''Here is my hand, your grace. If you can forgive me, I can easily forgive you, and I would be happy to continue as your reader.''

Simon found her hand and took it gratefully in both of his. ''Thank you, Miss Ware.''

They stood there, both feeling the intimacy of the moment. Simon willed his hands not to go to her face, although he suddenly desired above all things to ''see'' her.

Judith broke away first and in her attempt to restore things to normal asked, ''Do you wish me to continue with *Pride and Prejudice*, your grace?''

''Ah, yes. Please, sit down. May I ring for some tea this morning?''

''Thank you, your grace, I would like that.''

Simon moved more confidently, Judith noticed, and instead of taking his usual place on the sofa, he pulled the other chair closer to the fire and sat down, after ringing for Cranston.

''We left Elizabeth and Darcy in Pemberley Hall, I believe,'' said Judith, relieved to be dealing with the fictional problems of a man and woman. ''She was mortified to be found there, and afraid that Darcy would think her forward. Do you remember?''

''Yes,'' said Simon. ''And Darcy was quite different, was he not? Making an effort to be more easygoing and thoughtful? Pray continue, Miss Ware.''

And Judith proceeded, in her clear voice, to lead them back to Derbyshire and into a world where another man and woman stood confused and attracted to each other. Miss Austen's elegant prose had as calming an effect as an intricately constructed piece by Bach, and both Simon and Judith were relieved as the slightly overcharged atmosphere between them became more comfortable and everyday.

After Judith had read for over an hour, she finished a chapter and looked up.

"I think we should end here today, your grace, and continue next week?"

Simon paused thoughtfully, and then spoke, "Miss Ware, I have a request to make."

"Yes, your grace?"

"Now that I am attempting to resume as much of my old life as I can, I realize I will need to be read to more often. My secretary will be able to fill me in on estate matters. But if I eventually plan to take my seat in Parliament again, I must have the newspapers and other materials read to me. I do not wish to eliminate literature, but I would like to know if you could give me more time. It would, of course, mean an increase in your salary."

Judith was torn by her growing desire to spend more time with Simon and her knowledge that since nothing could come of their relationship, it would be foolish to become more involved.

"I do have responsibilities to my brother as his housekeeper, your grace. And I also want enough time for my art. I am not sure I can spare the time."

"On the other hand, you could contribute more money to the upkeep of the household. Would that not outweigh some of the other considerations?"

Judith thought for a minute. She could conceivably give Simon one more morning a week without placing too much of a burden on Hannah, and surely, knowing the danger, she could protect herself from growing too fond of Simon.

"I could come one other morning, your grace. Is there anyone else you can find for the rest of the time?"

"There are a few of my footmen who read and whom I could call upon for the papers, at least. What if you came Tuesdays, Wednesdays, and Thursdays? Would that suit?"

"Why, yes, I suppose so. Does this mean you do not wish to finish Miss Austen's novel?"

"Good heavens, no. I am most eager to discover how things sort themselves out. But it will mean less fiction and more fact, I am afraid."

"Well, then, that is settled," Judith said as she rose to leave. "I will see you tomorrow, your grace."

"Until tomorrow." Simon rose and reached out his hand.

''If you would be so kind as to give me your arm, Miss Ware . . . I need to consult with Francis in his office.'' Simon was not sure why he made this request, since he was moving around the house quite confidently now.

Judith moved quickly to his side and he placed his hand lightly on her arm. She was unsure of how to proceed, and started walking as hesitantly as though she were the one without sight.

''You can walk at a normal pace, Miss Ware,'' Simon said with a trace of amusement in his voice. ''Actually, I am getting quite expert at getting around, but now and then I find I get tired of concentrating so hard and keeping a picture in my mind of where things are and how many steps it is to the door. My memory is improving, but every once in a while I trip over something I could have sworn would not be there.''

Judith listened to Simon joking about himself and found it hard to believe this was the same man she had met a few weeks ago. The despairing self-pity was gone. The anger? She could not imagine that it would completely disappear, especially as Simon came up against things he could not do. His sense of humor had returned, however, and something else had happened also. If Simon had seemed mature to her years ago, she now knew that it had been merely the first flowering of his personality. Now, having been tested, he seemed more real. And having accepted his blindness, humor was his way of protecting himself and keeping others from taking it too seriously. ''If I can manage this, then so can you,'' he seemed to be saying. He had faced his terror and humiliation, and survived.

If Judith had been at all self-conscious about his blindness, she knew she would never be again. She admired his hard-won matter-of-factness and could only respond in kind. If she had ever felt a hint of condescension for his weakness or excessive pity, it was gone. He was a man of strength and integrity, a man who happened not to see, not a ''blind man.'' And as she walked with Simon down the hall toward Francis' office, Judith realized how much she loved him. Not the Simon of her earlier fantasies, not the Simon who needed her, but this Simon, whose light touch on her arm made her feel more than any arms around her in a waltz or the few kisses she had allowed stolen when she was seventeen. She was glad Simon could not see her face, or her flustered movements pulling on her pelisse after she left him with Francis. He would immediately have known. She left quickly, torn between her desire to stay forever and her knowledge that it would be best for her never to return.

19

Although she alternately dreaded and anticipated her mornings with the duke, for the most part Judith found them not as painful as they might have been. Both she and Simon were in agreement about politics, and reading parliamentary speeches gave rise to many lively discussions about the Corn Laws, Ireland's independence, and the beginnings of protest in the north. The novel reading came to a halt after they finished *Pride and Prejudice*. Judith was, after all, relieved to keep to essays and current events, for poetry and fiction were too personal. Both she and Simon were happy not to be confronted with images of men and women and intimate moments, lest it remind them of moments they had shared. They were forming an intellectual companionship and becoming fast friends, or so they both would have answered if questioned. Neither wished to look too deeply into his or her heart. Judith was beginning to think that perhaps she could begin to see Simon only as a friend and somehow suffocate her feelings of love by not acknowledging them. Simon, on the other hand, was far less conscious of his response to Miss Ware. He was throwing much of his returning energy into discovering just what he was still capable of.

A few days after his ride with Robin he had requested his valet to lay out his buckskins and boots. "For I am going to try riding again, Martin."

He rose early and had one of the footmen bring him to the courtyard in front of the stables. The night before he had requested that the groom have Petite Chance saddled for him. She was one of his first mounts. They had grown up together, Simon liked to think, and he had retired her, fat and placid, at the age of twelve. She was waiting, saddled, when he arrived. He ran his hands down her face and scratched behind her ears.

"Well, old girl, are you ready for me? Have you got the line, John?"

"Yes, your grace. Do you need a leg up?"

"I hope not." Simon felt from the reins to the stirrup, and pulled himself up lightly. He gathered up the reins, squeezed the mare's sides, and they moved forward at a slow walk. Simon tried to relax and find his balance. He felt more insecure than he had driving, and it took him a few circles of the yard before he could let his body take over. He was slowly beginning to find that when he forgot he was supposed to see in order to do things, when he concentrated less on his not seeing, and instead on—well, he supposed one could call it "sensing," all his activities became easier. As he and the mare warmed up, going from walk to slow trot, he realized riding was an excellent way of practicing the feeling of moving out from some other place than his eyes and head, for one's balance in riding depended upon shifting one's center from the head to the lower body. Simon had noticed that when he became angry and frustrated— which of course he did often—at his inability to see, he tripped more and lost his way more easily. If, on the other hand, he let his hands and ears and larger sense guide him, as he was doing now, he moved more easily. It wasn't that he forgot his blindness, but that he was not concentrating on it.

John brought the mare around in a wider circle and Simon kicked her into a canter. After half an hour, he pulled her in and dismounted.

"Thank you, Chance," he said. "We may not go over any more jumps together, but we may yet get out of this yard!"

For a week, Simon got up early and rode, forgetting for long stretches of time that he was on a line. The duke did not know it, but he was being watched and secretly cheered on by nearly every member of his staff, from the kitchen maid to Martin. Simon had always been a respected and well-loved employer, one to brag about to other households, but now he was gaining a reputation for miraculous powers. He had oriented himself to the whole house and was moving about with little help. He was back on horseback. But what awed the servants the most was his growing ability to recognize them before they spoke. Simon would catch a whiff of body odor or soap or cheap perfume, and greet a footman or maid before they had a chance to identify themselves. Often, when he was in a room alone, he could sense the arrival of someone before the person announced himself. Simon knew, of course, that these abilities were not magic or miraculous, except that nature seemed to enable one to compensate for the loss of one sense by an increase in the acuity of others.

When Robin called later that week, Simon met him in riding clothes.

"Well, Robin, are you ready to make a spectacle of yourself again, with me on a lead line?" Simon quizzed.

"Have you been riding, then?"

"Yes, I've been practicing in secret. But I'm not sure enough of myself to ride Tamburlane yet. Can you stand the further humiliation of Chance?"

"I can if you can." Robin laughed.

"Then let us proceed. I've had her brought up to the front door. All you have to do is manage your own horse and her line. Can you, do you think?"

"If you are trying to insult me, your grace, you are succeeding," said Robin with mock hauteur. "You would think that I'd get us entangled in trees or around young ladies!"

They set off slowly through the crowded streets, the lead line slack between them and unobtrusive. When they reached the park, it was beginning to get crowded. Robin chose some of the out-of-the-way paths, so they could perfect their partnership. The major's horse was skittish and restless, but nothing fazed the old mare. She twitched her ears if Robin brushed against her, but held her gait steady. Simon was glad he had not ridden his stallion the first time, out of pride. He most likely would have fallen on his face, he thought. With Petite Chance he felt secure, and that enabled him to relax and enjoy the feeling of free movement riding gave him. With Robin holding the line, he need not worry about bumping into anything or anyone.

"I think I need to let him out, Simon. What about it? Do you want to wait here?"

"Not a chance. Just keep the line loose so she can follow at her own pace. Can you keep him to an easy gallop?"

"I'll try." Robin's horse needed no encouragement, but Simon prayed as he slammed his heels into the old mare's sides. She responded well, and they enjoyed a controlled gallop for several minutes before Robin pulled up.

"How was that?" Robin asked.

"Wonderful!" Simon's hair was windblown and he had more color in his face than he had had since his return. "I can't tell you what it feels like to experience even the illusion of being in charge."

"Weren't you the least bit nervous?" Robin asked as they turned and walked the horses back. "I closed my eyes for a moment, and couldn't take the disorientation and the feeling of rushing into darkness."

"I am, or could be, scared all the time, Robin. But I am getting used to it. And you don't ride with your eyes, after all. It is a matter of trust, and that is the hardest part."

"I am not sure that I could ever have that trust," said Robin.

"It is damned hard at first. But one has to choose: some degree of freedom through relying on others, or no freedom at all. I don't find it easy, I can assure you. I never knew what a proud man I was."

"You? Proud? You are one of the most unassuming, least arrogant men I have ever met."

"Ah, yes! Well, that kind of pride I am relatively free of. But there is a much more stubborn kind, my friend. One that says: I am sufficient unto myself, I am strong, I can handle anything life hands me, I don't need anyone. Well, I need you to hold that line, and it is hard to admit. But it would be far harder not to ride or to drive—or go to my first assembly, for that matter," said Simon, changing from his serious tone. "I need you even more next Tuesday to lead me through the Duchess of Ross's musical evening. Were you planning to attend?"

"I am invited, but I'm not as fond of music as you are, Simon, so I had not yet decided."

"Can I impose upon you again?" Simon turned in the saddle and reached over for Robin's arm. "Could you stand the boredom of one evening? I promise I won't drag you with me all the time, but for this first *sortie* I would certainly like your company. It will be a small gathering and I should know most of the guests well. I can sit and listen as well as anyone, so for a first outing, it suits me."

"Of course I'll go," said Robin. "Just promise to dig your

elbow into my ribs if I start to snore while the *signorina* is singing.''

"I believe it is going to be a piano and violin playing sonatas by Mozart," Simon said, grinning at his friend and imagining his expression.

"Oh, lud. You will owe me for this one, Simon."

"And, no doubt, you won't let me forget it." Simon was relieved that Robin was complaining in his old way. If his old friend could feel comfortable doing that, then he could trust him not to let himself be imposed upon. He knew eventually he must ride at times with his groom and find other acquaintances to help him get about on social occasions, but for these first attempts at returning to more or less normal life, he needed Robin with him so he could occasionally let down his guard.

A week later Simon found himself climbing the steps of the duchess's house. Robin was guiding him and giving him sottovoce directions, and Simon was silently praying he would not disgrace himself by tripping or running into other guests who were also being announced by the butler.

"We made it in all right," muttered Simon. "I feel like I did before my first battle, Robin. I am shaking in my boots."

"Well, no one would guess."

The Ross butler greeted him warmly. "It is good to see you, your grace. May I say that we all here are happy to know you are here tonight."

"Thank you, Tyler," Simon said, touched and surprised by the genuine welcome in the man's voice.

Robin brought Simon over to where the duchess was receiving her guests. She was a small, plump, motherly woman in her forties. Her only son had died at Talavera, and she lavished her maternal concern on his friends.

Simon was one of her favorites, and also her godson. Like the rest of his friends she had visited and continuously been turned away. She had awaited his return patiently, convinced his strength of character would win over despair. When she had seen him driving in the park, she decided to risk an invitation. She purposely invited people Simon knew well, to make his

entry back into society as easy as possible, should he choose
to attend.

Tears came into her eyes as she watched the duke make his
bow to her. She could imagine his state of mind and took his
hands in hers and declared her intent of keeping him a prisoner
if he did not give her a proper greeting.

Simon went down to give the diminutive duchess a kiss on
her cheek as she reached up to him, resulting in a gentle bumping
of heads and shaky laughter from both of them. The duchess
touched his cheek gently with her hand and then patted his arm
and told him to hurry in. She knew it was fashionable to be
late, but the violin player was temperamental and liable to walk
off if they did not start on time.

As Simon walked into the music room, he was ready to turn
and leave. He was convinced that all eyes were on him and that
the light drone of conversation he had heard stopped and then
resumed more animatedly. His terror at feeling exposed came
back full force, and only the realization that he could not find
his way out by himself, and Robin's hand on his arm, got him
down the aisle and into a seat. The room became very silent,
and he heard the chair being pulled out from the piano and the
violinist tuning up. The audience applauded politely, and the
duo began with a sonata by Mozart. Simon began to lose himself
in the music, and his fear subsided.

However temperamental the violinist was, he certainly had
genius. The duo's rendering of Mozart was exquisite, and
selections from Handel so pleased the audience that they
demanded an encore. Even Robin managed to stay awake.

After the encore, the artists disappeared and guests began to
move toward the reception and light supper that was to follow.

Simon found himself looking forward to eating. He had been
so nervous all day that he had eaten little. He turned toward
Robin. "I am sure there is some young lady here that you would
rather be escorting to supper, Robin. I appreciate your
patience."

"If you don't stop being such a gudgeon, I will knock you
down. There is no one with whom I would rather be than you,"
Robin said with mock gallantry.

Simon punched him in the arm and relaxed.

Supper was not such an ordeal as Simon had feared. Robin was on his right, and on his left the duchess had placed Lady Brant, a matter-of-fact young woman who had been married several years to an acquaintance of Simon and Robin. She was most unobtrusively helpful in serving Simon, and he appreciated her comments on the location of the food on his plate and the approach of footmen clearing courses. She knew music, and Simon found himself enjoying her comments on the musicians.

After supper, the duchess, who enjoyed both male and female conversation, had the gentlemen rejoin the ladies after only a short time. The musicians were the center of attention, and Simon found himself more at ease. After the first few minutes of awkwardness with old friends, people became more natural in his presence. His air of confidence, his easy requests for help when he needed it, put them at their ease. Only a few people, usually those who did not know him well, were offensive: speaking loudly or slowly to him as though he were deaf and mentally deficient, not blind. He found he was able to regard them with amusement, and a real pity, which surprised him. He realized that they, in a manner of speaking, were more handicapped than he was.

He was relieved, however, when Robin asked him if he were ready to leave. After promising his godmother that he would not keep himself away from his friends again, Simon said a warm good-bye and thank you to Lady Brant. As he shrugged his shoulders into his greatcoat, he waited impatiently for Robin to do the same. When they reached the street, Simon took a deep breath and felt something release inside him.

"Let us go and get terribly drunk, Robin."

His friend was astounded. Simon had never been one for late nights and drinking, even when he was younger. But he sensed Simon wanted to celebrate what was, after all, a personal triumph. He hooked arms with Simon, tipped his hat forward, and swaggered down the street.

"I did it," said the duke later, his voice beginning to slur after their second bottle of champagne. "Do you know, I have never realized how much you need your eyes to hear people.

It was exhausting to keep track of who was speaking to whom. Maybe that toadeater Crooke was right to raise his voice.''

"Dear God, he sounded like he was talking to an idiot child and not a grown man. I was tempted to knock him down.''

"Well, fools are few and far between. But Lady Brant was a dear, and the duchess her inimitable self.'' Simon rubbed his forehead and he and Robin laughed at the memory of the duchess's and Simon's attempted kiss.

When Simon and Robin returned to Grosvenor Square, Martin had the door open even before Robin lifted the knocker, as though he'd been waiting for them. As a matter of fact, Martin, Francis, and Cranston had been waiting, and with every hour they had become more apprehensive. Francis had hoped that the evening had not been disastrous, and when he saw the duke was drunk, he worried that Simon had turned to the bottle to erase the experience of a ghastly evening. When he saw Robin and Simon laughing together, he sighed in relief and turned away from the top of the stairs to seek his own bed.

"Well, Robin, we were a success. I thank you for your company and hope to ride with you soon. G'night,'' Simon said, suddenly drowsy. "I will try to stumble up stairs without waking my household.''

Robin smiled at the members still awake whom Simon could not see, and Martin came forward and took the duke's arm. "Here, your grace, let me help you.''

"Thank you, Martin.''

Robin left Simon in the capable hands of his valet and returned to his own house to sleep off the brandy and champagne.

20

When Judith arrived the next morning, she was shown into the library to wait for the duke.

"His grace has been a little later rising than usual, miss. He will be right with you."

"Thank you, Cranston." Judith was a bit concerned, since Simon was always there to greet her. She hoped he was not suffering from the return of his headaches. A few moments later, she heard his step and looked up from the *Gazette* and almost laughed aloud. She had seen her brother after nights of celebration, and she recognized the walking-on-eggs step and pale face of a hangover.

"I apologize for keeping you waiting, Miss Ware. I had rather a late night and am not at all used to it. My celebrating seems also to have brought on a headache," Simon said ruefully. "I am afraid we will have to turn to poetry or something light. I am in no condition to think about or debate politics."

"Would you rather I left and came back tomorrow?"

"No, no. Why don't you find something familiar, so I don't have to concentrate. I assure you, Miss Ware, my suffering is all the more intense because it is unfamiliar. I do not often drink too much."

"You do not have to explain yourself, your grace," Judith replied. "I am happy to know that you are going out and that it was an enjoyable evening."

"Enjoyable? Yes, but exhausting also. But the first time is the hardest."

Judith pulled out a much-thumbed volume. "What do you think of Shakespeare's sonnets, your grace?"

"Ah, yes. I know some of them almost by heart. I would enjoy that. But not every one of them."

"I will read my favorites, and if I skip over any of yours, please stop me."

"Agreed."

Judith scanned the pages quickly. She had always found some of the sonnets tedious, particularly those imploring the poet's young friend to beget an heir She began to read selectively, and was soon lost in that familiar state where the poet's self and her self seemed to merge. His words were the very words she would have spoken, his feeling of unworthiness and diffidence hers. It did not matter that she was a woman and the poet a man. He seemed to speak with her voice. She forgot to whom she was reading, and read as though addressing her lover.

" 'Who is it that says most? which can say more/Than this rich praise, that you alone are you.' "

Simon could hear the feeling in Judith's voice as she read. He had little doubt that she was speaking for herself. He was surprised to find himself disturbed and annoyed by that fact. He realized he had never really thought about what her life was outside this room: where she lived, with whom she discussed ideas, with whom she laughed, and whom she might love and be loved by. He had so enjoyed their company, and only thought of her as his reader, that he had not seen her as separate at all. The truth was, as she had pointed out, that in this room they shared something special. Barriers of class and sex seemed to disappear. He had no doubt she benefited more than financially from the arrangement. But now he realized he had gained more than that reader for whom he had advertised weeks ago. He had begun to count on her presence. The days she did not come were longer and duller. She had become more like a companion and friend than employee. He would like to think he was impartially interested in her personal life, but the truth was he did not want to lose her presence in his life.

" 'Let me not to the marriage of true minds . . .' " Judith began.

"That is at least one poem about steadfastness and equality in love the poet gave us," said Simon. "He wrote more than I had remembered about a lover's insecurity in love."

"I think the experience of love has room for both. Surely there must be a great feeling of humility at the wonder of being loved, as well as a belief in equality and constancy?"

"And have you felt that insecurity or humility, Miss Ware?"

Judith was surprised to hear a little of the old sarcastic tone in Simon's voice, and was puzzled. She could not know the duke was experiencing the pangs of jealously. Simon was not fully aware of it himself. He only knew that he was not sure any woman could now love him because of his obvious "impediment." Miss Ware was, no doubt, acquainted with other men—friends of her brother, perhaps. For all he knew, she was engaged to one of them, a poorer man than he, and one of no rank, but a whole man. All of a sudden the burden of his sightlessness was back tenfold.

"Why, yes, your grace, I suspect most of us are lucky enough to have experienced the kind of vulnerability that love entails. It is surely a bittersweet part of life, but one I would not miss."

"I fear my headache is getting worse," Simon said abruptly. "I will send you home early today."

Judith murmured the startled hope "that he would feel better," and left. She had expressed herself far too openly and easily and didn't quite know what to make of Simon's hostility. For that is what his impatience and ironic tone had seemed like. She went home and had a short but good cry in the privacy of her bedroom, which relieved her immensely and enabled her to view Simon's abruptness more objectively, as the result of his late night and drinking.

Simon, who could not indulge in a similar relief, decided to ignore all affairs of state and estates and commandeered his footman to take him for a walk. He walked quickly and easily now when on someone's arm, hesitating only when they came to a curbstone. He was becoming adept at using a walking stick to feel for obstacles, but today he depended only upon James.

He was ashamed of himself, he decided. He had snapped at Judith because of his irritability from the night before. And, he had to be honest, because he found, to his surprise, he did not wish to think of her in love. And how did he wish to think of her? As a plain spinster, serving her brother and reading to him for the rest of her life? She is bound to marry, if only not to end up as a maiden aunt in charge of her nieces and nephews. Surely I could not want so warm and intelligent a woman to be condemned to that?

Simon realized that Miss Ware had become an important part of his life. He looked forward to what he thought of as "her" days. He enjoyed the reading not just for its own sake, but for the opportunity it afforded him to hear another view on things. Judith's honesty and her willingness to speak her mind were as appealing as her clear voice and ability to get to the meat of an article or speech.

We have more than a business relationship, thought Simon. We have a friendship, and I don't want her someday to move out of my life. I need her. And the only way to keep her in my life is to marry her.

He had, of course, no thought of romance. He had given up all hope of that. But we have respect for each other, we enjoy each other's company, we share a sense of humor. And I have something to offer that could outweigh the fact of being married to a handicapped husband. I can offer her position and fortune as well as friendship. Surely that makes it not such a bad bargain. Most marriages, after all, are based on far less mutual liking and respect. And I want an heir, he thought suddenly, surprised at the intensity of his desire, for he thought he had resigned himself to his cousin's eventual succession. I would not force myself on her, but surely we could work out a partnership that would serve us both.

Having so rationally sorted out his feelings, Simon meant to waste no time. He intended to present his proposition to Judith the next morning, before he let his conviction weaken.

After her cry of the day before, Judith had scolded herself for her missishness. I respond with far too much sensitivity. One bad mood of the duke and I am overset. He is only a man, after all, and it is unfair to romanticize his bravery and not allow him bad moods. When she returned the next morning, therefore, she had put the incident out of her mind and busied herself finding her place. Then she realized the duke was restlessly pacing back and forth behind the sofa, his hand running along the back as he turned. He reminded her of a caged animal.

She sat down and watched him pace a few minutes more. She was reluctant to break the silence. He obviously had something on his mind and she would wait until he was ready.

"Miss Ware?" Simon had finally stopped and turned to face her, as he located her by her voice.

"Yes, your grace?"

"I have done some thinking since yesterday. First, I wish to apologize for my bad temper."

"There is no need, your grace. I had quite forgotten it, and so should you."

"Thank you for your tolerance." Simon's tone was cool and rather businesslike, covering up his nervousness. "I have something I wish to ask you."

"If it is for more reading time," she broke in, "I fear I would not be able to give it to you." Judith was unable to think of anything else Simon would want from her.

"No, it is not as your employer that I wish to speak," said the duke. His tone softened. "It is as a friend. I hope that I may consider us friends?"

"Oh, yes," Judith said warmly. "I am happy to hear we share the same view of our relationship."

"Well, then, I have been thinking of how we may be of some help to each other."

Judith had no inkling of what was to come. If Simon did not want to increase her hours, then what other service could she render? Advice on another employee? Advice on a matter of the heart? Perhaps he had formed a *tendre* for some lady of quality and was afraid to approach her. Judith's hands grew cold as she realized they had been speaking of marriage the other day. She felt as if she were on the edge of an abyss, waiting to find out if she was to jump.

"I would like you to consider becoming my wife, Miss Ware. I can offer you my friendship, and security and position. I know this may seem rather sudden," Simon said, after a moment of dead silence while Judith sat in shock. "I could think of no gradual way to approach this, and once I was convinced, I wished to convince you. After all, we know and like each other better than many couples do before they marry."

Judith was speechless. If she had ever entertained the fantasy of an offer from the duke—and she had—her fantasy was one in which Simon interrupted her reading of a love lyric to tell her how much she had come to mean to him and then reached over to pull her into a passionate embrace. She would have had to refuse, of course, because of the difference in their stations. But she had never imagined a scene where he would discuss what sounded more like a rational arrangement than a loving union.

"I don't quite know how to answer you, your grace," Judith said slowly.

"You do not have to give me an immediate answer, Miss Ware. I know this is sudden, and perhaps all the advantages I can offer you do not, after all, outweigh the disadvantage of a blind husband." Simon wanted that objection, which to him was the crucial one, out in the open.

Judith was beginning to get angry. Simon was correct, there was an unprecedented intimacy between them; they had spoken of it before, that feeling of equality and companionship that existed in the world of Simon's library. He had, she knew, a warm regard for her. But he sounded as though he had been weighing the pros and cons of the match in some imaginary scale where his blindness was outweighed only by his wealth and position. On which scale they were equal only with regards to outside measurements: her lack of money and position balanced by his handicap.

"You speak of friendship and of advantage and disadvantage, your grace, but not of love?"

"Oh, I do not expect love, Miss Ware," Simon said, rushing in to reassure her. "One of the facts I had to accept with my blindness was that I would never figure in any woman's romantic dreams."

"And friendship is enough for you?"

"It will have to be," Simon answered quietly.

"And what would I get, to outweigh, as it were, a handicapped husband?"

"You would have my faithful companionship as well as all the advantage of my wealth and power. As you know, I intend to resume my seat and play an active role in politics, and your interest in reform, would, I am sure, give you an additional reason—"

"Well, that is not enough for me," interrupted Judith. "Perhaps you do not expect love in a marriage, but I do. You speak as though you are offering me an honor, as I suppose in a way you are. But underneath you are insulting both me and yourself. You make the assumption that no woman of your own rank could love you, and therefore you are willing to settle for a poor gentlewoman whom you think dependent upon your favors. And you assume becoming a duchess would be more important to me than who my husband was, or how he felt about me."

"You make it sound as though I am proposing a typical marriage-mart interaction," said Simon. "I assure you I was thinking more of the fact of our friendship. I was thinking, after yesterday, of a marriage of true minds.''

"I agree that friendship need be a part of marriage. But certainly one would wish a husband and wife to be bringing more than their minds to such a serious step. In your offer is the suggestion that each of us is in some way unmarketable, that we need to settle for a rational union. Well, I wish for friendship in marriage, but I also want a more passionate kind of love, however shameless that makes me, and if I do not find a man who can give me both, I will live alone.''

Simon had been so sure she would see the mutual advantage, the way he had, that he was completely floored by her response. Was she expecting him to claim he loved her? It certainly did not sound as though she loved him. He was so convinced no woman could love him passionately that he could not even begin to guess what lay behind Judith's anger.

"Miss Ware, I see I have made a complete mull of this. I did not mean my proposal as an insult. It merely occurred to me that a friendship was a good basis for marriage and that we both need each other, in different ways.''

"Need! Oh, I see. You protect me financially and I take care of your needs for a reader and a . . . breeder.''

Simon was shocked and rather angry himself by now.

"That is not how I meant it at all. I would never have imagined you would take it this way.''

"You have a very poor imagination, then! You are operating under several false assumptions. One is that a marriage—or, yes, even a friendship—is founded only upon a mutual and equal meeting of needs. You think you need me, your grace, to read, to converse with, to provide female companionship and eventually an heir. You think that because I need security and my own household, I would take you despite your blindness.''

"So it *is* my blindness that is the obstacle.'' Simon's face was wiped clean of all expression.

"Oh, you are such a great fool,'' Judith cried. "You are blind and deaf to what is right in front of you. Your sense of inferiority keeps you from seeing what you don't need eyes for.'' Which is, she thought, what is right here in this room, between us.

"I did not realize you considered me a fool,'' Simon said stiffly.

"Your grace," she said, speaking more calmly, "I do appreciate that you value the friendship between us enough to consider marrying me. But as much as I value it, I could not marry without love. Marriage, after all, is a union of bodies as well as minds." Judith was blushing, could Simon have seen her. "I am convinced a husband and wife should be equally delighted in each other physically as well as mentally. I know very few are lucky enough to find this in marriage, yet I still hope for it myself. I am sorry you have given up that hope. I think you have come to terms with your blindness most courageously. But I think until you learn that you are still attractive to women and that you are free to choose, rather than be resigned, no woman's heart would be safe with you. She would never know whether you wanted her for herself or only because you did not believe in the possibility of having anyone else."

"Perhaps what you say may be true in an ideal world, Miss Ware. But here in our world what is found attractive is appearance, grace, and strength. I no longer move with grace. I am dependent. No, hear me out," he said as Judith started to protest. "I cannot see. I have made my peace with that. I will never sink back into despair, although I know I will continue to feel it occasionally. I am, however, helpless. I cannot move across a strange room without someone to guide me. I could not dance with my wife. I could never compliment her upon her appearance, or indeed upon the beauty of our children. I cannot win a woman's admiration by my horsemanship. I shall always be, at some level, angry and ashamed, and I cannot always hide that."

"I cannot believe that you, of all men, think so little of women. Of course there are many to whom those things would matter. But I never imagined those sort were intimates of yours. Do you think all women value a man because he can put a hole in the middle of the bull's-eye at Manton's? I suppose some women are superficial enough to care that you could not see their new gown. But that you would think passion is dependent upon externals . . . It is as though we have been brought up in different countries and speak a different language."

Simon had revealed more of his feelings than he had to anyone, having been carried away in the heat of the moment and the openness that was the chief characteristic of their friendship. He could, in his resulting discomfort, only fall back upon the role of employer.

"I am sorry I have distressed you by all this, Miss Ware. I most certainly would not have made my proposal had I not thought you might be receptive to it. I did not, though you obviously think it, expect an immediate and suitably humble response. I am afraid, however, that we have gone too far to return to our comfortable companionship. I apologize both for upsetting you and for having to deprive you of this income. I feel honor-bound to continue your salary until you find something to replace this position. You will, of course, receive high recommendations."

Judith sat completely still. Under the circumstances, it would be impossible to continue in the duke's employment. She had said too much to ever be able to go back to an easy companionship, pretending his offer had never occurred. Had there truly only been friendship between them, a polite offer might have been politely rejected, and after some moments of embarrassment, she might have continued as his reader. We would never have flown at each other if there were no stronger feelings, she thought. It is his damnable blindness that gets in the way. And now I will never see him again. She did not know how she could bear it. And yet she could not have accepted him. She knew that. His offer would have given her what she wanted above all: to be with him. But she was convinced both of them would have been settling for far less than they could find with each other. How could she take advantage of his insecurity? He had to discover that he was, with or without sight, still capable of attracting women. He wanted to be safe from the insecurity and vulnerability of love. Well, thought Judith, no one could be safe, or protect himself from that lover's humility of "You could not possibly love me," by substituting a false humility of "You could not possibly love a blind man." She would not help him cut himself off from that experience and, at the same time, accept half of what she wished for him. She was, she realized, more of a gambler than she thought: all or nothing.

"I am happy that I have been of service to you, your grace. I feel privileged to have formed this friendship and am only sorry it must end. I cannot, however, take a salary for something I have not done."

"You must at least take a month's pay in severance," said the duke.

"All right, your grace." Judith stood up and was surprised to find her legs shaking. She almost sat right down again. 'Would you ring for my wrap? I would rather not wait in the hall for it."

"Of course," Simon said, and then stood, waiting for Martin to bring Judith's pelisse.

When she was ready to leave, she turned to him and reached out her hand to grasp his. "I wish you well, your grace." She turned quickly and left before Simon had time to respond.

He stood there, listening to her steps. The sound of the front door closing behind her echoed throughout the house, making it feel empty and cold.

When Judith got outside, she found that what had begun as a sunny day had turned, in typical London fashion, into a cloudy, wet one. The clouds now scudding across the sky, were spitting rain. There was no hackney in sight. She was glad. She could not have faced anyone and felt driven to some activity. She decided to walk at least part of the way home. After a few blocks, the rain became heavier, and she pulled her pelisse around her, wishing she had worn her old cloak. The rain dampening her hair began coursing down her face, mingling with her tears. Her slippers were becoming wet cardboard, but she was almost glad of the discomfort, since it distracted her from the pain of leaving Simon. She was vaguely aware of rude stares and comments as she walked, but she was so lost in her misery that it took some minutes before she heard a familiar voice addressing her.

"What the deuce are you doing out in this weather, Judith? Get into my carriage before you catch your death." Robin had been on his way to Simon's when he noticed her bedraggled figure. "I thought this morning was one of your mornings with the duke?"

"It is . . . was . . . Oh, Robin, he asked me to marry him." Judith started sobbing.

"There, there," Robin said soothingly, giving her a hand up. "I would have thought you might be happy at that? Perhaps I have been wrong in thinking you have come to care about Simon?"

"I do, but Simon does not love me. Perhaps he could, but he doesn't know that yet. No, he asked me to have a sort of marriage of convenience. In his heart, he does not believe a blind man is lovable, and he sees us as being mutually useful to each other.''

"Would that be such a bad beginning to a marriage?''

"Robin, I love him too much to accept an offer when he believes no one else will. What kind of marriage would that be? I want him to ask me as a whole man.''

"I didn't think his blindness would bother you, Judith?''

"Lord, you are as bad as he is, and you take me so literally. I don't mind that physical dependence, except for his sake. That is nothing. No, it is his sense of willingness to settle. The old Simon would not have settled. He was no coxcomb, but he was aware of his attractiveness to women. If he married me now, how could I ever trust his feeling for me? He sees it as a good bargain: my lower status weighing in the same as his blindness. Surely you see I could not accept!''

"Yes, I begin to understand. But how will he ever be convinced he has much to offer any woman?''

"Only by meeting someone else of his own rank who is attracted to him as he is. The irony, of course, is that that will not restore him to me, but take him away altogether.''

"I cannot think of any woman he could meet who would be as right for him, Judith.''

"There will be someday. The more he resumes a full social life, the more likely it is to happen. And there is nothing I can do.''

"Let me take you to Barbara,'' Robin said.

"Thank you, Robin, but, no, I'd rather go home. I will come and visit soon, but for now I need to be alone.''

"Whatever you wish, my dear.''

When they reached Gower Street, Robin gave the reins to a small boy who was standing about on the corner, and walked with Judith to the door. "Take care, Judith. We will see you soon, I hope?''

"Yes, Robin, I am not one to go into a decline, I assure you,'' said Judith, attempting a smile.

Robin kissed her lightly on the top of her head and rescued his team from his new ''groom,'' who was so intent on fending off two friends who wanted in on the job that he had almost forgotten the horses themselves.

21

H annah opened the door just as Judith was turning the handle.

"You are back early, Judith," she said with some surprise, for Judith was more likely to stay more than her two hours with the duke than to cut them short.

"Yes, Hannah, and I fear I am back to plague you until I find another position. I will not be returning. The duke and I have had a disagreement."

Hannah looked at Judith's face and knew the disagreement went beyond the political or literary. She had not seen such a look on her face since Judith's father died. She asked no more questions and, putting her arm around the girl's shoulder, drew her in and shut the door behind them.

"You are soaking wet, child," she exclaimed as she felt Judith's dress.

"Yes, I was walking home until Robin picked me up."

"Go upstairs immediately and get into something dry, or you'll catch your death. I'll make us a pot of tea."

"Yes, Hannah." Judith smiled to herself at Hannah's mothering. Since they had moved to London, she had been treating Judith, at least, like a grown woman. (Stephen, of course, being her "baby," would probably never be anything else in Hannah's mind, even when he reached fifty!) At this moment, however, she was very glad to feel taken care of.

She pulled off her wet dress and stood shivering as she toweled herself dry. She pulled on an old wool gown. Her shoes were probably ruined, she thought as she slipped her feet into a pair of slippers.

When she got down to the parlor, Hannah was there, stirring up the fire. The old Staffordshire teapot that Hannah had brought with her was sitting on the table. Instead of milk, Hannah had brought a lemon, and the translucent slices were neatly arranged on a celadon plate. For one moment, Judith forgot Simon, in her appreciation of the still life in front of her: amber tea, blue-green plate, thin wheels of fruit, and thick slices of brown bread. No matter how miserable I am, there is always this, she thought—"this" being the ability to be caught up in a moment that revealed the beauty in commonplace things. She thought of Simon, who could not find any solace in what was to be seen around him, and the tears, which she had been holding back since meeting Robin, started to roll down her cheeks.

Hannah turned and saw Judith standing there, gazing at the tea tray. She quickly moved over to her, and pulled her against her bony chest. Judith's ear remembered the feel of Hannah's sternum, and a tendril of her hair caught on a button, just as it had when she was younger and turning to Hannah for comfort. She let herself go and sobbed away as Hannah stroked her hair, murmuring soothing phrases.

Judith at last pulled back and winced as her hair pulled free from the button. "Oh, Hannah, now you are all wet, as though you had been out in the rain! I am sorry, but I needed that cry."

"Here, blow your nose," said Hannah, thrusting a napkin at Judith, "and then sit down and have your tea."

Judith obeyed and Hannah poured her a cup. She squeezed some lemon into it and stirred in a small teaspoon of honey.

"There. That should keep you from getting a cold. And lift your spirits." Hannah was trembling with curiosity, but would not lower herself to ask. Either Judith would tell her the details or she wouldn't, but she would find out in any case, for nothing could remain hidden for too long in such an informal household as they kept.

"Well, Hannah, you deserve to know what I've done," Judith said after a few sips had warmed her. "I've refused a duke!"

"Humph. You refused the squire because you didn't love him. I don't know that it's being a duke makes that much difference."

"You are right. It is not his being a duke that makes the difference. It is the fact that I love him."

"And why, then, did you refuse him?" Hannah was secretly relieved on one point: Judith had fallen in love. She had been as worried as Stephen that her isolation and lack of portion would discourage offers. And that her intelligence and independence might keep her from feeling anything closer to passion than warm regard.

"Because he doesn't love me. He only asked me because he thought it would be a fine marriage of convenience. No, I do him an injustice. He would be a kind and faithful husband, I am sure, and would expect the same from his duchess. But he no longer expects any woman to respond to him passionately, and so he is only looking for a full-time reader, after all."

"If you love him, why not marry him in the hope that he will come to love you?"

"Because I am convinced Simon cannot love anyone until he knows women can still be attracted to him, that he is, indeed, still lovable. So here I am, sending him off to find love with someone else. I won't even see him again. The only way I was ever likely to see him in London was the way I did: as his employee."

"Major Stanley and Lady Barbara are his friends. Surely you will have news from them and could even run into him at their house?"

"He doesn't know we are acquainted, and they can hardly introduce me without exposing our small deception. No. I shall have to make up my mind to never seeing him again. And now I am also again without an income."

"Surely he would not have sent you off with nothing?"

"No, as a matter of fact, he offered to pay my wages until I found a new position, but I would accept only a month's severance pay. I suppose I will end up tutoring or teaching young ladies to draw, after all. But I don't have the heart to start looking again."

"And so you shouldn't. We certainly have enough to run the house. I think you should give yourself some time before you go off to another position. You need to get back to your own drawing, and spend more time with the Stanleys. You must, it seems, avoid occasions when the duke might be there, but I see no reason for you to continue your stubbornness about accepting invitations from those you meet at Lady Barbara's."

"Perhaps you are right, Hannah," she said thoughtfully. "Perhaps I will accept an invitation to call or to a small dinner. It would keep my mind off the duke. Barbara has offered me a gown, and I could use some of my wages for a walking dress or two instead of more books. It would be something to look forward to, now that there is nothing else."

Hannah nodded in agreement. She was convinced Judith needed to be with her peers, not just to help ease her heartache, but also for enjoyment. Lord knows, the girl has had no fun in her life for the past three years, she thought. She has not danced or flirted, and her work with the duke would hardly fit into the category of light entertainment. They had obviously both needed the intimacy, but a lasting attachment must move out of the hothouse atmosphere of two together and survive exposure to the outside world. It will be good for him too, she mused further, to miss her and not take her for granted. From what she has told me, he does need to find his way socially again, and this he can do only alone. And eventually they very well may encounter each other by accident at a dinner party or musical evening . . .

22

On Thursday morning, Francis was surprised to see the duke still at breakfast at ten o'clock. Judith was usually a few minutes early, and Simon was always in the library waiting for her.

The duke heard him in the hall, and called out, "Is that you, Francis?"

"Yes, your grace."

"Can you join me for a cup of tea?"

"Certainly." Francis sat down and the footman in attendance poured him a cup and offered him muffins from the sideboard.

Simon nodded to the footman and said, "You may leave us," and sat silent for a moment, staring in front of him.

"Is there anything in particular that your grace wanted?" Francis asked.

Simon started. "I am sorry, Francis. Yes. I wish you to write out a draft to Miss Ware for a month's wages. And write her a letter of recommendation for me to sign. She will no longer be reading for me."

Francis took a minute to absorb this news. As far as he knew, Judith had been a very satisfactory reader. Francis was usually busy when Judith came and went, but on the occasion he was in the hall when they were saying good-bye or greeting each other, he had seen that the duke and his reader were on comfortable friendly terms. He was grateful to Judith for her part in Simon's recovery, and had grown to like her very much. She always had time for a short conversation with Francis himself. He could not imagine what could have happened to upset what was obviously a satisfactory arrangement for all concerned.

"Was Miss Ware unhappy here, your grace?" Francis did not want to press the duke. If he wanted to let down the barrier between employer and employee, he could, and he often did.

But Francis was never the one who took the initiative. He left it to Simon to confide in him.

Simon sighed. "No, Francis, it isn't precisely that. Tell me honestly: if you were a woman, would you consider marriage with a blind man?"

Francis was not sure what the question had to do with the matter at hand, but Simon was clearly inviting him to answer as an intimate, and it was also clear that Simon was considering a painful reality. Francis had no illusions about the *ton*. As the younger son of a country squire, he himself carried no value on the marriage market. No parent would wish his daughter to contract an alliance with someone who had no inheritance, no matter what his prospects as the secretary of a nobleman. Money and rank were the first considerations in most minds.

After fortune and position, appearance was of the greatest importance. What most of society shared was the belief, however illusory, that they were above the common herd. Appearance was all, and any falling away from outward perfection that might remind them of their own vulnerability was shunned. So Simon's question, obviously already answered in his own mind, was one that Francis knew emerged from a real concern. He was not about to dismiss it with a glib, optimistic answer. He spoke thoughtfully, "I think many young women would not, your grace. I would guess a particularly conventional young lady and her family would be looking for 'perfection.' And even some less superficial woman might still draw back from the difficulties. But I would think an intelligent woman in love with the man would not see his blindness as a reason to reject him."

"Perhaps you are right, Francis, but I am convinced, rightly or wrongly—and perhaps it is self-pity—that it is unfair to ask a woman to take on such a burden unless there is more to offer in return. I suppose you are wondering what all this has to do with Miss Ware? I asked her to marry me and she refused."

Francis was less surprised than he might have been. He had, upon a few occasions, felt something between the duke and his reader. But it was not done, for someone of Simon's rank, to consider a woman in his employ, no matter how gently bred, as a wife.

"I am not quite sure what to say, your grace. I am surprised, of course, since Miss Ware is clearly not someone you would have previously considered choosing for your duchess."

"You are right, Francis. Despite my radical politics, I am more bound by family feeling than I thought I was. But this is not before Waterloo, it is after. I am different, and it seemed as if Miss Ware and I were good companions and had something to offer each other. It seemed a fair bargain: wealth and position in exchange for a blind husband."

"And Miss Ware's opinion on the question?"

"Gave me another show of her independent mind, Francis. Accused me of insulting her, of insulting both of us. She claims that until I again believe myself an attractive man, my feelings for a woman cannot be trusted. That I was acting out of some sort of pride."

Francis wished Miss Ware had accepted the duke's proposal. He suddenly realized that of all women, Judith Ware, with her straightforwardness and sense of integrity, was precisely what Simon needed in a wife. Rank be damned, thought Francis, surprising himself. She loves him. No woman who didn't would have turned down such an offer. And he may even love her, but he most certainly does not know it.

Simon might not have been aware of the depth of his feelings for Judith, but over the next few weeks he certainly felt her absence. Now that he was truly preparing himself for his return to politics, he had to have another reader. Another advertisement was placed, and this time several male candidates presented themselves. Mr. Whitehedd, remembering his unconventional hiring of Miss Ware, and having no other information about her departure other than she was unable to continue her post, surveyed the applicants and, for no reason known to himself, chose the most nondescript of them: a Mr. Wiggins, who had previously been employed in a small firm that had closed on the death of its founder and owner.

Mr. Wiggins was in his early fifties and wore a muffler that seemed to take hours to unwind when he arrived. He smelled musty to Simon, as though he had been sitting on a shelf for the last thirty years—which, considering the nature of a clerk's job, he had. His reading was perfectly satisfactory, if a bit colorless. He showed no initiative, nor did he venture any opinions of his own, but followed Simon's wishes to the letter. Simon had to admit that the amount of reading they did together was more than he and Judith would get through, since she was wont to stop and make comments on the speeches they were reading. Whether serious or humorous, Simon always responded, and they would find themselves in many a discussion that drew them away from the task in front of them. Not that it was a waste of time, thought Simon one morning as he listened to Mr. Wiggins reading in his uninflected, even tone. *Our arguments helped refine my thinking, and while we most often agreed on ends, her views came from a different vantage point and gave me another way of looking at an issue.*

The days on which Judith had read had had a different feel to them. Simon had not realized it, but on Tuesdays, Wednesdays, and Thursdays, he awoke with a sense of anticipation. While Mr. Wiggins was certainly satisfactory, he certainly aroused no feelings of enthusiasm in the duke. To Simon, who depended upon smell and voice and nuances in tone to get a sense of a person, Mr. Wiggins had all the personality of a ledger.

Mr. Wiggins had become an expert at invisibility as a clerk, and the only thing that had given him the courage to apply for a position in a nobleman's household was depression. He and his wife had no children to help support them, and this salary was all that stood between them and the poorhouse. Like Judith, he had pictured himself reading for an older man, blinded by age, and was surprised to find his employer so young. Since his picture of young noblemen was greatly colored by the caricatures of the day, he had not expected to like the duke. But he was very moved, as he told his wife, by the young man's acceptance of his handicap.

"He has not let it embitter him, my dear, and far from being proud, he is everything that is gracious. He can find his way about the house, and even rides. He is quite a radical. I enjoy reading for him, and he has even set me to taking notes on articles and speeches. If only we had more like him, who took their responsibilities seriously . . ."

As always, it was impossible for anyone in regular contact with Simon not to feel affection for him. So Mr. Wiggins continued arriving and leaving punctually, unwinding and winding his long muffler, gradually feeling comfortable enough to accept a cup of tea, and later regaling his wife with the sights and sounds of Mayfair. After a few weeks, Mr. and Mrs. Wiggins began to feel protective toward Simon. His blindness made him human and less remote, and the fact that he was without close family aroused their dormant parental feelings.

Simon, of course, would have been embarrassed, particularly since he had no feeling for Mr. Wiggins at all, except a recurring disappointment that he was not Miss Ware.

In the afternoons, Simon met with Francis on estate business and then either went riding or driving with Robin. It was getting colder, and fewer people were out in the park, because of the weather and because the *ton* was preparing to return to the country for the holidays. Simon did not mind. He found it a strain to be attentive to every sound and be careful to acknowledge people. While he did it well, to recognize mere acquaintances by voice wore him out, and yet it would not do to slight anyone. But since the riding itself was exhilarating and freeing, he continued to go out every day. In the evenings, however, he was selective. So far he had been able to avoid social gatherings larger than dinners and musical evenings. Since he could, in truth, do nothing but talk, and since he needed an escort to dinner, he felt perfectly justified in avoiding the balls and routs he was invited to. This week, however, he was going to attend his first ball. He was not looking forward to it because, as he told Robin, "I will be relegated to sitting out dances with chaperones, wallflowers, or even worse, retired generals who will want to refight the Peninsular campaign with me. But I am planning my speech for the spring, and I need more contact with the politically influential. But for God's sake, don't let go of me, Robin."

Simon was dressed for the evening as simply as fashion dictated, in black knee breeches, black coat, and only a sapphire winking from his cravat. He had regained all of his lost weight, and the daily riding had ensured that it was regained in muscle, not fat. His sandy hair fell quite naturally in a Brutus. The only other jewelry he wore was his signet ring. While he was not as classically handsome as Robin, whose blondness was the ideal, he looked quite attractive. He had no look of a blind person about him. He worked hard at not staring blankly, and was now moving fairly confidently, even in unfamiliar surroundings, with the arm of a friend or servant, and occasionally with his walking stick. When they reached the door, however, after a long wait in the crush of carriages, Simon, listening to the hustle and bustle around him, was almost ready to return home and never attempt this again. He knew what it would be like: a crowd of people on the stairs, and in the ballroom the noises of the orchestra and dancers and conversations. All would combine to disorient him, since he depended upon his ears so much. If Robin was jostled aside, he was lost, and the fear of possible humiliation made him dig his fingers into his friend's arm as they waited on the crowded stairs.

Robin, of course, had no intention of losing Simon. "Don't worry," he joked under his breath, "I'm holding on to you so neither of us gets lost." Trying to relax the duke, he continued in his vein, making outrageous comments on the more ridiculously affected members of the *ton*, and finally felt Simon's grip on his arm relax as they passed through the receiving line and into the ballroom.

The ballroom itself presented another problem. Robin had no intention of leaving Simon with either the dowagers or the elderly ex-military. He sought for and found a group of their friends who were in the far corner, debating politics and arguing over who was the most pushing mama of the Season. It was generally agreed that Lady Hyde, who had four daughters to marry off, none of them particularly attractive and one at least decidedly plain, was, as Archie Clare put it, "a royal pain in the arse."

Simon realized he had something to be thankful for, and jokingly said, "Well, at least I am spared all that. No mother is going to be pushing her daughter in my direction."

His friends laughed and then Viscount Devenham said, "No, no, Simon, I'll lay odds that Lady Hyde approaches you this evening with her third daughter, Lady Alice. She would calculate your blindness as an advantage, because you will not be able to see how plain her daughter is."

They all laughed, including Simon, and began to make bets with one another. Underneath his enjoyment of the teasing, which meant his friends were at last at ease with him, was a discomfort with their underlying disregard for the reality of those who did not live up to fashionable standards. He found himself looking at them all through Judith Ware's eyes. Critical as he had always been of his society, he could not help but have absorbed some of its basic attitudes, one of them being that the main reason for marriage was an exchange of properties and titles, not love. If a husband and a wife liked each other, that was an unexpected bonus, but love was a luxury the rich could not afford.

Now that Simon was no longer a good "catch," now that his worth, which had been taken for granted, would be weighed against his blindness, his eyes were more open to what had always been there, unseen because so familiar. He had been lucky enough to have parents whose marriage included respect and love. But he had visited friends whose parents rarely saw each other. Coming from homes like that, it was no wonder that the young men he knew were so cynical; and living in a society where survival for a woman meant connection with some man, no wonder young girls and their mothers pushed to find the best match they could. Simon's position was now as vulnerable as any plain woman's or son of an improverished peer.

He was brought back from his musings as he realized the orchestra was tuning up for a country dance, and several of his friends were muttering about doing the pretty and leaving to partner the most attractive miss they could find. Simon touched Robin on the arm and said, "Please don't let me hold you back from enjoying yourself."

"I am going to skip this one," answered Robin. "Let me get us a glass of punch."

Simon stood there, feeling his old fear of being exposed flood back. He was only a part of the scenery, but felt his anxiety mounting as he waited for Robin to return. I cannot depend upon him like this, he thought, I must get used to being alone. He heard a rustling noise and smelled a combination of heavy perfume and acrid body odor as he felt someone approach.

"Good evening, your grace," said an older woman's voice.

"I saw you standing alone here, and said to my Alice—make your curtsy, Alice—that you should not have been left so." The woman was talking loudly at Simon, as some people tended to do, as though he were also deaf or lacking in wit, and he stepped back to get away from the voice and almost tripped on a chair behind him. Lady Hyde, for that was of course who it was, immediately grabbed his arm and clucked solicitously.

"You see, you do need someone with you," she said stridently, and pushed her daughter forward. Poor Alice, who was not even eighteen, and the despair of her mother and sisters for her lack of attraction, was red with embarrassment. She was used to her mother's insensitivity, but this rudeness and presumption was the outside of enough. She was so sorry for Simon that she was able to summon up the courage to face down her mother.

"I am certain the duke is very capable of handling himself, Mama," she said in a low voice. "We did not mean to disturb you, your grace," she said swiftly, rather aghast at her own temerity. "I am sure you were just waiting for Major Stanley to return."

So her mother had been waiting to pounce once he was alone, thought Simon. Well, Dev would win his bet. He laughed to himself. He could not be angry with Alice, but her mother was making him feel slightly ill, what with her loud voice, which made it difficult for Simon to listen for Robin's return, and her offensive smell. He turned away from her in a direct cut, toward her daughter, and said, "Yes, Robin has gone for a glass of punch. Perhaps you would be so kind as to give me your arm and we will go in search of him?" Anything, thought Simon, to get away from her mother.

Alice was surprised the duke would ask for her help, but then realized what he was about. It would get them both away from her mother in a way that would leave the older woman feeling successful in her maneuvering and not likely to be harsh to her daughter later.

"I am not sure how to go on, but I would be happy to take you," said Alice.

"Just let me rest my hand on your elbow, and steer me away from walls and tables, my dear, and we will do fine."

Alice offered her arm to Simon and walked slowly at first and then more naturally as she realized the duke was following her easily. She was trembling, never having been so close to a man before, but Simon was chattering reassuringly and asking her for observations on the ball. She was soon more relaxed and, by the time they reached the refreshment table, had quite forgotten that she, the despair of her mother, was talking quite naturally to a sophisticated older man.

Robin saw them come in and almost laughed aloud to see Simon with the plainest Hyde girl. He walked over quickly, intending to rescue his friend, but then realized that the two of them were chatting away quite comfortably. So when he handed Simon the glass of punch, instead of dismissing Alice, he offered to get a glass for her.

Alice had not sat on the sidelines for a Season and done nothing. She was a shrewd observer, and she described dresses and personalities in equal detail. Simon found he was genuinely enjoying her company. Robin often described the general scene to him, but was not interested in who was dancing with whom, or who was wearing what. Alice was able to help Simon ''see'' Viscount Earlham's high collar, which made it almost impossible for him to turn his head, and the oversized turban that almost extinguished the Duchess of Crewe.

''Oh, and there is Lady Diana Grahame,'' sighed Alice. ''I do admire her. If I were beautiful, Mama would not be so constantly displeased with me.''

Simon felt a rush of sympathy for the girl. She may be plain, he thought, but she is not stupid or dull, once her self-consciousness wears off. And she is genuinely kind.

''You are quite an attractive woman in ways that are not on the surface,'' Simon said kindly. ''You are obviously in a difficult family situation, and yet are still able to consider another's feelings. You stood up to your mother tonight, didn't you?''

''Yes,'' said Alice wonderingly.

''I find you a witty, observant companion,'' Simon continued, ''and I'm sure that anyone who looked below the surface would also.''

''Thank you, your grace,'' said Alice, knowing that super-

ficiality was more common than blindness. She was hardly likely
to have much chance to demonstrate her better qualities while
under her mother's wing, but she was grateful to Simon for his
kindness.

"Now, you admire Lady Diana, do you? What is she wearing
tonight? And who has she given her waltzes to?" Simon was
interested for Robin's sake.

"She is dressed splendidly, as usual. Tonight she has on a
sapphire-blue gown, just the color of her eyes, and it sets off
her black hair to perfection. She has spent most of the evening
with a cluster of young men, but as usual, it is Viscount Devenham who monopolizes her time."

"I have heard he has a *tendre* for her. Is the feeling mutual?"

"I am not sure, your grace. She seems to allow him his
attentions and is everything that is kind to him, but . . ."

"But what?"

"I am not convinced her kindness is anything more than just
that. She is known for flirting outrageously, but with Devenham, I think she is not encouraging, but only being sympathetic
to his obvious lovesickness."

"You are most observant, Lady Alice."

"I have had time to be, your grace," she replied simply.

"Yes. Well, I will introduce you to some of my younger
friends, and perhaps you will have less time on your hands and
spend more of it dancing."

Alice flushed with pleasure, not so much at the thought of
dancing with eligible young men, but at the duke's kindness.
No one had been kind to her for a long time.

Robin returned at that moment, bringing with him, as though
on cue, not only the punch, but young Lieutenant Scott, whom
he had instructed to rescue the duke. The lieutenant bowed and
asked for Alice's hand for the dance that was being struck up.

She nodded shyly, but just before she left, she touched
Simon's arm and whispered, "I enjoyed our time together, your
grace."

Simon smiled. "And I too. I trust that we will have another
occasion to further our friendship."

Alice went off, her face alive with pleasure, which caused
her partner to look at her in some surprise, for her animated
expression made her almost attractive.

"Do you mean to court her?" Robin asked incredulously.

"Of course not. But she is good company once she is away from her mother. She was not embarrassed to help me, nor overly solicitous, and gave me quite a detailed picture of the ball—quite different from yours, Robin. I enjoyed her and would like to get to know her better. I know you brought Scott over to rescue me, but I was in no need of rescue, I assure you. In fact, I would like you to encourage a few other junior officers to dance with Miss Hyde. Now, however, I would like you to take me into one of the empty card rooms and go off and dance a few dances."

"A headache, Simon?" Robin was immediately concerned. "We can go home, if you like."

"No, I am fine, just a bit overwhelmed by all the noise. I don't want to hold you back, nor stand out like a grand prize for all the desperate mothers. Just find me a small room where I can rest for a few minutes, and I'll be up to socializing again."

23

Robin led Simon into one of the anterooms off the main ballroom. There were a few chairs, and Simon sank into one gratefully and shooed his friend back to the dance floor. He could still hear the rise and fall of conversation, but it was muted. As he heard familiar tunes being struck, he had found his foot tapping and felt real pain that dancing could never be a part of his life again.

I will certainly confine myself to dinners, thought Simon. It is one thing to know one's limitations, quite another to be surrounded by dancing.

As he sat there, feeling more and more of an outsider, he heard the door open and shut abruptly, and the rustle of silk, and then an exclamation of surprise and chagrin. Whoever had entered had expected an empty room. Simon was both annoyed and amused. He needed a few minutes to himself and had no desire to make polite conversation. But it was quite clear that his lady was as put out by his presence as he was by hers.

They both started to speak at the same time. "I beg your pardon, your grace. I had thought to find this room empty."

Simon stood and bowed in her direction. "You only uttered what I was thinking, Lady Diana." Simon smiled. He had recognized her voice, which was distinctively low. "You are looking lovely tonight, my lady. That blue just matches your eyes."

Diana, in her customary unselfconscious way, said, "However did you know what I was wearing? Can you still see colors then, your grace?"

Simon laughed. Only Diana would have responded so naturally, without thinking. "No, I am afraid I was just teasing you. I had an informant this evening who described the Incomparable. It seems you still hold your title."

"You startled me. I was truly sorry to hear of your misfortune, your grace, and did not mean to be insensitive just now.''

"I know that, Diana. May we go back to the old informality? Come, sit down and tell me what has driven you into hiding. I have good-enough reason to be away from the ballroom, but surely you have a full card and some disappointed young man is searching for you.''

"I am trying to escape one particular young man, your—I mean, Simon.''

"Would that be Viscount Deverham?''

"Yes. How did you know?''

"I have heard the odd bit of gossip about . . .''

" . . . Lady Diana's latest outrageous action?''

"No, I wasn't going to say that. But I do know that you have shown a decided preference for his company.''

"I have been encouraging him," Diana said. "I don't know why I should be admitting this to you. But I have to tell someone or I will end up being cruel to Dev, who, Lord knows, does not deserve it, and confirm my reputation as a heartless flirt.''

There was more than self-satire in Diana's tone, thought Simon. There was a real sadness. "You do not care for him?''

"No. Oh, I care for him one way, although my actions certainly don't seem to prove it. I did not mean to end up hurting him. It was just that his adoration came along at a time when I needed it. Now, that makes me sound the complete egoist, doesn't it, if I weren't convinced he is only infatuated.''

"When I was on leave last fall I thought you and Robin . . . ?'' Simon was not sure how to continue. "I was not here for long, but it seemed to me it was more than a flirtation," he said hesitantly. "Forgive me, I shouldn't pry.'' Simon was not sure if he had not gone too far, but at the same time, he wanted to know what had happened to interfere with what had seemed to him an ideal match.

"I don't mind," Diana said. "Yes, we were both quite serious, though neither of us made it public. Robin asked me to marry him before he left. I refused, we quarreled, and it was over, just like that.''

"Why did you refuse him?''

"I don't know. Yes, I do. I felt pushed. I had never felt such strong feelings for anyone, and I was quite terrified. Had he not suddenly been called up, it would have all progressed at a more normal pace, but I felt rather like a horse refusing a jump. I needed to be brought around again, but we had no time. It was jump now or lose him. You see, he thought that I was afraid he would come home seriously wounded and that I wanted to wait until I saw him return whole. I was furious he thought me so shallow. I thought he should have known me better if he loved me. So I refused to explain further, and he left believing I cared so little for him that I needed insurance. As though I would not have loved him however he returned, crippled or blind . . .'' Diana gasped. ''Oh, my awful tongue. I am sorry, but I keep forgetting.''

''And thank you for doing so,'' Simon reassured her. ''It is a welcome change from those who treat me as though I had lost all my faculties, instead of just my sight. I have been hiding here precisely because it is quite wearing to be only regarded as the Blind Duke. So . . . Robin left without knowing that you loved him?''

''Yes. When I realized that he could not possibly know every corner of me even though he loved me, and that all we needed was some time to understand each other's position, I was frantic. I sent him a letter, but it was returned unopened. I never even knew whether he returned it or had never received it. At any rate, he is home now and never even speaks to me, except when politeness demands it and then in the most daunting of polite tones.''

''And so you welcomed the viscount as a suitor?''

''I truly do enjoy his company, Simon. But I was so intent upon proving to Robin that he could not hurt me by his coldness that I quite forgot the effect on Devenham. And now I am more entangled than I ever intended to be.''

''Do you think that he is truly in love with you?''

''He thinks he is,'' responded Diana. ''I am an 'older' woman; I am considered a bit fast, so that only increases the attraction. But he doesn't really know me.''

''So you flirt with Dev and Robin wastes his time with Lady Lenox. What a comedy it would be, were it not so painful for all of you.''

"If it is a comedy, it is unlikely to have a happy ending. I shall refuse Dev, but that will not bring Robin back to me. It is clear he has no feeling left for me at all."

It was not so clear to Simon that this was true. He had felt Robin stiffen every time the viscount was with them. Were he indifferent to Diana, surely he would not care with whom she flirted? But he was not sure the fact that Robin still cared would make a difference. He knew how proud his friend was. It seemed ridiculous to Simon, such misunderstanding and misplaced pride. But of course Robin had not believed Diana had truly loved him.

"I wish there were some way I could help you, Diana. I would like to see Robin happy, but I fear there is not much I could say to him." Simon heard the strains of a waltz, and trying to cheer Diana, said, "Surely your card is full and some young gallant is looking for you?"

"Devenham put his name down for every waltz"—Diana laughed—"and that is why I took refuge in here. There is no need to give more fuel to the gossips than is necessary. I am quite content in here with you, Simon. Unless I am intruding too long upon the privacy you sought? I quite forgot you were also seeking sanctuary."

"Please stay, if you wish to. I am enjoying your company," said Simon. "And it keeps my mind off myself. I must confess to a little self-pity tonight, as well as fatigue."

Diana's spirts had revived. The relief of confiding in someone had eased her conscience, and no longer preoccupied with her own problems, she looked closely at Simon for the first time. She noted one finger beating time against his thigh. She remembered dancing with him in her first Season and what a graceful dancer he had been, and she could not resist one of her sudden surges of enthusiasm. "*You* shall have this waltz, your grace," she said boldly.

Simon started to protest.

"I remember you as a wonderful dancer. No one can see us here. Let me roll back the carpet and push back the chairs." She proceeded to do so while Simon stood there, feeling both trapped and tempted. Diana was unconsciously and naturally flirtatious, and he was surprised at his response. He felt that current of attraction that may pass between men and women who know they are unsuited for anything more serious, but who enjoy each other's company all the more for it. Simon had forgotten how enjoyable that feeling was.

"Now," said Diana, standing in front of him, "the room is clear and we have perhaps twelve feet on either side of us as a dance floor. We shall have to pretend we are in a crowded ballroom and keep our circles small, but we are good enough to do that. Put your arms around my waist, Simon."

"Perhaps you should lead on our first try."

"Yes, maybe you are right. Oh, what a scandal this would make," Diana said as she awkwardly at first, then more skillfully, guided Simon around their small floor. Simon was stiff for the first few minutes, afraid that he would bump into a wall or a table, but as he began to trust Diana's lead, he relaxed and found his dance legs returning. Halfway through, he felt sure enough to clasp her closer to him and take the lead away from her, and by the end of the waltz he was feeling almost as natural as he had last winter. They both were breathless when the music stopped, and so excited that their experiment had been successful that neither of them heard the soft knock at the door. Diana's back was to Robin, and Simon had not heard him, so he had a moment before they knew he was there. A moment to see his best friend with his arm around Diana's waist and Diana laughing up into Simon's face. He had not thought he could feel so empty until now. If Dev made him feel angry and jealous, he was still sure it was unlikely to come to a match. But Diana and Simon? Well, wasn't it what they all thought Simon needed? A lady of quality who would make him realize he was still attractive? And hadn't he already faced the truth that Diana could never have loved him and sent him off to war the way she had? So why should he not be pleased for both of them?

Robin cleared his throat and, sounding more polite than Simon had ever heard him, said, "Excuse me for having intruded. I only came to see if you wanted me for anything, Simon."

Simon was too exhilarated, and he felt too natural with Diana to imagine what Robin might be feeling. He only saw an opportunity to bring them together.

"Thank you, Robin, but Diana and I were just waltzing. I'm

afraid I stepped on her toes a few times, but she was kind enough to overlook it. One dance is enough for me tonight. Why don't the two of you go out and enjoy the next one? I am sure she would welcome a more adept partner?"

Neither Robin or Diana could easily get out of the dance, as Simon well knew, without being openly rude to each other. And since both wanted to pretend indifference, they were left with no alternative.

"I will be back directly," Robin said, wanting to strangle Simon, both for dancing with the lady and for putting him in such an awkward position.

"Thank you, your grace," Diana said. "Perhaps on another occasion we may waltz again?"

"If you save one for me, I will gladly partner you," Simon said. He smiled to himself as he heard Robin and Diana uttering polite nothings as they walked out the door.

"I shall be back soon," Robin repeated, wasting an angry glance on Simon. Simon might not have been able to see his friend's face, but he could certainly sense his annoyance. He was glad, for all that, that he had forced the two together. Indeed, he thought, all they need is enough time and they will realize they still care for each other. And I will do my best to engineer another encounter.

When Robin returned, Simon innocently asked him to bring him over to Diana to bid her good night and thank her. "For it felt wonderful to waltz again, Robin, and I would never have attempted it without her encouragement. Of course, I will have to confine my dancing to anterooms, but I believe I will make sure I am down for one waltz an evening with the lady, if she will have me."

Robin could not refuse to lead Simon over without looking foolish. He had chosen not to confide in his friend about what had occurred between Diana and him and the reasons for their estrangement. Indeed, he had made it sound like they had only indulged in nothing more than a light flirtation, so he could hardly blame Simon either for his response to Diana or for throwing them together. Nevertheless, he found himself jealous and resentful, and ashamed of both feelings. I am acting the dog in the manger, he thought. She rejected me, and I accepted that; indeed, I was relieved by it when I realized how shallow she is. I do not want her, he protested to himself, so why should Simon not enjoy her company?

When Simon had made his farewells, he and Robin decided to walk rather than wait for the carriage. They were both quiet. Robin felt a certain constraint because of his mixed feelings. Simon, on the other hand, was enjoying the memory of his encounter with Diana. She had inspired in him a certain playfulness, a letting-go as they danced, that had been missing from his life for months. Two years of campaigning and then his months of recovery had seemingly wiped out his capacity to just enjoy life. All of his energy lately had been focused on proving his independence and finding a renewed purpose in life. Aside from riding and his companionship with Robin, he had, he realized, become too serious. Diana had given him some moments of carefree pleasure. The remembrance of moving confidently to music again and holding an attractive woman in his arms made him want to see her again. It was because Diana was attached to Robin that Simon had enjoyed her company so much. They both could and had flirted with each other, knowing it meant nothing beyond the moment. Simon was planning to call upon her, for his own enjoyment and, he hoped, slowly and subtly bring her into contact with Robin.

Simon's thank you to Robin was therefore rather distracted, and Robin's ritual disclaimers less wholehearted when they reached the house. But they planned to ride the following afternoon and so each went to bed reassured that nothing had changed, while somewhere, under the surface, aware that everything had.

24

While Simon was relearning the waltz, Judith was relearning discipline. During her three years as governess, in spite of—or, now she thought, perhaps because of—her limited hours to herself, she had taught herself to keep a schedule and made sure that she had had some time for her art every day. She had no illusions about herself: she had some talent, but not genius. She knew what her limits were: no large oils, though she longed to be capable of them, but small, detailed pen-and-inks and watercolors. She was excellent at nature drawing and had notebooks full of sketches of birds, trees, and "weeds," as the children used to call her pictures of wildflowers. London was hardly the place for a nature artist, particularly a female one. Taking her sketchbook to the park was possible in the early morning, before many were out, but up until now, most of her mornings had been taken up by her reading for the duke and riding with the Stanleys. A long day tramping around Hampstead Heath would have been just the thing, but was dangerous alone. And so, between getting the house in good order and her post with the duke, Judith had been neglecting her drawing.

She found it difficult to get up, particularly in the middle of the week, and know there was no possibility of seeing Simon. She missed him terribly, more than she would have thought possible. They had developed a friendship unlike Judith had ever had with a man. Close as she was to her brother and however much she enjoyed Robin, neither of them knew her as well as Simon. How amazing, she thought, that someone you have known only for weeks, could know you better than a brother. Even her intimacy with Barbara, deep and long-standing as it was, was quite different from the intimacy developed in the duke's library. Barbara and she created their closeness by long talks over tea and the conscious sharing of their feelings.

Although Simon and Judith had certainly built their friendship with words, it was in the silences between that Judith was most aware of their connection, and this connection was something not created, but seemingly discovered, having been in existence before they met, only waiting to be found by them.

And so, at first, she had to make herself go through the motions: setting aside some time in the mornings and the late afternoons, when the light was what she wanted; only adding one more day of riding; and going off by herself to find the right tree or a small bird puffing its feathers against the cold. Inside, she worked on still lifes: three apples, two whole and one sliced open crosswise to expose the star hidden in its center; Hannah's hands kneading bread; or Stephen's profile as he sat by the fire in the evening, engrossed by his work. There was some solace in realizing the world was still there, waiting for her to see it. As she filled her sketchbooks, she could not think of Simon. Imagine missing this, she would think as she drew a winter tree, branches feeling like her own veins. Or the pink-tipped white flesh of an apple. I would die if I lost my sight, she thought as she rediscovered it. All of London would not be enough to destroy in her rage, and Simon had only laid waste one library.

Through Robin and Barbara she heard about Simon. He had hired a new reader, they said, and surely must be missing her, since this Mr. Wiggins seemed to be a nondescript man and hardly the reader Judith was. The duke was riding with Robin, as usual, and beginning preparation for a speech on the Corn Laws. And most astonishingly of all, he was attending the occasional ball and had actually waltzed with Diana Grahame.

"In fact," said Barbara one afternoon over tea, "Simon has been in Diana's company quite frequently. Except for his never failing to spend some time with plain little Alice Hyde, Diana is most definitely his most frequent companion. And I am not sure if I am pleased or not. Dev is devastated—and I don't mean to be humorous," chided Barbara as Judith laughed at her phrasing. "I can't help but be relieved that Diana is not serious about him, but he is convinced his heart is broken and he will never love another woman. And maybe he won't . . ."

"From all I have heard," Judith said, "I think this was

certainly a case of infatuation, sudden and all-consuming. He had never been in love before, had he?"

"No, not since he was ten and in love with the Honorable Melissa Norfolk, who came to his birthday all in pink and white and was afraid of everything. Dev hovered over her all afternoon—it was quite touching and just as infuriating as it is now, I must say!"

"So even then you cared about him?"

"Yes, even then, the more fool I," Barbara said.

"I think," said Judith slowly, "he must have been drawn to Diana for some other reason than the obvious attraction of the older woman. He is quite warmhearted, the viscount, and likes to be the protector, I think."

"Well, no one could use a protector less than Diana," protested Barbara. "She managed to jilt Robin when they had almost come to an understanding. And that is the other thing. I am happy to see Simon enjoying himself, but it must be a strain on Robin. He accompanies them riding and is usually Simon's companion in the evenings. I know he does not mind being Simon's guide, but it means he is constantly with them. I have seen Simon and Diana laughing, and Robin just standing there with a polite smile fixed on his face. Of course, he has never admitted his feelings to Simon, so it is not Simon's fault . . . but what a tangle! No one is happy but that harpy."

Judith raised her eyebrows. "Surely too strong a word, Barbara. After all, we cannot know what she is thinking or feeling. Although I certainly wish I did. I know Simon needs to discover he is still attractive to women, but I hate it that he does it with someone other than me."

Judith went home that day as unhappy as she had ever been in her life. It was all very well, she thought that night as she lay in bed, to have grand ideas about love and freedom, but why had she sent Simon out to find out how lovable he was? Why was she such an idealist? If the price of integrity and honesty was loneliness for the rest of her life, she was not sure she was prepared to pay it. It was one thing to see Simon regularly and know he could never be a husband or lover. Their enjoyment of each other's company made it easy to live in the moment, and then go home and dream he would fall in love with her and sweep away all social barriers with the force of his feeling. In fact, she thought, looking at herself honestly, I reacted as much out of hurt pride at having my daydreams shattered as I did out of care for Simon. Judith blushed in the darkness as she realized how she must have sounded to him. He had been realistic; she hadn't. She had been living for some sort of dream of what marriage might be, when marriage wasn't even likely for her at all. Simon's offer of companionship was the only offer she would ever receive. Why hadn't she accepted it, as Robin had suggested, in the quite realistic hope that friendship would develop into love? But, no, she was still too much of a green girl who read love sonnets and believed that they described real life.

To know that she herself had sent him out to fall in love with a more suitable woman out of pride and romantic idealism, hurt in a particularly devastating way. Giving him up because there was no possibility of ever having him generated a pain that was, in a way, rather soothing. I could have lived on dreams of "what might have been" quite happily, she realized, going to his library and reading to him for twenty years. This pain was different. It felt like a scouring of her insides, a burning-off of old illusions, with no promise of a new life. She felt like a burned-off field, one that would remain unplanted, dead, and dry.

In addition to the desolation, she felt a stirring of jealousy. Why should Lady Diana be loved by Simon? She had her choice of anyone; she had rejected Robin; she had encouraged Dev; she had money, rank; and Judith had nothing. Her art! Small consolation at this time of night.

It seemed to Judith that all the hurt at losing her father and being forced to work as a governess and all the buried anger at her lost freedom were rising up in her, swelling her throat until she could barely swallow. When at last the tears came, they came in great wrenching sobs. She buried her face in her pillow and let them come, until she fell asleep against the cold, wet linen.

When she awoke the next morning, she looked and felt awful. Her eyes were still swollen, and she had to bathe her face for a few minutes before she was presentable enough to go downstairs.

Stephen looked up quickly from his paper to greet his sister and stopped in midsentence.

"Whatever is wrong, Judith? You look dreadful."

"I am fine now, Stephen. I just had a restless night." Judith had not confided in her brother. He was, as young men are, quite absorbed in his work. She had not spoken about the duke very much, but Stephen could see she found the position satisfying and stimulating. They would often find themselves discussing politics after dinner on the days Judith had been to read, and his sister, who had always been more conversant in literature and art, was becoming an astute commentator on the domestic economic situation. Stephen was too young and too oblivious to emotional subtleties to think more about Judith's obvious enjoyment of their new life together.

He would never have dreamed that his sister would be thinking of the duke as anything but her employer. A companionable and sympathetic one, to be sure, but the social distance was great enough that Simon would not imagine bridging it. He knew something had caused a disagreement, but Judith had chosen not to burden him with the details of her dismissal beyond a bland "It was mutually decided we would no longer suit. The duke needs someone now who is more familiar with parliamentary language," was the way she had put it. She had not wished to tell her brother of Simon's offer and her refusal. And it all seemed so fantastic now, the offer itself and her scruples, that she wished to forget she had ever met the duke.

"Why don't you go back to bed, my dear, and let Hannah bring you some chocolate? It looks like you need a day devoted only to rest and pleasure."

"I may rest later. But right now, I think I need some strong tea." She took nothing from the sideboard but a muffin, and barely nibbled at that.

"Well, I am off," Stephen said as he folded the *Gazette*. "I am likely to be late again tonight since we are still working on that difficult brief. Are you sure you are all right?"

"Yes, Stephen, please don't be concerned." Judith smiled, not wanting him to pry into her unhappiness further. "We will see you later."

Judith spent a restless morning, unable to settle down to anything, housework or painting. Finally she grabbed her woolen cloak and, telling Hannah that she would return for tea, decided to see if a visit to Hatchards would lift her spirits.

At Hatchards she immediately sought out the latest Minerva romance. I am not up to anything heavier, she thought, and noticed a new novel by Mrs. Hazeltine. Delighted, she started to page through it, and was quite caught up in the first few pages when she heard Simon's voice. She stood as still as a deer caught in torchlight, afraid she would be seen, forgetting Simon could not see her. Then as she realized she would remain unobserved, she turned, ready to pull the hood of her cloak up to avoid the gaze of John, the footman who often accompanied the duke. It was not John with Simon, but a stranger, an older man quite smothered in a long muffler. Judith realized this must be the reader who had taken her place.

Simon was asking at the desk for Miss Austen's latest, and the clerk pointed Wiggins toward Judith. "I shall be right back, your grace," he said awkwardly as he let go of Simon's arm. He was not used to guiding the duke and was so careful that Simon was ready to scream.

Wiggins approached the table where Judith was standing, and hesitantly asked her if this was indeed where *Emma* was located. She nodded, and Wiggins picked up a copy.

"Do you read many novels, miss?" asked Wiggins, surprised at his own boldness in addressing a strange young woman, but from her worn cloak, he guessed she was not a young lady of quality, and he was very nervous at what seemed to be his next reading assignment.

"Yes . . . yes, I do," said Judith distractedly, gazing at the duke.

"I am a reader for his grace, and I have never read a novel," said Wiggins. "I am very nervous about reading anything but straight prose."

"Never read a novel?" asked Judith, looking at him for the first time. "How sad."

"Sad? I have never thought about it that way, but I have never had the time. I have been a clerk my whole life, you see, and am used only to things of a practical nature."

"I see." Judith smiled. "You will have a treat in store for you, then."

"Do you have any advice, ma'am, as to how I should read

a novel aloud? I wish to go on pleasing my employer, but I am afraid I will not be able to read dramatically enough.''

"I suggest you read it as though the characters were real and the author was next to you, gossiping about them. You need not be a Kean to read in an entertaining manner. I never tried to sound too dramatic when I read to him, and his grace seemed perfectly satisfied.''

Mr. Wiggins looked up from *Emma* in surprise. Judith was so distracted by Simon's presence that she did not even realize what she had said. But Wiggins, who had heard a few scattered comments from the servants about his predecessor, knew this must indeed be that ''nice little Miss Ware'' who always had a smile for even the lowest housemaid and whom the duke had dismissed for no known reason.

"You had better get back," said Judith. "The duke is beginning to look restless.''

Simon was indeed wondering what was keeping his reader. He could hear customers talking around him, and he felt his usual anxiety about being left alone in a strange place. It was galling to stand and wait, knowing he could not move without making a fool of himself, and so, when Wiggins returned, his tone was rather sharp. "Did you find the book?''

"Yes, your grace, yes, and I am sorry I took so long.''

"Well, let us pay for it and get home," Simon said, determined never again to go into a public strange place without a friend to accompany him.

Judith watched them leave and then went up to make her purchase. She was shaken by seeing Simon.

Mr. Wiggins was distracted on the way home. He wondered why the duke had dismissed so nice a young lady and why she had looked so sad. As he told his wife later, she was a small, wrenlike girl who reminded him of his sister Joan: frail on the outside, but inside, tough as an oak.

"And how did your first reading of the novel go?" asked his wife.

"Quite well, I think, once I warmed up and got into the swing of it. I think I will take a bit from my next wages to join a circulating library and treat you to a reading of Miss Austen too!''

Mrs. Wiggins was delighted, and was privately convinced

that the demise of his former employer had been a blessing in disguise. For years her Joseph had come home, head aching and body stiff from bending over his work, with barely enough energy to eat his supper and chat in front of the fire before they took themselves off to bed. But now her husband had energy to spare when he came home. He had new sights and sounds to chat about, and new ideas. His eyes were clear again, instead of red and strained, and his walk to the duke's house was beginning to make him feel younger. The salary was generous; it almost matched what he had been making as a clerk, which meant they did not have to draw upon their meager savings. The servants were welcoming and often asked him to share a light luncheon with them before he went home. It is an ill wind, thought Mrs. Wiggins. I am not happy that that poor young man has lost his sight, nor that this young woman lost her position, but my Joseph deserved something good for all his years of drudgery, and I am glad he has finally gotten it!

25

S imon had thrown himself so thoroughly into his political
preparations during the day, and into a more active social
life at night, that while he had occasionally found himself
thinking of one of their discussions, at first he had managed
not to think of Judith. At the moment, he found Wiggins a
satisfactory if colorless reader, and Lady Diana very pleasant
to be with.

While he and Diana were enjoying more than a little frisson
of excitement from their flirtation, Robin became more and more
aloof. Instead of using the opportunities Simon was trying to
give him to reestablish a relationship with Diana, Robin excused
himself and sought out Lady Lenox. He cared too much for his
friend to interfere in what he thought was becoming a romantic
attachment. Diana was perhaps what Simon wanted, after all:
a sophisticated woman of his own rank to support his career.
Judith hadn't stood a chance, thought Robin. Perhaps there had
been some feeling between the duke and Miss Ware, but now
it seemed as though he had forgotten her existence.

Simon and Diana continued to enjoy each other's company.
Because it was clearly understood by both of them that the
flirtation was only that, they were free to enjoy it. There was
an undercurrent of physical attraction that both were aware of
and both comfortable with, since there were clear boundaries
on the relationship. For Simon, it was wonderful to know that
he could kindle attraction in a woman, despite his handicap.
Judith had been correct, although he was still not aware of it.
His helplessness had led to a certain resignation and he had lost
his sense of himself as a man. He had never been one who
needed to dominate a woman, but he did need to be able to take
the initiative and respond to a woman's physical vulnerability
with a feeling of strength. Simon could sense Diana's tension
when Robin was with them, and her pain as he continued to

address her with a cool and precise courtesy, and he felt protective of her, as well as stimulated by her.

Simon was, in fact, a little annoyed with his friend. He assumed Robin could tell this was nothing but a growing friendship with the frosting of a light flirtation. He kept trying to generate conversation between the two, but neither would proceed beyond monosyllables. He was not able to just walk off and leave them alone together, so their meetings were always in his presence. On the second occasion he had suggested Robin take his dance with Diana, he was dismayed by the cold refusal on account of a prior engagement.

As Simon gained confidence, however, his thoughts returned more often to his former reader. He would be in the middle of a particularly vapid conversation and plan to recount it to her so they could both laugh at it, or he would hear a voice that had the same timbre as hers, and, for a moment, was convinced she was nearby. The more he enjoyed Diana's company, the clearer it became to him how well-suited she and Robin were. She was intelligent, but not with Judith's passionate brightness. Her interests, though wider than many ladies, were narrower than Judith's. She had never wanted for anything and had never wanted a life different from what she was born to. In her first Season, she had been considered a bit wild and continued to have that reputation, but Simon knew her rebelliousness was only skin-deep. Once she was settled down she would be a wonderfully content wife and mother.

The duke found himself annoyed with Miss Ware all over again. It was so clear they were well-suited, sharing a critical stance toward their society and a sense of humor. Now that he had acted as rescuer to both Lady Alice and Diana, Simon felt less of a burden, more conscious of his attractiveness, and he was beginning to be more sure he would be quite happy with Judith as his companion at any of these social occasions.

Robin was not the only one affected by Simon's supposed conquest of Lady Diana. Or *by* Lady Diana, Barbara would have said. "She has interfered with and spoiled all of our lives," said Barbara one morning as she and Judith set out on a shopping trip.

"How is the viscount these days?" Judith asked sympathetically.

"No longer visibly brokenhearted. He has thrown himself into late-night gambling and drinking, and then visits me the morning after, looking pale and blue-deviled and clearly expecting me to be the good little Barbara who always cheered him when he fell off his pony or got into trouble with his father. Well, I won't do it this time. With him, of course, I have been quite cool and sensible, and said that clearly Simon and Diana are well-suited and seem to be happy together, which, of course, infuriates him. He wants me to tell him that she'll get bored with Simon and turn back to him."

"Do you really think the duke is in love with her and she with him?" Judith asked quietly.

"It certainly appears so. They are together at every occasion."

Judith felt a most painful mixture of love and jealousy. I can't really feel happy for him, she thought. I should, if I really loved him . . . But I don't. I want to be held in his arms, and I want to be the one who convinces him he is attractive still.

In the quiet of the duke's library, reading and talking, Judith had given free rein to one part of her feeling for him. She had let herself care for him with her mind and heart, but had been, she saw now, terrified of her growing attraction to him. She had refused to entertain her fantasies, her desire to trace his lips with her fingers and pull his face down to hers, or her need to be held by him, to bury her nose in his shoulder and take in the smell of cloth, cologne, and Simon. She had been frank and open with him in many ways, but she had carefully controlled her physical response, putting up a barrier that might well have made it hard for him to have thought of her as anything but a companion and friend. I was so careful, she thought despairingly, and I don't know how to flirt or let a little of the physical enter in to a relationship. No wonder he offered me companionship without passion. How could he have been attracted to me if I never let my attraction to him anywhere near the surface? And he probably wouldn't be attracted to me. Lady Diana is far more sophisticated and beautiful. Of course, he can't see how beautiful she is, but I'm sure he can *remember* it, she thought, a bit wildly. Compounded with her sickening feeling of jealousy was her increasing sense of foolishness, of having ruined her own chances, whatever they might have been.

"And now Robin is miserable and won't admit it because Simon is his best friend and I must listen to Dev complain and never let him know my own feelings, and you, my dear friend, are sitting there looking as though your heart were broken." Barbara's voice broke through Judith's distraction. "You must let me buy you something for Christmas, Judith, and you must come to the Rosses' ball with us," said Barbara impulsively. "You have met them at our house and they especially invited you. You need to get out and meet people. You cannot go into a decline over this."

"I assure you," replied Judith, "that I do not intend to go into a decline. It is painful to hear about Simon, but if he is happy, then how can I begrudge it to him? And, yes, I will let you buy me a dress, and I will go to the Rosses' ball. I need something to look forward to for the holidays." Judith was tired of resignation, and all her good resolutions against socializing flew out the window.

"At last! I agree, we may as well throw ourselves into the frivolous pursuit of the perfect dress, if the perfect man will take no notice of us!"

The two women made a determined descent upon Madame Céleste's and the Pantheon Bazaar. Barbara selected a pale-blue embroidered silk. She and the dressmaker, one of the few genuine Parisian modistes in a trade where every other seamstress adapted a French name and accent, took more time with Judith. She brought out lighter colors first, but they did nothing for Judith's coloring.

"*Un moment*, I have just the dress," she said suddenly, and sent her assistant to the back. The young woman returned, carrying the richest dress Judith had ever seen. It was forest-green velvet, cut simply and with the wider skirts that were becoming popular. As it was slipped over her head, she stood there trembling, thinking how wonderful it would be to own such a dress. "It is a bit large in the waist and the bodice, for it was made for someone else, who in the end decided against it. But of course I will alter it to fit *mademoiselle*. And, of course, it will not be too dear, since it was originally made for someone else," said Céleste shrewdly, guessing from Judith's appearance that price might be a consideration.

All three stood back to look at Judith's image in the mirror. The deep-green brought out the green flecks in her eyes and the milky whiteness of her skin. "Even my freckles look better," she said, and all of them laughed.

"There is something quite pagan about that dress," said Barbara, "and it quite suits you."

"Yes, doesn't it?" Judith turned slowly to admire it from all angles, and she felt transformed.

"A simple ruby necklace and earrings and no other jewelry," said Madame Céleste.

Judith laughed. "A garnet pendant from my mother and a small garnet ring is what it will have to be."

"Hmpph! Yes . . . but red it must be."

"And now, Madame, you have a pelisse that will compliment this, I am sure?"

"Oh, no, Barbara, I have my wool cloak. I can't take anything else," Judith protested.

"Nonsense. That cloak will do on a rainy day, but not for an evening out. I insist. The dress is from me, but Robin wanted to give you something too."

"You are both too kind, and I am quite corrupted by the dress, so I can protest no more," said Judith.

They found a corduroy cloak in a lighter shade of the green, banded in black velvet. Judith was by now quite light-headed at the prospect of owning such fashionable clothes. She did not notice Barbara whispering to Madame, adding two more dresses to the order, a wine-red kerseymere round gown and a sprigged muslin. Barbara knew her friend well enough to restrain herself from adding more.

She whisked Judith out and they headed for the Bazaar, where Barbara and Judith bought gloves, stockings, and a reticule that seemed made for Judith's new kerseymere. By that time the ladies were exhausted. They had originally planned to have a cup of tea and pastry out, but decided to return to the Stanleys', where they could sort out their packages.

Judith arrived home a few hours later, laden with assorted parcels, and could not even open the door. Hannah answered her ring, but was unable to take anything, since she had been baking and her hands were floury. Judith let everything spill out on the sofa and told Hannah about the ball and the shopping. Hannah smiled at the expression on her face. She looked like a child as she rediscovered what was in each bundle.

"Wait until you see the dress! I look quite elegant, and the cloak compliments the dress perfectly. Barbara and Robin were much too generous."

"Nonsense. They have been wanting to give you something, and they can well afford it. I am sure that you will be a success at this ball."

"Maybe not the Incomparable of the evening, Hannah, but I am looking forward to it. I have been moping about too long. It will do me good to socialize a little. I'll have a party or two to remember in my old age.

"I shall be right back to help with dinner." Judith gathered up her bundles and started up to her room. Once there, she sorted out gloves and stockings and put them away, then stood for a moment looking out her window. The garden was now completely dead. The rosebushes had wrinkled brown hips hanging from them, but all else was sere and bare.

"We must get some Christmas greens," and the thought of pine boughs reminded her of the dress. "I wish Simon could see me. I felt so different in it. More sure of myself." She imagined Simon's hand around her waist and waltzing with him, and her pulse quickened just dreaming of it.

She shook her head as if to clear it of such unrealistic fantasies and turned from the window to go downstairs to the more prosaic tasks of setting the table and making the gravy.

26

T he Duchess of Ross's ball was one of the last of the Little Season. Some of the *ton* had already left for their country homes to celebrate the holidays, so there was not a great crush at the door or on the receiving line. Nor would there have been, for her grace was a rarity, more interested in her guests' comfort than in her own prominence as a hostess. She provided good food, dancing, and a select group, so that one could enjoy a waltz, whist, or a stimulating conversation on the latest Tory scandal.

She had been watching Simon and Diana together and rejoiced to see the duke begin to enjoy himself at larger social gatherings. Diana had made a difference, and tonight Simon was looking infinitely more relaxed. The duchess knew it was most likely a flirtation that she was watching, for she was an observant woman and remembered Robin and Diana on the dance floor just a year ago. *That* had been more than a flirtation; she was willing to stake her emerald necklace on it.

What had happened, she couldn't begin to guess. She was an old friend of all concerned and shook her head at the comedy of errors being enacted in front of her: Barbara thinking herself in love with Dev all these years, Devenham convinced of his undying passion for Diana, Diana in love with Robin, and Robin in love with Diana. And Simon? Was Simon in love with anyone, or was he not yet ready? And who would be right for him? I must be on the lookout for someone, thought the duchess as she turned to greet newly arrived guests.

Robin, Barbara, and Judith had arrived early. Judith felt as though she were moving in a dream. She had, as the vicar's daughter, attended the local assemblies and been to small dances at the squire's home, but country socializing was nothing compared to this. The jewels and the dresses were dazzling. She watched Barbara be swept away for the first country dance and was quite prepared to hold up the wall, when some young man approached her. At first she was worried she might have forgotten the steps, but she was able to relax after the first few measures and by the end even exchange a few polite words with her partner as they were brought together by the figures of the dance.

After that first dance, Judith noticed that of the steady stream of men who came her way, many were of the military, and when Robin came to claim her for the first waltz, she teased him about sending his subalterns on a rescue mission.

"Rescue, be damned," he said. "I may have sent one over, but after that I was beseiged by all the young lieutenants. They all wanted to know who the goddess in green was. Truly, Judith, you look wonderful, rather like a druidic priestess. You stand out from all the bespangled girls in their whites and pinks and silver and gauze. No wonder you are a success."

"I must admit it is thrilling, Robin. I am glad the two of you persuaded me, and I can't thank you enough for your generosity."

"Nonsense. It was nothing."

After their dance, Robin offered Judith his arm and took her in for some refreshment. Neither of them, therefore, was present when Simon and Diana arrived. Robin had made his excuses to Simon earlier in the week, saying only that he had promised to escort a friend of Barbara's, and could not go with him. Simon had a footman come along and lead him through the receiving line, but was able to dismiss him soon afterward when Diana came up and took his arm to lead him to the ballroom.

When Robin and Judith returned, there was Simon, laughing in the middle of a small group of guests, with Lady Diana on his arm. The shock of seeing him quite took Judith's breath away, and she felt Robin stiffen. Judith was ready to turn and run before Simon could see her, and then she realized once again that his ease of movement made one forget his blindness. She was safe as long as she was not introduced to him, and she knew she could avoid that. She let her breath out in one long sigh, and Robin looked down at her.

"As bad as that, Judith?"

"I fear so, Robin. And you?"

Robin looked surprised, but forsook his usual humorous stance for honesty. "Yes, I find it most painful. Simon is my best friend and I can hardly begrudge him happiness after all he's been through, but sometimes it is almost too much for me when all three of us are together."

"She is certainly very beautiful." Judith could not help noticing the way Diana's arm was tucked under Simon's, and the way he turned to her as she spoke, leaning down as though what she had to say was the most interesting observation he had heard in years.

As country dances were struck up, Judith could not help noticing how Diana and Simon took the time to stroll along one side of the room as though they were discussing something intimate. They wandered in to get some punch, and Judith, although she was thirsty again, refused Robin's offer to lead her in, and sent him in alone. She was standing there, awaiting his return, when her hostess approached her.

"Are you enjoying yourself, my dear?" asked the duchess.

"Yes, yes, indeed. I am very grateful you included me in your invitation."

"I was happy to. Any friend of Robin and Barbara's is welcome," said the duchess in her matter-of-fact way. "You knew Barbara from school?"

"Yes, we attended a seminary in Bath together."

"And you returned home afterward? Have never been to London before?"

"No, I did not return home. My father died and I was forced to take as post as a governess. But I doubt I would have made my come-out in any case, since my father was only a country vicar, with but distant connections in London."

The duchess raised her eyebrows in surprise. Judith waited for a set-down or a polite retreat, and was pleasantly surprised when the duchess asked with genuine interest, "And are you on holiday now and visiting the Stanleys?"

"No, I am now in London for good. You see, my brother finished his degree and is studying law. We both had planned to set up house together when he came down from Oxford."

"And now you are a lady of well-deserved leisure." The duchess smiled warmly.

"For a short while, your grace. I did have a position for a little while, and am looking for one again, to make a little extra for luxuries like the theater and books. I must be boring you with all these details. And it is hardly polite to speak of job-hunting at a ball," Judith said, suddenly aware of the humorous side of this encounter, for she had utterly relaxed her guard in the other woman's genuine interest.

"I admit it is not a common topic, but I find it far more interesting to listen to an obviously intelligent young woman than some of the hen-witted ladies here tonight. I see you have achieved a certain popularity with the military, my dear."

Judith laughed. "I fear that was all Robin's doing."

"Not at all. You are quite lovely in that dress, and something out of the ordinary. I do hope you will come and drink tea with me some afternoon?"

Judith flushed with pleasure and surprise. "Thank you, your grace, for your kindness. If you mean it and are not just being polite, I would enjoy it very much."

"You are plainspoken almost to a fault, I see." The duchess laughed and Judith blushed at her own bluntness. "I do mean it. You will receive my card, but now I must spend some time with my other guests, much as I am enjoying our chat."

Judith was promised for the second waltz to a young subaltern, and as the music began, she noticed that Robin was with Lady Lenox and Barbara actually dancing with Dev. Neither Barbara nor Dev looked particularly happy, however, for one of the couple who had been standing near them was Simon and Diana, and Dev's last-minute invitation to Barbara had been an instantaneous reaction to the sight of Diana and the duke gliding off together.

Simon was enjoying his waltz, as he always did. By now, he and Diana were expert at making it seem as though he were in charge, whereas, in truth, the gentle pressure of her hand on his back enabled them to avoid catastrophe. "We have been lucky so far, Diana," he said as they whirled around the room, "but I am almost glad the Little Season is just about over, so I can relax."

"You can't fool me, your grace. You enjoy the risk!" On a more serious note she observed that Barbara and the viscount were dancing together. "They do not look particularly happy, I must admit, but now perhaps Dev will seek her out more."

"She has loved him since she was a little girl. And he has never regarded her with anything but a brotherly affection," said Simon. "I think it will be a few years before he learns to appreciate her . . . if he ever does."

"Oh, look . . . I *am* sorry, I am always forgetting," Diana said, terribly embarrassed.

"It is all right, milady, people forget all the time," said Simon in a teasing tone to lighten the tension. "What did you see?"

"I was just going to point out Lieutenant Graves' partner. I did not catch her name, but she is a friend of Robin and Barbara."

"Perhaps if you describe her, I will recognize her. Robin spoke of escorting a friend of his sister's, and I have met many of Barbara's friends over the years."

"She is not beautiful," replied Diana.

Simon chuckled.

"No, no, that is not a catty comment. She is, in fact, rather plain. Reddish-brown hair, freckles, small and slim. But she is quite striking all the same. She is dressed in an exquisite green velvet gown, which quite sets her apart from the rest of us."

"No distinguishing features?" asked Simon. "No squint or pug nose that would jog my memory?"

"No."

"Well, she is probably someone I have never met, or only briefly. Do you wish to be introduced?"

"No, I don't want to be eclipsed, your grace."

"The Lady Diana eclipsed! You in your—what did you tell me?—silver-tissue gown, looking like the goddess of the moon herself, no doubt."

"I wonder what extravagances you would utter could you see me." Diana laughed. "If I look like the moon, then this woman is of the earth . . . there is something pagan about her."

"And you accuse me of extravagance."

"No, truly, Simon, there is an air about her of oak groves and standing stones."

"Well, then, we'd best stay away from her lest she put us under a spell. She might cause us to fall in love."

"Oh, it would not take a very powerful spell to do that," Diana said.

The two of them continued in that vein for a while. It was a game they played, knowing there was a slim possibility one of them would end the game and begin to play in earnest, yet also knowing neither of them would. Simon, in fact, was beginning to find it less and less amusing and more frustrating. There was most certainly a current of attraction, and there were times during an evening when he was tempted to pull Diana off into an alcove and give way to the feelings she sometimes aroused in him. Except, of course, he could not see the damned alcoves and could hardly picture himself bribing a footman to lead him to one or asking Diana herself. His sense of the ridiculous lightened his desire to release, with a few passionate kisses, some of the sexual tension between them. On the other hand, he knew there was nothing else he wanted from the lady than that release. His feelings ran no deeper than friendship, gratitude, and attraction. As he began to realize he need not be condemned to a bachelor existence because of his blindness, he found himself wanting more. He thought about Miss Ware more often. Not just to contemplate her astute observations on the *ton*, but also her equally astute observations on politics and poetry. As he remembered some of their more intimate conversations, he began to realize that an attraction had been growing that he had not been aware of at the time. She had had the potential of becoming more than a companion. After all, there would not have been such anger if there were no strong feelings, he thought, becoming angry at her all over again. Had she only agreed to his proposal, they might have discovered deeper feelings for each other. Or he might have discovered them. She certainly had never said she cared. Had she, wouldn't she have wanted to be with him in any circumstances?

"Don't you agree, your grace?" Diana asked.

Simon was brought back from his daydreaming by Diana's voice, which was both amused and a bit annoyed at his distraction. He quickly agreed, apologizing for his lapse of attention, and they moved out of the ballroom and into the refreshment room.

Judith, who had been very conscious that Diana seemed to

be looking over at her, was greatly relieved when they left. They had not been introduced, but Diana might have heard her name over the course of the evening. If Simon found out that Miss Ware was at the ball, Judith did not want to be anywhere near him.

The ball ended uneventfully, however, and both Simon and Judith went home strangely dissatisfied with what had been, after all, a very enjoyable evening.

Judith had found it thrilling to be found attractive and in demand, yet knew that only Simon's attentions would have made the night a triumph. She went to bed certain that the duke was going to propose to Diana. She had wanted him to discover he was still lovable, but it seemed to her he had succeeded all too well. She sank into a sleep punctuated by dreams of her disrupting the duke's wedding, wearing green velvet robes and muttering curses in some ancient language.

27

J udith had almost forgotten her conversation with the duchess, when a few days after the ball she received a short note inviting her to tea. She was touched that she had been remembered, and relieved that she had accepted all of Barbara's gifts, since she now had an appropriate gown to wear for her visit.

She was looking forward to tea for two reasons. She had enjoyed the older woman's interest in her, for, aside from Hannah, she had no motherly figures to turn to for comfort. And since the duchess was not put off by her honesty, it might be possible to get advice and perhaps some help in finding another situation.

Judith found her enthusiasm beginning to drain out of her on her way over. Perhaps she had mistaken the duchess's kindness, after all? Why would a duchess take notice of a veritable nobody like herself anyway? By the time she reached Grosvenor Square, Judith had given up her plan to ask for advice and had decided to drink her tea and leave quickly.

When they sat down together in the morning room, the duchess was afraid that the subdued girl, responding in monosyllables, was the only companion she would have for tea, and did her best to put Judith at ease. Judith, however, could not seem to relax, until the duchess, in desperation, asked her if she were fond of novels, and receiving a nod, asked if she had read the new book by Miss Austen. Judith's face lit up, and her grace saw a little of what had attracted her to the girl in the first place.

"Indeed yes. I am just now finishing *Emma*. Have you read it, your grace?"

"No, but I am eager to. How does it compare to *Pride and Prejudice*?"

"It is quite a different sort of book. Or rather, a very different sort of heroine. Emma is as lively and intelligent as Eliza Bennet, but she is also a bit spoiled and too sure of herself. I don't know if I like her at all—she makes me feel uncomfortable.''

"You do not think that women should be too sure of themselves?''

"Oh, dear, I do not know how to answer." Judith laughed. "Perhaps I feel uncomfortable with Emma because in her I can recognize some of my own pride.''

The duchess looked at her inquiringly. "Go on.''

"Emma is always convinced she knows what is best for others, and she acts on that belief and changes lives. I can think of several times when I forcefully expressed my opinion, thinking I knew what was best for myself or another. In the heat of the moment, it seemed the right advice. Now, I am not so sure. I think I have learned a little humility. It remains to be seen if Emma does." Judith smiled, to lighten her observation.

"And was this recent, your lesson in humility? I should have thought it would be hard to survive three years as a governess without it.''

"Oh, yes, you are right. When you are at someone else's beck and call, no matter how kind the employer, one's self-esteem is surely diminished. But I think I am talking about another kind, one that goes deeper. For me, it takes the form of a rather rigid idealism. Love should be this way, and no other. A perhaps misguided sense of integrity has ruled my life. It would have been far better if I had given in to what I feared was a misguided heart . . ." Judith paused. "I should not be prosing on like this. You do not need to be burdened with my dilemmas. But I do tend to get carried away, especially when the listener seems truly interested.''

"As indeed I am. When was it that you realized that you would have been better to follow your heart?''

Without thinking, Judith blurted out, "When I saw Simon with Lady Diana.''

"Simon? The Duke of Sutton?''

"Oh, dear! Yes.''

"Do you know Simon?''

"I was his reader this fall.''

"So that was the position you mentioned the other night."

"Yes. I suppose that I had better explain, or you will think me quite mad." Judith told the story as concisely as she could, ending with her refusal of Simon's proposal. "So, you see, if I hadn't been so sure of myself, I might be with him now. Instead, I was convinced I knew what he needed and sent him out to find love, which he has so obviously done."

"I am not so sure," said the duchess. She was surprised, but not shocked at Judith's revelation. *The poor girl doesn't realize how much good she has done Simon*, she thought. *He came back to life because of her outspokenness and integrity, her willingness to be honest with him. The pity is that now she has begun to realize the depth of her feeling for him, and now that he is feeling more sure of himself, there is no easy way to bring them together.*

"I have known Simon and Diana for many years, and my impression is they are both enjoying a flirtation, nothing more. You were right, my dear. It did restore something to Simon to discover he could still be attractive to a woman. And this flirtation of theirs gave Diana the opportunity to discourage Viscount Devenham and remain safe from other suitors."

"Do you really think so, your grace?" Judith so wanted to believe her, but was afraid the duchess was only offering false comfort.

"I do. The question remains, however, how to resolve this comedy so that all end up with whom they belong. I am convinced, by the way, that you most certainly belong with Simon and he with you."

"How can you say that? You hardly know me!"

"I was struck by your forthrightness the other night, and today has only confirmed my first impression. Simon needs a woman to love him passionately, yes, but more than that he needs a good and trustworthy friend. You can offer him both love and a companionship of the mind and spirit, a rare thing in this day and age. I would be quite envious had I not something like it with my dear Harold. Do not underestimate the value of your time together, or his proposal to you. It may have sounded too rational, and he may not have spoken of love, but I know Simon well, and he would never have proposed marriage where there was no feeling. He is too warm a man; his parents married for love, and that memory has stayed with him.''

"If all that is true, your grace, then it is even worse than I thought. I made him furious with me. I can hardly knock on his door now and inform him that I have changed my mind!''

"No. But you might meet at a small dinner party here.''

"Oh, no, I could never risk that. He would recognize me immediately!''

"Of course. Why do you think I suggested it?'' The duchess laughed.

"But why would Miss Ware be invited in the first place?''

"Because you are a friend of Barbara's and because I enjoy your company. Oh, Lady Diana will come too. We shall have all the actors assembled.''

"No, I cannot do it,'' Judith said. "I thank your grace, but I could not bear to see him and have him ignore me or, even worse, berate me.''

"Ring a peal over you for what? For caring enough about yourself and him to do what you thought was best?''

"I think, your grace, he would be angry because I knew him too well. And because I deceived him. I never told him I knew the Stanleys or that our acquaintance helped me win an interview for the situation. He will think I acted as some sort of spy.''

"My dear,'' said the duchess, taking both of Judith's hands in hers to stop her wringing them, "do you love Simon? Would you be willing to be married to a blind man, knowing the difficulties it would entail?''

"Oh, yes, I do love him. I never realized how much until I saw him waltzing with Diana.''

"And you are going to spend the rest of your life dreaming about what you might have had together, instead of taking the risk of getting what you want? Or do you want to remain safe in your dream world?''

Judith pulled back as though she had been slapped.

"I know that I sound harsh. But I am offering you a chance to see Simon again, to stand up to his anger and to ask him for what you want.''

Judith hesitated a moment as she took in the duchess's words. "You are right, your grace. I am terrified that I will lose. But

I would hate myself for the rest of my life did I not take the opportunity you are offering me. I don't know why you should care to go to all this trouble for a virtual stranger, but I am grateful.''

"Because I love Simon as though he were my own son, and I would like to see him happy—and because I would like to bring you into the family. Now, when should this famous party be," mused the duchess, releasing Judith's hands and letting her regain a little of her composure.

"As soon as possible, before I lose my courage." Judith laughed.

"It does need to be set within a week or so," agreed the duchess. "There are not many people in town at this time of year, and the closer to the holidays, the more who will be gone into the country. I think I will try for Tuesday week."

The dinner invitation arrived at the Wares' a few days later, and Judith, who had successfully hidden her heartaches, wondered what to tell Stephen. It would be relatively easy to explain the dinner invitation. What would be more difficult would be to explain any outcome, good or bad. For if Simon refused to have anything to do with her, Judith knew she could hide her feelings no longer. And if he did? Well, that would be as hard to explain! And it was bad enough to have to meet Simon. But to have Diana and Dev and the Stanleys there seemed the outside of enough. It is inviting disaster, thought Judith. I am glad that I am not the hostess for this infamous party.

When Stephen returned home that night, Judith took down the heavy white envelope from the mantel and handed it to him.

"What's this, Judith?"

"I am invited to the Duchess of Ross's for dinner next Tuesday."

Stephen smiled at her. "One evening out, and you're a success, eh? And who is the duchess?"

"A friend of the Stanleys, and also the godmother of the Duke of Sutton, I believe."

Stephen was immediately more attentive. "The duke? Does she know that you were once employed by him? Won't it be a bit awkward?"

"Yes, she knows. She also knows I fell in love with him, Stephen."

Stephen's fingers, which had been lightly fingering the engraving on the invitation, became still. "I thought there might have been more to your dismissal than you told me. Why did you remain silent?"

"I didn't want to upset you. And I felt that the less I spoke about it, the sooner I would forget him."

"Will the duke be at this dinner?"

"Yes. And Lady Diana Grahame, to whom he has been paying marked attention, and Robin, who is probably in love with Diana, and Judith Ware, who loves Simon, Duke of Sutton!"

"Why do we need a novel tonight." Stephen ran his hand through his hair. "We are right in the middle of a comedy. Or is it a tragedy? Does the duke love this Lady Diana?"

"The duchess thinks not. Oh, Stephen, she is a dear woman, but I think even she has taken on too much. But she met me briefly at the ball, and I had tea with her this week. She likes me, and was so warm that I could not help revealing to her who Miss Ware really was. She challenged me—said I should be willing to meet Simon under everyday circumstances and see if there might be a chance he cared for me. I think she is right, I must do this. But I am terrified."

"I quite understand, but if I were you, I wouldn't miss this dinner for anything."

Judith laughed. "You know, it is quite dreadful, but a part of me can stand back and imagine what Miss Austen might do with a scene like this. I wish, however, I were the author, and not an actor in the drama."

"At least this way, you will have acted on your own behalf, Judith. It may not change the outcome, but at least you will not be hating yourself for not trying."

"That is why I finally agreed to this scheme. Come, let us finish off another chapter of our novel, before we retire."

28

S imon was too caught up in preparing his speech to refine much upon an invitation to what was for him practically a family dinner. He was pleased Robin and Barbara would be there, for he had not seen them as often as usual these past few days. Robin had made his apologies upon a few occasions that Simon had asked for an escort. The excuses were legitimate, but Simon worried if his friend were not tiring of being his "eyes." On the one hand Simon was grateful Robin was honest with him, but on the other hand, the duke had the uneasy feeling that the growing constraint between them was due to something else. He had about given up on pushing Robin and Diana together. Perhaps his friend had never been in love with her? Or Diana might be right that she had killed off his feelings for her, thought Simon. He would never have imagined Robin would see his flirtation with Diana as anything but that. He was unusually sensitive, for a man, to others' feelings, and his blindness made him rely upon this sensitivity even more. But his blindness also hampered him in ways he could not have anticipated. He had never before realized how much depends upon small things like a lifted eyebrow or an averted gaze, as clues to one's companion's moods. He could feel the constraint between Robin and Diana and the slight stiffness in Robin's manner to himself, but could not see the tightening of his friend's jaw when Simon spoke of Diana in flattering terms with the intent of rekindling Robin's interest, or the pain and longing he could not keep from his eyes when Simon and Diana were waltzing.

For himself, he was happy the holidays were approaching. He was almost finished with his research and could work on his speech with Francis. He had been invited to Ashurst and had accepted. Leaving London meant a break in his flirtation. He wished to remain friends with Diana, but knew he could propose nothing more. Whenever he imagined offering marriage to her, it was not her voice he heard coolly accepting, but Miss Ware's passionate refusal. He would find himself irritated all over again. He missed her, damn it, and at the same time resented her for being right. For he knew now she had been correct in her assessment of him. He had asked her out of self-doubt, not love. The time he had spent with Diana had restored not only his belief in his own attractiveness, but more important, his own responses to an attractive woman. Simon was a realist. He had no illusions that his former "value" on the marriage market would ever be the same, or that he was likely to inspire a passionate response in young debutantes. But he was more confident that he held some attraction because his own feelings toward a woman had been restored. Because he could now imagine himself arousing a passionate response, he found himself thinking of that last scene in the library, wondering what would have happened if he had pulled Judith to him, if he had "seen" her, traced her face until he found her lips . . . Of course, he thought as he pulled himself out of these fantasies, I have no idea whether she had any such feeling for me. I may have been right; despite her protests it may have been my blindness that put her off. Although she was always honest to a fault, he mused, and then he dimissed both Diana and Judith as he got back to work.

Robin had agreed to meet Simon Tuesday night. When he arrived at the duke's he handed his coat to Cranston and said, "Tell his grace I am here and ask him to join me in the library. And bring us both a glass of brandy."

"Yes, Major Stanley."

Cranston knocked at Simon's door and informed him that Major Stanley had arrived and was awaiting him in the library.

"Thank you, Cranston." Simon was perhaps the only person looking forward to the evening, since he had no way of knowing what his godmother was about. He walked downstairs by himself and paused at the library door for a moment.

"Robin?"

Robin stood up and greeted him and Simon moved toward

his voice. "You are a bit early. Would you like a drink before we leave?"

"I took the liberty of asking Cranston for some brandy for us both."

Simon sensed the tension in his friend and wondered again if Robin was tired of acting as his escort and guide. He decided it was time to ask. He moved over to the fireplace and, leaning against it, cleared his throat. "Robin, I have noticed that over the past few weeks you seem constrained with me. It is hard for me to ask this, but I wish you to be honest with me."

Robin stiffened. Was Simon going to ask if he approved of Diana as a future duchess? Well, better to get the worst over with. "Of course I will be honest. Do you want to know if I can wish you happy?"

"What?" Simon said, confused. "For what?"

"Well, I had wondered if you and Lady Diana . . ." Robin paused to let Simon fill in the rest.

"If Lady Diana and I what?"

"This *is* an intimate dinner at your godmother's house."

"Oh, Lord, no!" Simon laughed. "You haven't been thinking we've formed an attachment to each other? All these weeks? No wonder you have been rather removed. Here I have been worrying you are sick of leading me about, and you have been convinced I was courting Diana."

"Well, I can hardly be blamed for thinking that, since half the *ton* does also," said Robin stiffly. "And how could you even imagine I would get tired of being with you?"

"Not tired of being with me. But of being so responsible for me."

"Not at all," said Robin, even more remotely. "In fact, I am insulted you would even think so."

Simon moved toward his friend and put a hand on his arm. "Robin, I thought you and the lady might still have an interest in each other. I kept pushing you to dance with her and you kept refusing or being so ungracious about it that it cannot have been pleasant for either of you. I enjoy her company enormously. Who would not? She is utterly charming and has been very good for me, Robin. I can't explain it, but I thought I would never enjoy that sort of flirtation again. I was still afraid

no woman could see beyond my blindness. But while there is
certainly an attraction there, there is no serious feeling. You
avoided us whenever you could, so I gave up believing that you
still cared for her. I thought you were impatient with my
dependency upon you. *Do* you still care for her?''

''Yes. Yes, I do, damn it.''

''Are you sure it has all been jealousy, and not a touch of
boredom with squiring your friend?''

''I swear to you, Simon, that any time I find it inconvenient
or am the least bored, I will let you know.''

''Thank you.'' Simon let go of Robin's arm and took a sip
of brandy. ''Well, then, where are we? You know I do not love
Diana, nor she me. She was most certainly not in love with
Devenham, since she was so grateful to me for providing her
with an excuse to escape him. What we don't know is whether
she loves you. And it is you, my dear friend, who is going to
have to find the answer to that question.''

Robin groaned.

''I will play no go-between, I assure you,'' Simon said.
''Tonight you must stay by my side and actually converse with
the lady in more than monosyllables. You might even ask her
to ride with us in the morning. I will then become conveniently
tired and have my groom bring me home.''

Robin laughed. ''What a tactician you are! Won't that look
a bit obvious?''

''Who cares? You have wasted enough time. Now, let us
finish our drinks and go, before we are late. My godmother
has no patience with tardy guests.''

Robin had been so caught up with his own dilemma he had
completely forgotten the fact that Judith would be there until
they were almost at the door. By then it was too late to worry
about it. Whatever happened, at least he and Simon were back
to their old closeness.

29

The duke and Robin were among the first to arrive. They were shown into the drawing room, where the duchess's nephew, the Marquess of Worthington, and his wife greeted them. Then Diana was announced, and although Robin had promised himself that he would try to be more open with her, he found himself greeting her very formally. The men began to cluster together, as usual, and the marchioness, very obviously increasing, motioned to Diana to join her on the sofa.

"For, once I am down, I cannot get up without help."

"So this is why we have not seen much of you this fall. This is your first, I believe?"

"Yes, and I am determined not my last. I have been feeling wonderful all along. The marquess is most attentive and stays home more than is fashionable to entertain me, so I was very happy with my aunt's invitation, since he is clearly enjoying the male company."

"Lady Barbara Stanley and Miss Judith Ware."

The noise of the conversation had drowned out part of the butler's announcement, so Simon only heard Barbara's name. Almost immediately afterward the last guest arrived, Captain Hunt, a friend of the Duke of Ross, whom the duchess had invited as a dinner partner for Barbara.

"Now we can go in to dinner," said her grace, taking advantage of the confusion of introductions and conversations to avoid any confrontations until after the meal.

She had thought a great deal about her seating arrangements. It was one thing to create the potential for a volatile situation by inviting *Dame Durden*'s crew, quite another to figure out how to seat them. So Simon and Judith were not seated next to each other, but across the table. It was an intimate-enough group that there could be some conversation across, but there would be no scenes this way, she hoped. It was almost impossible to seat the rest: as soon as she thought of one combination she had to scrap it and come up with another. Finally she decided to seat her niece and nephew across from each other, and have Diana and Robin together. It is time they said more than two words to each other, after all, she thought.

And once they were seated, Robin found that he had only Diana to talk to, since the marchioness was helping Simon orient himself.

Diana had no excuse to turn away when Robin politely asked her how she got on.

"Very well, thank you, Major Stanley."

Robin realized he had nothing else to say. Either he uttered polite inanities, as he had been doing for weeks—and he couldn't, for the life of him, think of any—or he made the effort to break down the barrier that had been between them for months. Maybe Simon didn't care for Diana, but maybe she had learned to care for the duke? He decided to compromise and ask Diana's opinion on the discussion begun in the drawing room, one on the increasing poverty seen around.

"I am utterly hopeless at politics, you know that, Major. I know what I feel when I see a single person in need, but I don't have the knowledge to make any generalizations."

Robin countered a little stiffly, "But you are an intelligent woman, milady. I am sure you and Simon have discussed serious matters."

"The duke and I discovered immediately that political sophistication and intellectual discussion are not my forte." She laughed. "We agreed early on to keep our conversation light."

"But you do have some opinions on returning soldiers, I recall." Robin could not stop himself, nor keep his tone neutral.

Diana hesitated before answering. She knew to what Robin was referring, although others would not. She also knew this might be her only chance to explain herself.

"I once expressed an opinion on the matter, yes, out of insecurity and fear. I changed my mind almost overnight, but I was never able to convey that to the person I most wished to. I was never given the chance." Diana lifted her eyes and looked straight at Robin. "I have regretted it ever since."

"Then you are sympathetic to the plight of the returning veteran?"

"Oh, yes, very much so," she answered softly.

"Perhaps we might talk further after dinner," Robin said with great control, considering his heart was racing.

"Of course, Major Stanley," answered Diana, looking down at her soup as though consommé was the most wonderful sight in the world. She was not sure why, at last, Robin was willing to hear her explanation, but he was giving her a chance and she intended to take it, if she had to propose to him herself.

Simon had not heard any of this, since he was preoccupied with getting his soup into his mouth without spoiling his cravat. He assumed that Barbara's old schooll friend was across from him, and was going to ask the marshioness to introduce them, when the marquess turned to Judith and said, "I understand, Miss Ware, that you have not been in London long? Do you find the city overwhelming?"

Simon's spoon was halfway to his mouth when he heard her name. He froze, and Judith knew that she had been found out. It was no use disguising her voice, which she had, in sheer terror, thought of doing, so she turned and answered naturally. "I did at first, but now that I have been here for a few months, I am a bit more used to the noise and crowds. I find it stimulating, although I do miss the country."

"And where did you grow up?"

"In Hertfordshire, my lord."

Of course, thought Simon. How could I have forgotten. She is Barbara's friend from the Christmas years ago. He remembered enjoying her company, but no clear details of her background. He placed his spoon carefully on the table, as though he were controlling his desire to throw it. So, it had all been a conspiracy. They had sent her to read to him. She did not need the position, if she was a friend of Barbara's. She has never been a governess, and is, no doubt, well-portioned.

Judith went on chatting while Simon fumed. If he had been asked why he was so angry, he could not have formulated a clear answer. He felt duped, for one thing. Robin had known who she was and no doubt sent her, and yet had let him go on and on over his proposal. They had all taken advantage of his blindness. Judith was not who she seemed, and if she had deceived him about her background, then what about her refusal? Damn it, he had worried about her, and here she was, attending balls and intimate suppers.

Simon leaned toward Diana and begged pardon for his interruption. He lowered his voice and said, "I have a favor to ask of you."

"Of course, Simon. What can I do for you?"

"I wish to have a private chat with Miss Ware. Can you see to it that I am introduced after dinner and get us to a corner of the room and leave us alone for a few minutes?"

Diana looked curiously across the table at Judith, who was feeling alternately cold and hot, ready to claim illness and run from the table, cursing all well-bred people who could sit and talk so politely.

"Miss Ware is the young woman I described to you at the ball. So you do know her, after all?"

Simon answered stiffly, "Yes, I know her from three years ago and would like to renew our acquaintance."

"I'll do my best at maneuvering, then." Diana was not at all sure that this would be a comfortable tête-à-tête, judging from Simon's expression.

Since at least half the party was in ignorance of Simon's relationship with Judith, they managed to be genuinely relaxed, while the other half cultivated that appearance. Simon concentrated on his meal and the marchioness's chatter and never once attempted to address Judith, although there were times during dinner when both of them were part of no conversation and had nothing to do but sit silently and push food around on their plates.

The duchess could see that Simon had become aware of Judith's presence, and she had no intention of postponing their confrontation. At the end of dinner, therefore, she announced that since they were all practically family, the gentlemen would join the ladies in the drawing room.

Robin was relieved, since he had no wish to face Simon's inevitable anger and was eager to speak to Diana. He led Simon in and was about ready to seat him when the duke objected.

"I would rather stand, Robin. Please fetch me a glass of port."

Simon's tone was cool, and at any other time Robin would have been offended, but he was relieved to have the reckoning postponed.

After all the guests were comfortable, the duchess turned to

Barbara and asked if she would be willing to play for them. She decided that since it was a small and familiar group, she would play the second movement of the Beethoven sonata she had been practicing and then perhaps a few songs.

The rest of the company, with the exception of Judith, had never heard the music, and sat expectantly. Barbara loved the andante and had worked on it enough so that she lost her nervousness almost immediately.

The company was quiet and so was Barbara after she had finished. The music left them serene and aching for something, thought Judith, as Barbara explained that the last chord led directly into the third movement.

"Perhaps in a little while you will play something else for us, dear," said the duchess. "Now, anything else would be anticlimactic."

The conversation started slowly, as though all of them were reluctant to break the mood of the music, and when Diana approached Simon, he found it hard to recapture the intensity of his anger from dinner.

"Miss Ware is in conversation with Major Stanley, Simon. If we walk over now, perhaps I can distract him and leave you alone with her for a few minutes."

"Thank you, Diana."

Judith saw them approaching first and instinctively reached out for Robin's arm.

"Simon, Judith and I were just discussing Barbara's performance. She was marvelous, don't you think?"

"I do indeed. And one does not hear Beethoven's music that often in England. I prefer him to others who are . . . How can I say it?"

"Thinner and less textured, your grace?" said Judith, deciding she need not give Simon all the initiative.

"Well said, Miss . . . Ware, is it not?" Simon's voice held all of the old sarcasm.

"Major Stanley, I would like some ratafia. Would you accompany me?" said Diana.

"Certainly," replied Robin, and squeezed Judith's hand before he moved off, having no choice but to follow Diana.

"I am quite surprised to find you here, Miss Ware. I had

no idea a lowly ex-governess would move in such exalted circles." Simon's sarcasm affected Judith more than a direct accusation would have done.

"I am surprised to be here myself, your grace," she answered quietly. "But the duchess kindly invited me for tea after her ball and then asked me to come tonight."

"Yes, and Barbara is an old friend of yours. If I am not mistaken, we spent a holiday together at Ashurst."

"Yes, your grace, we all enjoyed one another's company that Christmas."

"And yet you had forgotten, or never thought to remind me of it when I hired you? And what were you doing, letting yourself be paid for a position anyway?"

"I was doing exactly what I said I was: earning a little extra money to supplement our income."

"For what? An extra pair of shoes? Oh, no, my dear, you were sent there by my good friends, out of pity for me."

"I was not," Judith responded warmly. "Or not precisely. I told you the truth except for the fact that I knew the Stanleys and had met you a few years ago. Robin helped me convince Mr. Whithedd to get me an interview so he would have a firsthand account of how you were getting on, but I had already seen the advertisement and decided to apply for the position."

"Why, Miss Ware?"

"Because I needed the money and because I wanted to help you. I remembered you from that Christmas and did not like to think of someone I had liked and admired so shut off from everyone who cared for you."

"And so I was in the nature of a crusade?"

Judith was by now near tears. Simon's response was almost as bad as she had anticipated. But she felt a stirring of anger. She was being made out a criminal—and for a minor deception, which had, after all, worked out to Simon's benefit.

"You are purposely putting things in the worst possible light, your grace. I was a satisfactory employee, was I not? If I did pretend to be a stranger, it was because of your good friends' care for you, and my own."

"And if your background is what you claimed, then why did

you refuse my offer?'' Simon's anger was beginning to abate, and since it was, indeed, largely irrational, he was having a hard time finding a logical accusation to hurl at Judith. She was right, and as an objective observer, he would not have faulted her for a small deception that had wrought so much good. For some reason, he could not be objective.

"I refused for precisely the reasons I gave you. And I was right. You and Lady Diana make a striking couple, and I can see you have regained confidence in yourself. And now, your grace, I think we have said all that we have to say to each other. I wish to speak with the duchess a moment, so I will leave you.'' And Judith walked away, not caring that she had left Simon stranded in the corner until someone noticed him and came to get him. He heard conversation around him, but did not want to make a fool of himself by attempting to make his way toward someone and perhaps falling over a chair on the way. And so he stood there, with the growing realization that despite Judith's statement, they had not said all they had to say to each other; in fact, he reflected, they would probably need a whole lifetime to do so.

Why, I love her, thought Simon. It is as simple as that. And she was right. I never would have known it had she not turned me down. We would have had a calm, companionable marriage and I would have held myself back from her out of insecurity. I would have done my duty as a husband, but never would have believed that I could awaken a passionate response. Something dammed up inside him since returning to England was moving again. But did she feel the same? he wondered. He had no doubt she cared for him, but was she attracted to him? She clearly wanted a marriage of mind and body, but with him? She thought, as everyone must, that Diana had captured his heart. Well, he thought, I think after tonight that misconception will be cleared up. Robin and Diana should be able to reach some understanding. And then I will have to convince Judith of my feelings for her.

When Judith walked away from Simon, she blindly joined the marquess and his wife. The marchioness looked up and smiled, and her husband remarked politely, "I saw you conversing with the duke, Miss Ware. Are you acquainted?''

"I met him through the Stanleys, my lord." Judith looked back to where she had left Simon stranded. It serves him right to stand there waiting, she thought angrily, and then immediately was struck with remorse. "I am afraid I left him rather suddenly. Perhaps you could bring him over to Robin, my lord?"

"Of course," replied the marquess, and he joined Simon, who was beginning to wonder if he would spend the rest of the evening in the corner.

Judith was relieved when the party drew to a close. She thanked her hostess and, when the duchess looked at her questioningly, gave a small shrug of her shoulders.

I will have to invite her shopping with me, thought the duchess, and find out what transpired between them.

When Simon bade her good night, he said with a trace of irony, "I hope the evening went as you planned, my dear Godmama."

"Why, yes," the duchess said shamelessly. "Better than I had planned."

Simon smiled a rather tight little smile. On his way home, he wondered what Robin and Diana had said to each other, and if his godmother's matchmaking scheme had succeeded.

30

T he next day, after Wiggins had read and left, Simon was finishing a light luncheon when he heard footsteps in the front hall. A moment later, Major Stanley was announced, and Robin walked in. Simon could immediately feel the difference in him. For days he had been removed and even slow in his walk, but today his stride was energetic and the hand he placed on Simon's shoulder was as warm and affectionate as it had ever been.

"Join me, Robin? I'll have Cranston bring in more tea."

"All right. I am hungry. I ate very little before my ride."

"You and Barbara?"

"No. I rode with Diana."

"Unaccompanied?" queried Simon, raising his eyebrows.

"Unaccompanied." Robin laughed. "We finished the conversation we began last night and . . . Well, wish me happy, Simon."

"I do wish you happy," Simon said, a big smile on his face. "How did you manage to make this come about so soon?"

"I told you we had almost reached an agreement last spring, but she refused to marry me before I left. I was insulted and hurt—sure she didn't really love me enough to risk being married to whatever came home to her. She was more frightened of marriage itself, had I but known. She tried to get in touch with me. I sent back her notes and refused to see her, and of course, when I returned, there she was, leading Dev a merry chase."

"Whereas the truth was, he was in way over his head and she was using him to show you she didn't care."

"Yes. And then you. I was angry about Dev, but could not see him as a real threat. But you . . . How could any woman not prefer you?"

Simon was surprised. "Whatever do you mean, Robin? Diana cares nothing for rank."

"I am not speaking of rank, Simon. I am only a man of action. You are far more intelligent. No, let me finish," said Robin as Simon began to protest. "I am not saying that I am stupid, just that you are far more serious a person."

"I'll not have my friend insulted, even by himself," replied Simon.

"I am only saying we are different. And that I would think Diana would have found you hard to resist."

"But indeed she did, you great fool," said Simon. "Not that she had anything to resist, since I was not courting her. But she loves you precisely because you are a man of action, precisely because you are most happy in the country. She has no interest in politics and would be quite bored with my serious side."

"I know that now."

"Oh? That I am quite boring?" Simon teased.

"No, you clunch, that she loves me. I feel wonderful. I can't describe it."

"You sound like an exultant cock, crowing over his supposed rival."

"You have no regrets?" asked Robin anxiously.

"None, my friend. I am only funning you. And I wish to discuss with you another young woman," Simon said in a more serious tone.

"Judith?"

"Yes. Miss Ware. I forgive you all your small deception, for I know why you did it. But last night I lost my temper—she does have a way of provoking me to do that!—and accused Judith of full-scale deception."

"But her only lie was not revealing her friendship with us."

"I found that out, but not before I'd insulted her and made her furious." Simon leaned forward. "And now I discover I am in love with her. Have you any helpful suggestions for me?" he asked wryly.

"I would suggest that the first thing you must do is call upon her and apologize for your anger last night. Perhaps you might ask her to go for a drive with you? It would seem you both need some time to become at ease with each other again."

Robin decided not to tell Simon that Judith loved him. It was not his secret to tell. And a little of the normal insecurity of the lover would be good for Simon, he thought, in contrast to the morbid sense of inferiority he had come home with.

"You give good advice, Robin, I'll call upon Judith this afternoon."

"Do you want me to take you?"

"No, I will have my groom drive me."

"Good luck, then, Simon."

"Thank you, Robin. I believe I'll need it."

A few hours later, Simon's coach drew up in front of the house on Gower Street. "Take me to the door, James."

James led Simon up the steps and rapped sharply at the front door. Hannah muttered to herself as she walked down the hall. Some boy playing tricks again, no doubt, and she pulled the door open suddenly, ready to pick up her skirts and take after the imagined urchin. She was completely taken by surprise to see a gentleman dressed in the highest fashion standing on their doorstep.

"Is this the Ware residence?" James asked solemnly. He had grown tremendously in solemnity and dignity, thought Simon with amusement, since being designated Simon's guide.

"Why, yes," Hannah said. She was taking in Simon's gleaming boots and tightly fitting trousers and perfectly fitted bottle-green coat, and thinking Stephen would give his eyeteeth to look like that, when she finally looked at Simon's face and realized, from the way he was staring straight ahead, that this was the Duke of Sutton.

"Oh, my word," she exclaimed without thinking.

"I beg your pardon?" Simon said politely.

"Nothing. What can I do for your grace?"

It did not surprise Simon that he had been recognized. This must be the Hannah Judith had told him about, and she, of course, knew about him.

"I am looking to speak with Miss Ware. Is she at home?"

"No, she went out a while ago, to the circulating library."

Simon's face reflected his disappointment, and Hannah said quickly, "But she should be back any minute, your grace. Won't you come in and have a cup of tea? I am sure she will be back in time to join you."

"Thank you, um, Hannah, is it not? I am afraid I don't know you by your surname."

"Hannah is fine, your grace. Come in. Do you need my arm?"

"No, no, James has got me. Just lead the way."

Hannah led them to the small room on the right side of the house. It was hardly ever used, since they didn't entertain much, aside from Stephen's friends. There was dust on the mantel clock, Hannah noticed in embarrassment, but then realized that the duke could not see it anyway.

"Now you just sit yourself down and I'll be back in a moment."

James stood awkwardly by the fireplace. Simon had never required invisibility from his servants, like some of the nobility, but James sometimes found it difficult, as the duke's guide, to be present for Simon's needs, and not present, at the same time, for the conversation around him. This small house was less intimidating, but he, James, could not sit and have tea with the duke, and so he stood until Hannah returned with the tray. James was hungry immediately upon seeing the fresh scones, and shifted his feet. The sound reminded Simon of his presence, and he felt guilty about his thoughtlessness. He usually tried to be aware of James and let him join the servants whenever possible. Here, of course, there was no belowstairs, so he wasn't sure what to do when Hannah stepped in.

"Perhaps your footman would like to come into the kitchen for some tea? I shall settle him in and come right back to pour."

"Thank you, Hannah, that is very kind of you," Simon replied with a smile.

The duke sat poised on the chair. He could feel himself getting chilled, for of course, he thought, they would have no fire in an unused room. He could smell the tea and carefully reached out his hands to warm them on the teapot when he heard the front door open and Judith call out, "Hannah, I'm home," and then ask, "Why is the drawing-room door open?"

Simon heard what sounded like books dropping, as Judith looked in and saw him sitting there. "Your grace!"

"Miss Ware," Simon said, standing up.

"What are you doing here?" Judith asked, sounding annoyed.

Simon was about to make his carefully thought-out apology when she continued, "This room is freezing. We rarely use it. I suppose Hannah thought it was more suitable for your rank than the parlor. But why you should be chilled to the bone only because you are a duke, I'm sure I don't know. Thank God, we always keep a fire laid."

Simon could hear Judith at the fireplace and smelled sulfur as she lit the fire. She brushed her dress off and came over to him, saying, "Let me move the chairs closer to the heat." Simon stood up, and she had him wait until she had positioned the chairs and tea table before she led him to his seat.

The duke was enjoying himself. He was amused and touched by her immediate reaction, which in many a young lady would have been all injured dignity after the other night. Judith reacted in the moment, and her immediate concern was for his comfort.

"Let me hang up my cloak, your grace, and I will be right back to pour your tea."

Judith's initial reaction was giving way to a feeling of dreadful anticipation as she removed her cloak and smoothed her hair. One part of her wondered what on earth Simon wanted with her after the duchess's party. Another part of her, of course, was thrilled to see him there and was already spinning fantasies. " 'Down, wantons, down,' " she told herself. "You don't know why he is here, and you won't find out until you go back in there."

Judith sat down opposite Simon and poured his tea. "Would you like me to butter you a scone?"

"Yes, thank you, Miss Ware."

Judith handed Simon a napkin, which he spread on his lap, and then she placed a small china plate on the table in front of him. He was holding his cup in his right hand, wondering, as usual, if he could carry it off without dropping too many crumbs, or, God forbid, his cup, when Judith told him the location of the scone. She watched him carefully locate it, and marveled at the way he managed. There were some crumbs on his trousers, which he was not aware of, and lulled by their quiet absorption in eating and drinking, she almost reached over to brush them off and caught herself just in time. But his closeness made her remember that feeling of intimacy in the library;

she could not help wanting the right to do such homely things as brushing off crumbs.

" 'That way madness lies.' Goodness, I'm turning into Lear this afternoon," she told herself. "I cannot let myself drift this way."

Simon finished his tea and was warming up from the fire and his drink. He cleared his throat and said, "Miss Ware, I seem to have spent a large portion of our short acquaintance apologizing, but I do beg your pardon for my anger last night. I know now you were only guilty of that small deception, and I fear I was quite offensive."

"You were, your grace," replied Judith without thinking.

Simon was amused and relieved. An automatic "Oh, no, your grace" would only have made him feel worse.

Judith continued, "What hurt the most was that it seemed that you let one lie make you doubt what you came to know of me in all those weeks."

"I was very angry."

"I know, and I accept your apology. I offer you one for finding it necessary to deceive you. Perhaps you would have hired me anyway, but we all feared not."

"No, you were right, I wouldn't have let anyone in the door who knew me even slightly. But what I have also come to ask is if you would be willing to resume our friendship? You were right to refuse my offer of marriage, I see that now. But I hoped we could put that behind us. Perhaps we could go driving or riding together. If you are not embarrassed to be seen with me on a lead line, that is."

Judith's heart lifted and then fell, in the same moment. He does care, she thought, but only as a friend. Could she stand seeing him, knowing he would be looking for a more passionate attachment elsewhere? She would never know if she had a chance, however, unless she accepted.

"I would enjoy driving or riding with you, your grace," she answered quietly.

"You speak rather unenthusiastically," said Simon. "Forgive me for being so blunt, but I do not wish you to feel obligated in any way."

"Oh, no," Judith said. "I have missed our conversations and

welcome the opportunity to renew our friendship. I am just a bit tired right now.''

"Of course. And I have stayed far too long," he said, feeling for the table and putting his cup down carefully. He stood up, and at that moment Hannah returned, having timed it so they had had some time to be alone, but so that Judith had not been unchaperoned for too long.

"You are leaving so soon, your grace? Shall I call your footman?''

"Please, Hannah.''

Judith rose and followed Simon into the hall. She watched as James helped him into his greatcoat and gave him her hand when he turned and reached for it.

"May I call to take you driving on Friday afternoon, then?''

"Yes, I would like that very much," Judith answered, feeling his touch all through her body.

"Until Friday, then. Thank you for the excellent tea, Hannah. James?''

After the duke left, Hannah looked at Judith questioningly.

"He came to apologize, Hannah, and as you heard, to invite me to go driving with him.''

"He is an impressive young man, Judith. Quite confident, despite his blindness.''

"Yes, it is wonderful to see how he handles himself. And he is very natural about asking for help. I think that it is that realness, if there is such a word, that I care about the most. One feels that he is ultimately trustworthy.''

"A quality you both have in common, then, my dear.''

"Thank you, Hannah . . . Oh, Hannah, I am so happy that he has called—and so miserable!'' Judith laughed through her tears.

Hannah nodded. "He did not offer for you right this afternoon then,'' she teased.

"Oh, I know I am being ridiculous. But he seems only to want the old friendship back. So do I, but now I want more.''

"Do not write an ending at the beginning, Judith. Right now, he wants to be with you, that is clear, or he would never have called. Give it some time. Now, I must get back to the kitchen, and you may calm yourself by clearing the dishes out of the small parlor!''

31

The next morning dragged by for Judith. She was working on a still life of several pieces of fruit, a teapot, and half a loaf of bread. She would work for a while, then go off into a dream where Simon put his arm around her and drew her to him and kissed her . . . and she would find herself absent-mindedly picking at the loaf of bread or taking a bite out of an apple, which then necessitated several changes in her composition! She and Barbara were supposed to ride early in the afternoon, and Judith was looking forward to telling her all about Simon's visit.

It had started to snow by lunchtime, a fine dry snow. It was cold enough to accumulate a few inches, and Judith wondered if Barbara would cancel their ride. But no footman arrived with a note, and at two o'clock she heard the clatter of hooves and looked out to see Barbara waiting, with Judith's mount being led by the Stanleys' groom.

Hannah thought the two women foolish to be out in such weather, but had to agree with Judith that in the country one wouldn't have thought twice about it. "It is only a snowfall, and not a storm, Hannah. It just seems like more because we are in the city. I am sure we will not stay long."

Neither Judith nor Barbara spoke much until they got to the park. The streets were slushy and slippery, and they were concentrating on the horses, who were ready to play, thought Judith as she held hers in. Their winter coats held the snowflakes, and they looked more like wild ponies than prime Thoroughbreds. There was a great head-tossing and bridle-jingling until they were able to let them out into a canter. Being out in such weather made Judith feel a little girl again, playing in the snow, galloping around and shaking the snow off her hair as if she were one of the horses.

When they slowed to a walk, Judith was feeling wonderful:

warmed up and relaxed. She could see Barbara had enjoyed it as much as she had.

"I am glad we came. I was afraid you might not want to be out in such weather."

Barbara smiled at her. "Oh, no, I love it too. And as I suspected, we almost have the park to ourselves. We can pretend we're back in Sussex."

"When are you returning to Ashurst?" Judith asked.

"Next Sunday," answered Barbara. "I am surprised at how quickly it has come upon us. I only wish I could convince you to join us, Judith."

"I would love to, but this will be our first holiday in our new home, and I think it important to stay in London. Will Dev be home for Christmas also?"

"I don't know. And, do you know Judith, for the first time in years, I don't think I care."

Judith looked at her in surprise.

"I know, I should be hopeful, now that Diana and Robin have reached an understanding, but it is finally clear to me that he will never feel anything for me but a brotherly affection. I could go on hoping forever that he may change, but I cannot live like that for another five years of my life. I feel rather empty; not brokenhearted, as I thought I must be, but disoriented. It is as though I were a compass needle gone loose after being pointed in the same direction for so long. It is clear to me now that my love for Dev allowed me to be in love and have my music at the same time. I must have known there was no danger of him ever sweeping me off my feet and distracting me from my art."

"I have always thought . . . But now is perhaps not the time to say it."

"No, pray continue."

"I think you are too strong for the viscount. I could understand his infatuation with a woman like Diana, but I doubt he would ever turn to you in any romantic way. He needs someone to protect."

"I know you are right. I have probably always known it. Well, I suppose that I will feel lost for a while, but I cannot like it. Now, tell me about Simon."

Judith blushed. "He called yesterday to apologize. He seems to want to renew our friendship. But I don't think it is any more than that. I am not sure what kind of heartache I am letting myself in for.''

"Better heartache than nothing," advised Barbara. "I am sure it will all come right between you. You are clearly made for one another. Come, we'd better turn back before we get lost in the park!"

The snow was still coming down steadily, and the return to the Wares' was slow going, but Judith thanked Barbara for persevering despite the weather, for the exercise had been wonderful.

"Will you come in for a cup of tea?"

"Not today, thank you, Judith. Shall I see you tomorrow?"

"Only if it be in the morning. My engagement with Simon is in the afternoon."

Barbara smiled. " 'Oh, wonderful, wonderful . . . and after that, beyond all whooping.' "

"I think your enthusiasm is a bit premature, my friend," said Judith, trying to subdue the feelings of hope that rose with her friend's response. "I told you, it is more than likely he still only sees me as a friend. The more appropriate quote would be 'How full of briars is this working-day world.' "

"You have had more than your share of the briars, Judith. I think that you will be seeing some roses. You deserve them."

The next day was bright, dry, and cold. The snow had left a thick frosting on the ground and roofs. Later that day, of course, it would melt, and the soot and traffic would ruin the pristine whiteness. The streets were always filthy, though, and Wiggins had arrived at Simon's cold and wet. They were back to reading political speeches and commentaries, and Wiggins was sorry to leave the world of fiction.

Simon could not keep his mind on the reading. He was daydreaming like any schoolboy, imagining his arms around Judith, tilting her head back, kissing her full on the lips . . .

"Do you want me to continue with the next speech, your grace?" Wiggins was asking this a second time, after the long silence that had followed the first speech. Usually Simon asked him to take notes, or go back to a pertinent section, but either the duke was very involved with the ideas raised, or completely distracted, thought Wiggins.

Simon grinned in his direction. "I beg your pardon. I was obviously woolgathering. As a matter of fact, we may as well stop for today. I am quite unable to fix my mind on Lord Phillips' response to his opponent at all. Why don't you take the rest of the morning off? I shall see you tomorrow."

"Yes, your grace. Thank you, your grace."

After Wiggins had gone, Simon was not sure how he was going to make it through the morning. He was not riding and was too restless to sit with Francis. He was very pleased, therefore, when the butler announced Robin.

"I hope I don't disturb you, Simon?"

"I'm glad you've come, Robin. I was just about ready to jump out of my skin. Come in, sit down. Cranston, could you bring us some tea?"

"What has you blue-deviled?" Robin asked.

"I am about to begin my courtship of Miss Ware, and I must admit that I am too eager. I am looking forward to the holidays, Robin, when I will have time to woo her properly."

Robin grinned at Simon's nervousness. "You sound like a typical lover."

"It's all very well for you to say. You know you have Diana's heart. Will you come for a drive with me this afternoon? I have promised to take Miss Ware up with me, but I am sure that she would enjoy seeing us both." Simon thought this invitation to Robin was rather inspired. Having someone else in the carriage would make it easier for Judith to feel at ease, and make his way a bit smoother.

To Judith, of course, Robin's presence meant one thing: Simon was not romantically interested and had brought his friend along as a protector. She tried not to let her disappointment show as she was helped into the carriage. After all, it was not Robin's fault Simon did not love her, and she would have to save her despair for later.

Simon had ordered the old landaulet, since there were three of them, and he and Robin settled back to face Judith. They fell into an animated discussion of new farming methods as Judith listened. They were both good men, she thought, with a sense of responsibility that exceeded some of their contemporaries.

Simon suddenly realized that they were so engrossed they had quite ignored Judith, and he stopped midsentence to apologize.

"That is quite all right, your grace. I have enjoyed listening to you, and though I know very little about farming, was able to follow you very well. I was thinking how fortunate your tenants are, to have responsible landlords."

"Enough of business," Simon said, brushing off Judith's compliment. "You will be at Ashurst, Miss Ware?"

"No, your grace. I have been invited, but I do not wish to leave my brother and Hannah on the first Christmas in our new home."

"I understand," the duke said, not letting his disappointment into his voice. He had been sure that Judith would be present and had hoped that being together daily would enable him to discover the state of her feelings toward him. The two weeks with the Stanleys did not seem so inviting, now that he knew that Judith would not be there.

They had almost reached the park, and the sun, which had kept them a bit warm, was being obscured by clouds. "It looks like we are in for more snow," said Robin, glancing up at the graying sky.

"Are you warm enough, Miss Ware?" asked Simon as he himself began to feel the cold.

"For the moment, your grace."

"Well, we will not go too far into the park," said Simon. "We will have to keep our drive shorter than I had planned."

Judith was fairly subdued for the rest of the ride. Simon had not sounded at all let down by her holiday plans. In fact, he had probably only asked to be polite, she thought. She had looked forward to being alone with him this afternoon, and they had had no chance for personal conversation. She was almost relieved when they reached her door and the groom helped her down.

"Thank you for the outing, your grace. I wish you both a happy holiday."

"And you also, Miss Ware," Simon replied in the same formal tones. Had Judith heard him as they drove away, however, she would have felt quite different.

"Damn," he said as the carriage turned the corner, "I thought she was sure to be at Ashurst. Now I won't be able to see her for almost two weeks."

"I should be insulted, but I understand, Simon. Will you be traveling with us?"

"If you have room for me, Robin."

"We are bringing my father's coach, so you are very welcome."

"Till Sunday then," Simon said, when he dropped Robin off, and returned home, now impatient for the end rather than the beginning of the holidays.

32

J udith had hoped to hear from the duke again, and when he did not call before leaving for Ashurst, was even more convinced that her place in his life was as a friend and not as a romantic interest.

How can I ever hope to move beyond friendship if we never see each other? she worried. The fact that Simon couldn't see her was becoming more important. Now that she was aware of him physically, she realized he had been right: one did, quite naturally, wish to be seen, to be complimented, to attract by one's dress or the sheen of one's hair, or the green in one's eyes brought out by a particular shade of green. If he couldn't see her, then how on earth could he keep her in mind? And while she may be able to see him at the Stanleys', the initiative was all his. Judith felt her poverty and lack of position more keenly than she had ever done.

The holidays, which she had been looking forward to, were rather lonely, although Christmas Day itself was lovely. After breakfast they all attended services at the local parish, and although the day was foggy and cold, they were warmed by the candles, the sermon, and the realization that they were together as a family. After three years of being an onlooker at other families' holidays, Judith was happy to be returning to their own house, which smelled of apples and sage and onion from the small capon Hannah was roasting. They toasted one another, and Judith sat down to dinner in her green dress. Stephen's gift to her had been paints and brushes, and she had bought him a new scarf and gloves. For Hannah, they had both gone in on a coach ticket so she could visit her family. After supper, they spent the evening reading in front of the fire. But the next day, Stephen was back at work, and Judith was on her own. No Barbara to have tea with, no riding, and no hope, false or otherwise, that Simon might call. She painted, she read, she walked when the weather was dry, but the days after Christmas seemed to crawl by.

Toward the end of the fortnight, Judith was ready to cry in frustration. She decided she'd better take herself in hand and walk to Hatchards to survey the latest novels. The exercise and having a particular destination would do her good.

The bookseller's was quiet, so it was almost like being in a private library. The sight and smell of new books, as well as her walk, calmed her down, and she was quite lost in a collection of Byron's poems when she felt someone near her. She looked up, and across from her, equally engrossed, was Simon's reader. He looked up and caught her looking at him. She lowered her gaze, but could no longer concentrate on the words in front of her. Perhaps he was purchasing something for the duke's return. She looked up again and saw that what he was holding could only be the latest novel from the Minerva Press. The duke might enjoy Miss Austen, but Judith could not conceive of his tastes running to errant monks or dashing earls, so this man must be a devotee himself. Judith smiled to herself at the incongruous picture. To see an older man just as absorbed as the usual bevy of giggling young ladies, was amusing and also somewhat touching. He looked as though he had had a hard life, and perhaps a romance or two helped him escape his troubles. Surely that was a worthier result than confirming your ladies in their silliness.

I wish I were reading for Simon again, thought Judith. *I know that then I could tell if Simon loved me, or if it is only friendly interest.* As she watched the avid reader in front of her, she was suddenly inspired. Did she dare? Well, it was no worse than her original venture. She moved around until she was standing next to Wiggins. "I beg your pardon," she said.

Wiggins looked a little dazed as he lifted his head. He had been wooing Lady Lucinda Luxley and to be brought back to the reality of the bookstore was jarring. It took him a moment to recognize Judith as the young lady he had seen before.

"I know this is forward of me, but may I ask you a question?" she said.

Wiggins blinked in surprise and nodded.

"Are you employed by the Duke of Sutton as his reader?"

"Why, yes, miss. However did you know?"

"I saw you in here with him a few weeks ago and you spoke

to me briefly. I would like to talk to you privately. If you have a few minutes to spare, could we sit down to tea across the street? I know this seems a bit bold, but it is very important to me.''

Wiggins had liked Judith immediately. First of all, she was not Lady Lucinda, who though wonderful to woo in fantasy, would have been intimidating in a real-life version. Judith was wearing her old cloak, and her manner, though straightforward and direct and her request unconventional, was not what his wife would have called bold. He was sure that whatever she wanted to talk about had something to do with Simon. Her eyes were begging him not to refuse, and his curiosity was not going to let him rest, so he nodded his agreement, and out they went, heading for the tea shop on the corner.

"Shall we have some scones with tea?" asked Judith. Wiggins nodded, and they both sat silently until the tea and the warm triangles were set in front of them.

"I know this must seem rather odd to you," Judith began. "Perhaps I had better explain from the beginning." Without giving every detail, Judith sketched out her acquaintance with Simon. Wiggins liked her more and more as she spoke. It was clear to him that she loved the duke. He had no way of knowing whether the duke loved her.

"The duke has forgiven me my deception and called upon me since the dinner party, but I have no way to be in his company naturally, as a young lady of the *ton* might be.''

Wiggins had been nodding sympathetically during the story. Although Judith came from a good family, she had had to work for her living just the way he had. She had courage, he decided, for while he had never expected his life to be anything other than an eight-to-six position, she had been brought up differently. His clerkship, in fact, had been considered a rise in station by his family. His father kept a butcher shop, but recognizing his son's "scholarly" qualities, had sent him to school. Over his years as clerk, Wiggins had often wished he had taken after his father, for though butchering was messy, hard work, it certainly afforded some creative outlet, if only in cutting chops to the right size. And it afforded one the freedom to chat with customers and move from task to task. Hunched over his desk, raised high on his stool, Wiggins would sometimes see himself in a blood-splattered apron, bringing his cleaver down neatly to separate the leg and arm joints of the owner of the firm. But, however much he didn't like it, he had risen while Judith had fallen in station. He pulled himself back to the present as she continued.

"Perhaps I am too impatient, or too unladylike, but I cannot see how friendly calls from the duke or occasional dinners with the Stanleys will result in anything. I want something more like the intimacy that existed when I was reading for him."

Wiggins was beginning to get nervous. Was this young woman going to ask him to give up his position so she could see the duke more regularly? If she offered, why would the duke not accept? Who wouldn't prefer a vibrant young woman to a dried-out old man like himself? Wiggins had himself halfway home, preparing to tell his wife the bad news, when Judith leaned forward, saying, "I want to ask you a favor."

"Yes, yes, I agree. It would be better for the duke if you returned. I will hand in my notice, but I would ask for a few weeks more." Wiggins was about to push back his chair and rewind himself when Judith realized what he was talking about.

She put out her hand and patted his arm, saying, "Oh, dear, I've muddled this whole thing. Of course I would not presume to replace you. It is your position now and I am sure the duke is very satisfied with you. And now that he knows who I am, his grace would consider it improper of me to be there alone with him. He can't rehire the good friend of his friends."

Wiggins was wiping his brow with his napkin—a gesture that left a few crumbs—and sank back in his chair as though released from an awful tension.

"What I wish to ask is much easier, I think," said Judith. "When do you next read for his grace?"

"Tuesday next, and then on Thursday and Friday."

"Could you let me take your place for one day? I am sure if I had some time alone with him, I could tell if he has any deep feelings for me. If need be, I will ask him," Judith said suddenly and vehemently, realizing that she meant it, however shocking it sounded.

Wiggins let his breath out slowly. He had been foolish to let his fantasies run away with him, but he had survived so many years of drudgery by allowing his imagination the freedom he lacked that it was an ingrained habit by now.

"Do you think one morning will be enough?"

"I don't know," confessed Judith. "It will have to be, for he certainly will not let me return."

"What if he sent you away immediately?"

"I will deal with that hurdle when I come to it. He can hardly have me thrown bodily out of the house. And the very fact I am there will open up a conversation that goes beyond friendly politeness."

"I will do it," Wiggins, said, feeling like a character in a Minerva novel. She was the sort of woman that would do for the duke, he decided, and he would do his small part to help her.

"Oh, thank you, Mr. Wiggins. I could kiss you, right here—"

"Please don't," said Wiggins. He was not ready to step completely off the conventional path that was his life.

"Of course not!" Judith smiled. "Let us order another pot of tea and biscuits, shall we?" And over the second pot she began to draw him out. He told her of being the first in his family to read beyond the basic level required by a shopkeeper and how proud his father had been to see him settled in as a clerk.

"To him, I was better off because my hands were dirty with ink and not cows' blood."

As Judith listened, she began to sense that behind a rather odd exterior was a thoughtful person, leeched by circumstances, drained by years of subservience and deadening work. How could she ever have resented her time as a governess?

"You must be very happy in your position with the duke?"

"Oh, yes. I was surprised that he hired me, but his secretary told me I was just what he was looking for."

Judith smiled to herself. She could imagine Simon, determined to have a reader as different from Miss Ware as possible.

"It is agreed, then," said Judith, "that I will be at the duke's at 10:00 on Tuesday? I will tell Cranston that you are ill and I have come to take your place, and walk in boldly before he has a chance to wonder how we are acquainted."

Judith settled their bill and bade Wiggins good-bye at the door. She walked to the nearest cabstand, both tired and exhilarated. Tired, for it had been a long day, but excited, because she would soon be together with Simon, where surely the intimacy they had created would revive.

33

Simon's holiday was not as lonely as Judith's. For the first part of his visit, he found the time passing quickly and pleasantly. He and Robin and Barbara enjoyed their rides, which were fairly tame, due to the frozen ground. The evenings were spent in comfortable informality, except for their occasional socializing. There was a dinner at the local squire's, and the Stanleys entertained their neighbors with a small dinner and dance the day after Christmas.

By the second week, however, when Diana arrived with her elderly companion, Simon became more and more restless. They all went riding, but he was beginning to wonder if he were holding them back. They could not gallop as freely with one rider on a lead, and although winter riding was bound to be tame, Simon was feeling more handicapped than he had in London, where park riding was more restricted.

On Wednesday of the second week he declined a ride, claiming he was tired and would keep Miss Trueblood company, and then spent a wretched two hours alone while she napped. He could do nothing. The house, though familiar to him in the past, was still confusing. He had relaxed since his arrival and had let himself be led rather than take on the task of counting steps. He could not read to pass the time. All he could do was sit in the morning room feeling sorry for himself, a state he deplored but could not help but fall into from time to time. I should take up knitting, he thought in disgust. At least I would feel useful. He wanted to take a walk on the grounds *and* be alone, and of course, this was not possible. In the city he had not been as blue-deviled, but here, with no secretary and no reader, he was experiencing his limitations anew.

The evenings they spent at home were also dragging for him, now that Diana was here. The engagement was to be announced after the new year. Simon was genuinely happy for both of them, but they were naturally absorbed in each other, making up for the months of estrangement.

Simon could not keep his mind off Judith. He alternated between imagining passionate embraces and worrying whether his love for her was reciprocated. He was sure now of his feeling, but the depth of his love made him realize what he would be asking of her as the wife of a blind man. He wanted to return to London immediately, and at the same time dreaded their next meeting, for what if her feeling did not go beyond friendship?

Despite his ambivalence, however, Simon felt great relief on Saturday morning when he bade good-bye to the Stanleys. He was pleasantly surprised to learn that Francis had come down with his groom.

"I apologize, your grace," said Francis as they settled themselves in the coach, "but there were a few estate matters that needed your immediate attention, and I thought we could use the traveling time to deal with them?"

"Don't apologize," said Simon. "I am so grateful to have something useful to do and someone to talk to who is not in love that I will, no doubt, give you even more of a raise than I had planned."

"You did not enjoy your holidays, then?"

"Oh, I suppose I did, yes. It is only that it was difficult to keep myself occupied without Wiggins to read to me, or my own footman, and I suppose I just got bored. I find my blindness weighs on me when I am not feeling useful. It will be good to get back to my regular routine. But how was your holiday?"

"It was good to be with my family again," said Francis. "My father is getting older and I feel it necessary to spend as much time with him as I can."

"And your sisters?"

"All well, and the eldest quite happy in her marriage and increasing again."

"Tell me, Francis, and please be honest with me. How do you think a woman would feel about taking on a blind husband?"

Francis was of course aware of Simon's call on Judith and thought he knew what particular woman the duke had in mind. Thank God, he thought, he is thinking of asking her again. He framed his answer carefully. "I think that it would depend on

the woman. Some might believe, I am sure, that the advantages
of rank outweighed the difficulties. But if a woman loved you?
Then I think that your blindness would not weigh with her at all.''

"So you would not consider it unfair to ask her?"

"Are we speaking of a particular woman?" asked Francis
a trifle disingenuously.

"Of course, this is not hypothetical. Miss Ware, Francis."

"I thought you had already asked her, your grace?"

"Yes, and she refused upon the grounds that she did not want
a marriage of convenience. But I still do not know if my
blindness weighed in her refusal, despite her protests to the
contrary. And now I want to offer her a very different kind of
marriage, one based upon mutual affection."

Francis chose his words very carefully. He was fairly sure
Judith's heart had been the duke's the first time he asked her, but
he had no right to raise Simon's hopes or reveal what he could
only surmise were Judith's feelings. "I came to know Miss Ware
a little, your grace, and she impressed me as a young woman of
integrity, whom you could trust to be honest. If she said your
blindness was not a consideration, then I would trust her."

"So you think that I should risk asking her again, Francis?"

"I think you are, after all, in the position of any one of us.
There is always a risk involved in loving, blindness or no. She
may not love you, but you will never find out unless you ask."

"Of course you are right. Now I will just have to summon up
the courage."

Judith spent the days after her visit with Wiggins alternating
between hope and despair. In some daydreams she started to read
to Simon and in the middle of a love poem he would move close
to her and enfold her in his arms. In others, as soon as he heard
her voice, he stopped her and sent her home out of friendship.
She wondered why she had ever decided to go there alone. It was
a bold action that she was contemplating, and laid her open to
the worst suspicions. And how would Simon react? Perhaps he
would be shocked at her actions, or respond only with pity, send
her home, and never call again. At that thought, she almost sent
a note to Wiggins, calling the whole deception off.

By Tuesday, however, she had moved from agitation to an
almost numb determination. She and Simon could go on as friends,

but the only way she could think of to recapture any closeness
and show her feelings for him was to turn back the clock, reappear
as his reader, and hope his feelings had undergone a
transformation.

She dressed in the old cloak and red dress she had worn on
her first visit and took a hackney, so she would be on time. Indeed,
she seemed to have gone back in time, for she was feeling the
same nervousness at the door that she had in late September. She
rapped hard at the door and spoke quickly to Cranston's surprised
face.

"Mr. Wiggins has laryngitis, Cranston, and asked me if I could
come and take his place."

As she had predicted, Cranston was so surprised to see her again
that he never thought to question her acquaintance with Wiggins,
an unlikely one, surely. He let her in, took her cloak, and was
about to announce her presence when she put her finger to her lips.

"I would like to surprise his grace, just as a small jest . . ."

Cranston nodded and, after hanging her cloak, went down the
hall to tell the news to James, who, of course, passed it on to
the kitchen. Soon the whole house was aware that the nice Miss
Ware was here again. And what did it mean?

While the servants speculated, Judith was hesitating at the door
of the library, which was open. Simon was sitting in his usual
place with several newspapers ready, and he lifted his head and
called to the door, "Is that you, Wiggins? Come on in."

Judith walked in, holding her skirts close, so their rustling did
not give her away. What she could not know was that Simon
became aware of her presence almost immediately she stepped
through the door. The delicate scent of her cologne brought back
the memory of all their former meetings in the library, and Simon's
initial desire was to make one of Judith's wilder fantasies come
true. But he was curious to see why she had come. He wondered
where Wiggins was and whether he would be announced also,
and a little anxious still about her feelings for him. But why would
she have come if she didn't care?

"Sit down, sit down, man. Here are the *Chronicle* and the
Times."

Judith sat, unable to open her mouth. What would he say when
he heard her voice? How had she imagined that she could carry
this off? Why could she never remember that reality was always

different from imagination, and that while poets spoke of perfect communion, such communication was rare outside of the pages of a book? The greenhouse atmosphere that had protected them in the earlier days was gone. Too much had happened. Simon had returned to the real world, and so had she.

She had intended to enter silently, pick up a book of love poems, and begin reading something like Donne's "Good Morrow," pausing at a line like: "If ever any beauty I did see which I desired and got . . ." waiting for Simon to complete the stanza. All would be understood, all encompassed by the poet's vision and they would . . .

"Start with the *Gazette* please, Wiggins."

Judith was still rather paralyzed. Perhaps she should just whisper hoarsely that she had laryngitis and get out as fast as she could, hoping Simon didn't recognize her voice.

Simon wondered when Judith was going to open her mouth and what she would say to explain her presence. He decided to tease her a bit more, as she was clearly frozen into silence.

"Come, come, man, what's wrong?"

Judith tried to swallow, but her mouth was dry. She finally, after several attempts, got a few words out almost in a whisper.

"I beg your pardon, your grace, but it is not Wiggins. It is Judith . . . Miss Ware."

"Miss Ware! What on earth are you doing here? Alone, I gather?"

Judith's wits were so scattered that all she could say was "I don't know."

"You don't know if you are alone or not?" Simon felt perhaps this *was* a bit cruel.

"No, no—I mean, I don't know what I am doing here . . . that is, I thought I did, but now I see that it was all wrong to come."

"And where is Wiggins?"

"At home, your grace?"

"Is he ill? And however would you know? Are you acquainted?" Simon decided to continue his adversarial tactics a bit longer.

"Not exactly. That is, I saw him in Hatchards with your grace once, and then this past week, when I saw him again, I introduced myself and we started talking . . ." As Judith came nearer to the truth, she realized how forward she was going to sound. What she had done was too unconventional, and how could she ever explain it? ". . . And I asked him if he would let me come in his place today."

"And Wiggins agreed?" Simon asked, in the most forbidding tones he could summon up. He wondered if that would be enough to push Judith to open her heart.

"Oh, please, your grace, do not blame Mr. Wiggins. I persuaded him against his will. This was all my idea."

"I hope your persuasive powers are strong enough to convince me, Miss Ware. This puts us both in a very compromising position. You are here alone, without a chaperone, having called without an invitation, and you are no longer in my employ. Or did you think that my blindness would protect us from a scandal?"

"I didn't think at all," Judith said miserably, for, indeed, she had never thought that she was putting Simon in a position where any honorable gentleman would feel compelled to propose to her. What had seemed romantic looked only shabby now.

"Why did you come?" Simon asked quietly.

For a moment, Judith was dumb. What could she possibly say to excuse her conduct? She looked over at Simon and around the familiar room, which most likely she would never see again, and spoke, without thinking, what was in her heart.

"I came because I miss you."

"Miss me? We have just seen each other a few weeks ago."

"Yes, but . . . Oh, this is much harder to explain than I thought."

Simon needed to be sure, once and for all, what her feelings were.

"Please try."

"It is not the same, seeing you socially upon occasion or having you invite me for a drive. Here, in this room I somehow feel closer to you. I don't want only a friendship." What difference did it make now, thought Judith, she had nothing to lose, having lost it all by her stupid precipitous action. "I love you," she said through the tears that were falling and started to get up before she made an even greater fool of herself.

Simon had begun to move when she made her confession and was in front of her chair, on his knees, before she could stand up. He reached up to touch her face and felt it wet with tears.

"My dear, I am sorry for teasing you. I knew it was you the moment you entered the room. It was only that I wanted so much to hear you tell me you loved me so I could be sure you meant it." Simon began to trace Judith's face with his long fingers, and when he reached her mouth, he stood up and, pulling her up with him, guided her to the sofa, and finding her mouth again, covered it with his, all the while smoothing her hair gently with his hands. Judith closed her eyes, and they were both lost in a darkness that dissolved barriers and brought them close. She kept her eyes closed as they broke apart, and reached her hand up to Simon's face, to "see" it in another way. But she was too hungry for the sight of him, and her eyes flew open, and seeing his face bending down over her, realizing he would never see the love in her eyes, she quickly covered his mouth and forehead with light kisses, murmuring, "Oh, my dear love, I am so sorry. I don't think I realized it till now."

Simon knew immediately what she meant. "It is all right, Judith. If it doesn't matter to you, then I am only glad that out of a great loss has come such happiness."

"I want you to see how I love you," whispered Judith.

"I can feel it. And that is truly all that you will miss?" said Simon. "I will be dependent upon you, to a degree. I will never be able to compliment your appearance. Some people will, no doubt, say we made the marriage of convenience that I once offered you."

It was so wonderful to Judith have her love returned that she could not, in that moment, conceive of any greater happiness.

Simon pulled back. "We must stop . . . or I do not trust myself."

"Nor I."

They both sighed at the same time, and then had to laugh at themselves, which broke the tension.

Simon moved a little farther away, as though to weaken the current between them.

"Miss Ware," he said in mock-serious tones, "I am aware that having compromised you so thoroughly, I must now offer for you and will call upon your brother this evening."

"Yes, your grace."

"And you will marry me?"

"How could you have a doubt?"

"You know . . . No, you can't know, but you will find out, that it will be difficult. I am not always as adjusted as I appear. I still have moments of great anger and frustration and do not expect them to go away. Perhaps had I never seen, it would be different, but there are still moments that I feel that I will break through the barrier, and the knowledge that I never will see the ocean, or the Downs, or my children's faces can be quite overwhelming. I am saying this not to arouse your pity, but to let you know beforehand that marriage to me will present difficulties beyond the obvious ones."

"I know I cannot truly understand how it feels, but I am warned, and will do my best to weather the storms, Simon."

"I have just spent the most restless two weeks, just wanting to get back to you. And I was courting you, albeit rather slowly."

"You mean you were eventually going to ask me to marry you and let me make a fool of myself this morning," said Judith, a little real indignation mixed in with her teasing.

"Yes. I knew I had come to . . . No, had probably always loved you the way you wanted, but I did not know yet about you."

"Well, now you do," said Judith.

"Most certainly," said Simon with a smile. "How ever did you convince Wiggins to let you take his place?"

"I told him the truth."

"You told him that you loved me?" said Simon in astonishment.

"Yes, and he was most sympathetic, being a devotee of romantic novels."

Simon laughed. "Wiggins?"

"Yes," replied Judith more seriously. "He is not quite as colorless as he seems. He told me a little about himself, and I was quite ashamed of my complaining about a governess's lot. You will keep him on, even though you will have your first reader back?"

"Of course. He does very well with newspapers and speeches. I will have to make the effort to get to know him better myself. But enough of Wiggins, Judith. It is our life together I wish to discuss." And Simon reached out to pull her closer again, and their discussion quickly became the kisses and murmurings of lovers.

Epilogue

There was great speculation, of course, over Simon and Judith's marriage. Many people, as Simon had predicted, considered it a good bargain for both. The blind duke gained a companion, and the poor governess, in turn, became a duchess. The duke and duchess knew the truth, however, as did their intimate friends, and ignored the rumors that were rife after their quiet and some said hurried marriage.

Robin and Barbara were of course ecstatic, and Barbara, it must be confessed, a little envious. Robin and Diana were to be married in a large society wedding in June, and they were busily planning their lives together, so that she had two happily settled couples to watch.

The Duchess of Ross was of course convinced that she was solely responsible for Simon and Judith's happiness, but would have been in strong disagreement with Wiggins, had they ever had the opportunity to argue the matter. For he was triumphant after Simon told him of the coming marriage and thanked him for his part in the courtship. His grace was clearly happy, Miss Ware would make a wonderful duchess, and Wiggins' salary had been raised in the new year. When Miss Austen's *Persuasion* was published, and Wiggins had finished reading it to his wife, he could only comment that he was glad that the author, whom he had always admired, had, before her untimely death, at last become a romantic.